SOMETHING
AWAKENS

HOUSE
OF
DEATH
&
SHADOW

OLIVIA GOLD

Cover Design by Getcovers

Logo Design by MJ Design

Published by Olivia Gold.

ISBNs: Ebook 979-8-9919377-0-2

Paperback: 979-8-9919377-1-9

Pronunciation Guide

Meiora (Meye-or-uh)—Darci's cryarsh

Myzonia (my-zone-ee-uh)—Adrian's world

Oria (or-eye-uh)—Darci's world

Faolan (fay-oh-lahn)—boy

Stygo (sti-go)—pink fruit, cross between apple and berries

Zaiven (zi-ven)—small village near Adrian's house

Rizyrk (ri-zirk)—capital of Myzonia

Novundo (no-voon-doh) capital of Oria

Khitaen (kite-en)—God of War and Peace

Araina (uh-rain-uh) Goddess of Light

Luna–Goddess of Wind and Sky

Markyr (mar-keer) God of Fire and Ice

Cryirz (cry-irz) God of Night

To anyone who has ever felt like the villain in their own story.

In long times past before all that is
Death walked hand in hand with Life.
But in its greed, the God of Death sought to take more than it was allotted
Death searched for a place amongst the living.
But all that is and all that was could not coexist with monsters.
Life pushed back and Death was shunned.
War broke the ties between worlds, and the destruction from a war between gods and goddesses left the people devastated.
Death was banished.
Its role left corrupt and broken
Forgotten by man and gods alike.

—-A Myzonian Account

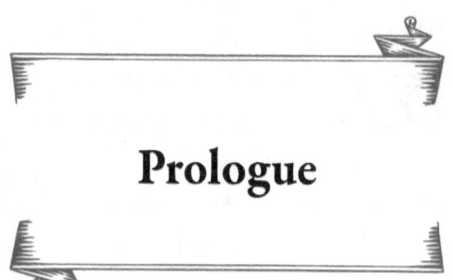

Prologue

Death was my friend once. I knew it deeply and profoundly in every corner of my being. The others feared its power—-feared what it could do if left unchecked. Not me. I was never afraid of it. Until it came for me; then left me behind.

I didn't want much—-to live a life of peace, to taste love. A life where shadows stayed hidden, and the ghosts of my past haunted someone else for a change.

But monsters come for us all eventually.

Someone screams. Wings beat the air somewhere far away. A chill crawls up my spine, and movement amongst the trees draws my eyes. Cold sweat wets my skin, and I see two white eyes watching me from the darkness. I smile, though the terror building within my chest makes the movement painful. I've been here before. I've seen him.

A sharp pain slices across my palms. I lift them slowly and see the fine line of blood growing from the fresh wounds. A bargain. A deal. Alongside the blood, a dark tendril of shadow escapes my flesh. Rage consumes me.

Betrayal. Poison. I snap my gaze back to the eyes drawing ever closer to me. A figure shrouded in black robes. No, a cloak. No, shadows. *Liar.* They don't belong to you.

The pounding of my blood echoes in my ears. A great winged beast flies overhead. More screams fill the air. A thousand shadows pour out of the forest around me, rushing toward every living being in their path. The cloaked figure draws closer, its movements light and ethereal like its floating above the ground. I know he's not.

None of this is real.

I whisper the mantra to myself, or I might simply think the words. Kiran screams at me to run. *Get out! Get out! Run!*

Everything around me blurs. My eyes burn with the ash and soot smothering the life out of this world.

No. We all burn here.

He grabs my hand. Doesn't he feel my blood? Something shifts. My mind collapses in on itself. I yank my hand back from this stranger. Who is he? Do I know him? Small versions of him parade through my mind. Who are they?

They fade and become wisps on the wind, disappearing. I try to hold the image of them, but they are like sand through open fingers.

But who is he? Who are they?

A door closes. Darkness falls upon me—-upon us. It feels wrong. It feels foreign. The fire in my chest suffocates and dies, pushed down by someone's will. No, not dead. Not really.

Shadows. There are so many shadows.

Death was a friend of mine until it left me behind.

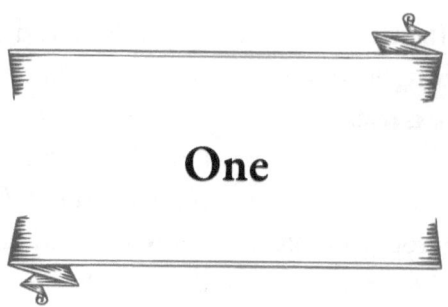

One

Darci

An omen of death and destruction follows me—-shadows teasing the corner of my vision. They dance in the corners of my eyes noticeably enough that I turn my head. There for a breath, then gone like a ghost. I get the strange feeling that I barely missed whatever was taunting me. Perhaps I blinked too often or waited too long to peer over, but it's always the same—a movement to the side and chills of trepidation living with me daily.

I see it again in the corner of my eye, but I focus on the task before me. I don't have time to wonder who's there or what they want. I don't have time to be going crazy. I ignore it and keep working on the bread dough under my hands.

I'm all alone now with only my memories to remind me of everything I've lost. Everything is different. War devastated my world. The proud land where I was born crumbled under the pressure of wealth, power, and greed. Some of it from within, no doubt. A lot of it came from the invaders—the dark forces swept in like a plague and stole the lifeblood of this land.

I wonder sometimes if there was more to it. If the shadows I see are a taste of what was responsible for our downfall. If something we cannot see with the naked eye exists—-a world within a world. Other places existing with magic and wonder unlike this one devoid of power and beauty. Those other worlds might simply be full of evil and darkness, too. It's nonsense. Magic isn't real, and why I see darkness flickering in my peripheral vision probably has more to do with the state of my mind than anything supernatural. Still, the thought nags at me from time to time. Those enemy forces moved quickly and without much resistance. We didn't stand a chance against their might.

My family crumbled to pieces because of the shadows. Children and a husband—all gone—leaving me alone with my thoughts and broken heart. Our friends and neighbors who survived the fallout of war fled this land and this town, surrounded by shadowy woods on our south and east and a vast ocean on the west.

No one bothers me here. No one comes this far out of the town. No one comes to my house.

I think the woods scare them away.

When the warriors invaded, they were subtle at first. They chose to come on foot through dark and wooded lands appearing out of the shadows like phantoms and demons. They invaded the obscure, seemingly safe towns, the towns not big enough to call a city. Those places where one thinks nothing bad will happen here. We were all painfully wrong. Whole communities vanished overnight. Children disappeared into the dark, lost to the woods and the armies camped there.

I live near the forest, and people's memories endure. No one risks their lives and their families by living here. It may be the most generous source of life we can access, but it is also the one most likely to steal it away. I don't blame them. I wouldn't live here either. But I have nothing to lose, and my memories are my punishment.

I notice movement again, and the sound of footsteps moving in the room off the kitchen. The sound startles me enough that I almost drop the dough. I squeeze my eyes shut, willing the shadows to haunt someone else. My skin crawls with goosebumps, but as I count to ten, the footsteps stop. Opening my eyes, everything appears normal again.

Maybe it is coming for me through the shadows. The shadows that took everything important to me when I failed to save those I love. Now, I would welcome the darkness with open arms, embracing death–unafraid and reunited with my family. At least, I think I would.

These thoughts plague me every day as I work to stay alive. I try to stay alert, but most days I feel numb. I can't help it. It is easier to feel nothing than to feel everything.

The sensation that I'm not alone sends shivers up my spine again. Another shadow scurries across my vision in the corner. I pause my work, remaining quiet and watchful, and shift my eyes to the corner of the room. I listen for any sound, any evidence someone or something is there. It is unsettling how I feel certain I saw someone move out of the corner of my eye; yet at the same time, I am certain nothing is in the room with me. Nothing is in the house. I worry the memories of my family escape my mind and come to life, for a moment. A part of my heart is still hopeful and longs to have them back in my home making noise and causing chaos, to the point, I'm delusional enough to believe they are here.

I wait a minute longer, not moving. It is eerily quiet, but I don't see anything.

I finish the dough, place it in the pan, and put it into the stone oven I've built along my fireplace. The new sovereign of this world prioritized the capital of Novundo for most resources. He is a tyrant who only wants the resources of this world for himself. He doesn't care if he cripples the rest of the towns and the people around him to do it. Rage flares to life in my chest for the briefest of moments. I breathe hard through my nose to calm myself. A tingling in my fingertips draws my attention, and I rub my fingers together to remove the sensation before holding my hands toward the fire's warmth.

My days are spent building fires, maintaining fires, cooking over fires, and staring at fires. I hate them and their smell.

A soft whoosh comes through the open window, and I'm reminded summer is over and fall is here. It is time to clean the garden and harvest the rest of what I have. We used to have longer, warmer summers. It wasn't unusual for us to still have warm weather for eight months out of the year, but when evil people use war and any means necessary to destroy things, it can change the weather for the whole world. Whatever forces they used to destroy towns released enough debris and darkness into the sky that the sun now spends a lot of its time obscured. A constant gray haze hangs over all of us, and the shadows on the horizon never fully leave.

I still think there was more to it than simply greedy people. I believe darkness and evil are more tangible than we think, and there might be a little bit of magic leaking into the world somewhere polluting us with death. This thought irritates my mind because it seems vaguely familiar, though I can't figure out why.

An hour later, the bread is done, and I venture to the nearest neighbor's house to trade. As I walk on the broken stone of what used to be a well-maintained road, I can't quite shake the feeling I'm being followed. Or that someone is watching me. The sensation frays at my nerves. The road to my neighbor's borders the woods for a mile. I periodically check to see if anything is causing a stir, but the woods are alive and happy with creatures—normal creatures. Squirrels scurry up trees; birds sing; the occasional deer meanders over a fallen log. There is enough noise to know that right now no danger is lurking nearby.

The downside to trees is the ever-present shadows. The movement of the branches swaying in the wind makes the shadows dance and makes me jumpy. My heart beats a harder rhythm. I can't distinguish between the trees' shadows and the shadowy movements lingering in my peripheral vision. Are they there? Or is it the breeze keeping me on edge?

Just as I step out of the presence of the woods, I hear them—-footsteps. My body freezes though my mind screams that I should run. I can't stop myself from looking over my shoulder. The shadow of a man stands in the distance obscured by trees. Who could that be? Who would be following me? Terror grips my chest. I turn quickly and trot farther away from the trees, hoping whoever is in the woods doesn't follow me. When I put a greater distance between me and the forest, I slow to a walk and listen. No footsteps. No sounds. I steal a glance behind me again, but no one is there. Maybe I imagined it.

It is a relief to escape the shadows of the woods for open fields. Some fields haven't recovered from the war and lay barren and burnt. Others managed to escape the war without any scars. Those are kind of beautiful now. Nature takes over what once belonged to it, and the former inhabitants are being forgotten. A smile touches my lips for a moment. Life prevails.

My neighbor's home, the McClanes, is rundown but clean. They've managed to keep it from falling to the ground and their small number of livestock keeps them from starving or being downright poor like me. I walk up the creaky porch steps and knock. Their old dog, Rust, dozes on the porch without a care in the world oblivious to my presence. At this point, I'm unsure if he is deaf and blind, a terrible guard dog, or simply recognizes my smell and finds me unworthy of his efforts to wake up. Can't say I blame him.

The latch clicks and the door squeaks as Mrs. McClane opens it to me.

"Hi there, Darci. Peace to Novundo. How are you today?" Her use of the customary greeting required in our land now grates on my nerves, but I try not to show it. She reaches out and pulls me in for a hug. She's almost like family to me. If I let myself get close to feeling anything for anyone ever again, she would be the one to stir it within me. Instead, I resist the sentiment.

"Peace to Novundo," I murmur. One does not snub the capital of our new world. Not if they want to continue living. I can't risk the possibility she would turn me in to the authorities. Even family can betray you. "I'm doing okay. How are you guys?" I smile slightly.

"Now Darci, how many times have I told you to call me Eleanor? We're doing just fine by the way." She pats my arm.

"I know. It just doesn't quite feel polite." I don't want to love someone else who might end up dead. "I have some bread I made this morning. I didn't know if you would be interested in trading for some eggs and goat's milk?" I unwrap the loaves to let her get a peek.

"Ooh, I think I can manage that. How many eggs do you need, honey? I just milked Greta and have a pint jar I can trade too."

"Whatever you can spare. Has Mr. McClane started hunting for the season?"

"Two dozen it is." She smiles knowingly. "He hasn't started yet, but he's getting ready to go out next weekend. You wantin' to join him again?"

I don't want to join him, but survival requires death. "Yeah, if he doesn't mind to have a tag-along again," I say sheepishly.

"Oh, you know he doesn't mind! Besides, what are neighbors for if we don't look out for one another?"

Eleanor McClane and her husband Rick are in their sixties. I'm not entirely sure how they managed to survive the attacks. They've never elaborated on those details. All I know is they lost one of their sons and his family in the war and their other son lives two days away. Two days is a long journey when this much uncertainty waits for us on the roads. I know she misses him. But she doesn't talk about him, and I don't talk about my life either.

"Just let me know when he plans on heading into the woods," I murmur. I cringe at my mistake. Most don't venture into the woods to hunt. They stay on the outskirts. Set up corn traps to draw the deer out and to easily kill them without having to cross the border.

Mrs. McClane's face pales, and I immediately try to backtrack.

"I mean, let me know when he plans on getting set up. I prefer to have another person with me when hunting. Makes it a little less lonely." I'm rushing my words, mumbling. I don't mind being lonely when I hunt, but Mr. McClane has more resources to draw the deer out of the trees. He always gets what he needs, and if I work with him, he'll offer to help me clean and prep the meat afterward. It's like I said. Survival requires death, but I don't care for this part of living.

"Now, don't tell me you've been wandering into the woods after meat," she scolds. "Especially all on your own?" Her concern taints the air between us.

"I try to avoid going into the woods as much as possible. But sometimes, hunger takes priority." We don't all have chickens, cows, and pigs from which to glean a little bit of meat, but I keep those thoughts to myself.

"I worry about you, Darci. You are far too young to be out here surviving on your own. Won't you consider coming and living in the small house next to the barn? You'd still have your own space, but you wouldn't be right next to those woods. And you wouldn't be all alone."

I'm not "far too young." I'm thirty, though I feel ancient. But I guess perspective is everything here.

"I don't mind being alone. I'll be fine." I hand her the bread. Today, I won't have to make a trip to town. Today, I can walk the two miles back home, instead.

"Alrighty, if that's what you prefer. You want something to eat? Maybe a drink?" She balances the bread in her hands and nods her head in the direction of the open door for me to follow her inside. I obey and hold the screen door open for her.

"No, it's okay. I brought a canteen, and I ate before I left." A lie. Her slight smile knows it, but she also knows food is limited and sharing is hard.

"Alright. I'll go grab your eggs and milk." She limps off toward the kitchen, and I hear her puttering around, grabbing cartons and getting the essentials out.

I stand quietly by the door and lose myself in my thoughts. Her living room is off to the right. An old red couch and armchair sit with tattered upholstery next to each other. They put in a stone fireplace in the far-right corner alongside the front window, looking out onto the porch. To my left is a closet door. Most likely a coat closet. It's cracked open slightly. The pale green paint of the room is faded and old. I sigh and glance back towards the kitchen.

My pulse jumps. There it is again in the left-hand corner of my vision. A quick scurry across the room. Almost as if it came out of the closet five feet away from me. I can't help it; I have to look. Nothing. No shadows move. Yet the hairs on my arms stand up and my skin is tingling. Its presence is stronger than before, for whatever reason. I need to get home. I need to start walking back so I don't have to be near the woods in the dark.

Mrs. McClane's uneven gait gets louder as she returns to the front door.

"Here you go, sweetie. Two dozen eggs and a pint of goat's milk."

I tuck them into my basket and cover them up with my towels. "Thank you so much. You saved me a trip into town."

"Well, that alone is worth coming this way. Would you like to stay and visit for a bit?"

I smile, "I really can't. I wish I could. But I don't want to walk home in the dark." Even Mrs. McClane can't argue. She pulls me into one more hug and opens the screen door. Mr. McClane is walking up the porch steps as I step out.

"Hey, Darci. You bring us some good bread again?" He shakes my hand firmly. His eyes are piercing, and it makes me a little nervous. Something about his gaze feels wrong.

"Sure did. I need to be getting on the road though now. Let me know when you plan on hunting, okay?"

"I sure will. I can always use some company when trying to get some meat for dinner." He pats me on the back. The gesture comes across as fatherly, but my muscles tighten involuntarily. I force a smile and walk down the steps.

"I'll see you another time." I wave to them both. Mrs. McClane gives me a wistful smile. I think she wishes she could take me in like another child–to not feel so deeply her separation from her son. Nevertheless, I don't plan on letting them get too close. We need each other to survive. Or maybe I need them more than anything. That's all this is. Humans helping other humans live.

I start down the road again—-this time heading home. I avoid resting even though I'm getting thirsty. I don't want to delay my return to the safety of my house. When I reach the woods, I take a deep breath and try to remind myself nothing is ever there and I am safe. Lies.

But the woods are not as benign as when I first walked through them. As I pass under the shadows of the trees, I notice a presence hovering nearby. In the corner of my eye, I see movement, and the shadow causing it lingers this time. I don't know why. It hugs the side closest to the trees. If I turn my head, I might not be alone anymore, and the thought terrifies me.

My gait falters only slightly, and I keep my eyes forward. If I run, will the strange darkness follow? I continue on the uneven ground, and the shadow never leaves. It stays resolute like a person waiting for me to acknowledge their existence. When I'm halfway through the wooded stretch, I realize something else. It is quiet, unsettlingly quiet. The creatures of the woods have gone still, and I managed to miss the shift until now.

I pick up my pace, and my heart pounds. My mind runs through all possible scenarios. All the possible ways of escape from this encounter. Is it a man or a beast? Could an enemy soldier be after me? Dread grows in my stomach, and it takes all my willpower to control my emotions.

As quickly as it appears on the edge of my vision it vanishes. I step out of the shadows on the road into the dim, fall sunlight. My home is not far, and the foreboding is gone. A bird squawks from the treetops. No shadows dance in my periphery.

I am alone again.

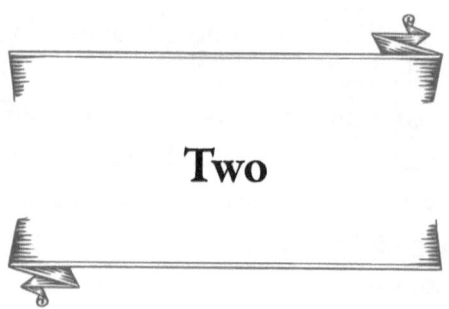

Two

I stumble into my house and slump against the door. The small home with a couple of bedrooms has never felt more welcoming. My heart calms after the strange events on the road. The dull gray of the walls seems darker than usual, but I think it's because the house is emptier than it should be. Sadness stains the walls and makes me feel that even the shadows can taste my sorrow. I take my boots off at the door because old habits die hard and carry the eggs and milk into the kitchen. The milk will be my protein source today. I'll save the eggs for other meals because they'll last longer.

The back of my house faces the woods. I keep the blinds closed now, but I know the hill sloping down to the shadows is there. I don't want to have reminders of how quickly death came to this house. Most of my life is lived in this small place with these painful memories of my children and husband. I should leave, but I would have to care, to feel something to justify leaving. I secretly hope death will come for me too.

Darkness settles into the corners of the house as the sun goes down. Walking to the wood pile next to the back door, I gather a few logs so I can start the fire for the night. The events of the day consuming my thoughts as I work. Once the blaze burns brightly, I settle into the chair with the goat's milk and some beans from the garden. The crackling fire and the soft crunch of fresh uncooked beans are the only sounds I hear. If there is one thing I've grown to hate, it's the eerie glow cast onto the wall by the fire's flames.

Shadows dance around me, leaving me unsettled and nervous. I'm being watched again; I'm not quite alone. I know this instinctively. The hairs on my neck stand up, and I pause for a moment from my chewing. I don't look up right away. I wait to see if the shadows move less predictably.

They don't, but the weight of another presence presses down my spine. I think it has become more tangible in the past few months. It wasn't like this, at first, when things settled down from the invasion. I thought I would be safe and forgotten here. What more could the enemy want? What more could they steal they hadn't already taken or destroyed?

This land is called Oria now, along with most of the world. When the kingdom of Khatum decided we all belonged to them, they swept in from the west and moved like monsters, taking what didn't belong to them. They were shadows of fear and death, and no one stopped them. Only a tiny island kingdom far out in the ocean managed to escape the bloodshed.

This was the last I had heard when I ventured into town, and the information was almost two years old by then. I'm not sure why Khatum spared that kingdom or how it avoided conquest. It stood its ground though, and Oria became what is today without them—a kingdom devoid of joy and peace and only caring for the elite in its society.

Now, I stay out of everyone else's way, and they avoid me too, and this is as good as it is going to get. I shake my head and take another bite of a bean. I've let my thoughts drift away from me again.

Shortly after the war ended, I saw the shadows maybe once a week. Eventually, they appeared once a day for the past six months. But there has been no change since then. Tonight, however, I feel it. I sense the presence of someone else, another mind sharing this place. The shadows on the wall begin to quiet. I'm left with only one shadow in the corner of my eye that won't leave me alone no matter what I do.

I glance to the left. At first, I'm not sure I see anything. Then, I notice a darkness moving on its own. It is denser and darker than the other shadows. It freezes the moment I look at it. I suck in a breath and hold it, my heart pounding in my chest. I have the strangest urge to reach out—to see if the shadow will return the gesture, but tonight, I am too afraid.

I quickly turn my gaze away again. Back to my jar of goat's milk, I bring it slowly to my lips and take a sip, trying to force the bean down that I didn't swallow well. In the corner of my eye, the shadow seems to inhale; and then it is gone. Is it living? Sentient? I try not to dwell on it, but now every shift in darkness I see makes me feel certain I'm not alone in this house. Whatever follows me is becoming bolder. The shadow seems as surprised as I am when I look at it. Almost as if it didn't expect me to notice it moving around the room. I can't explain how I discern emotion from a shadow. I *feel* it.

The rest of the night is quiet though tense. I decide it will be best to stay curled up on the chair instead of venturing into my room. I want to stay close to the fire. Close to the warmth and away from the impenetrable darkness. It's the first time in a long time that I miss filling the house with light, if only to dispel any dark corners that could be occupied.

After a couple of hours, I slip into a dreamless sleep until morning.

I STARTLE AWAKE WITH a headache and a sore neck. For a second, I forget why I'm sprawled across the chair, but the memory of the night before comes to me and I look automatically to the corner of the room. It's empty. No strange shadows or darkness of any kind. The sun is shining through the windows, and I feel the tension release in my chest as I exhale. Rubbing my face, I move to stand and stretch feeling every bit decades older than I am.

I walk to the front of the house and look out the windows. It's sunny and looks warm. An ache swells in my chest as I feel the deep loss more than usual today. The loneliness is starting to get to me. Maybe my loneliness is making me create these shadows. I'm imagining all of it—my mind's feeble attempt to remedy an issue that is slowly getting worse. Madness.

"I miss you." My voice is tight with disuse. "It's stupid because I know you can't hear me. But I miss you, and I'm tired. Tired of waiting to die. Tired of trying to live."

The words are spoken into the air falling flat and empty. None of them can hear me, but I miss them. I want to be a part of their world wherever they might be.

A sound scrapes along the floor of the other room. My heart immediately jumps into overdrive, adrenaline coming to the forefront. I turn quickly and look through the door into the room I'd been sleeping in. I don't see anything. It sounded like someone pushed a chair back across the floor. I tiptoe to the threshold peeking towards the kitchen on my right. The chairs sit in the same place they always have. My mind knows no one is there, but my mind screams I'm not alone in this house. Not anymore.

"I think it's time to go work outside today," I say to no one. I think. "Great, now I'm losing my mind entirely."

I walk to the front door, slip shoes on my feet, and step out onto the porch. The porch creaks under my feet. It has held up decently over the past couple of years, but the railing is wobbly and the wood protests a bit more than it used to. I grab my basket off the step and head towards the garden behind the house. A creak sounds from behind me back on the porch. I twirl around to face whatever is there, but no one stands on the porch. There are no shadows in strange places. I breathe deeply through my nose, blowing the air out between my lips. It's nothing. Nothing is there.

Unfortunately, the sunniest place for my garden sits only a small distance from the wood line which means two things. One, I have to get close to the trees and the memories I avoid, and two, the deer have easy access to my fruits and vegetables.

It's...inconvenient. I have a week of harvesting to do before the weather shifts dramatically. Time spent amongst growing things reminds me life persists even when circumstances deem it improbable. There is some peace to be found when my hands are in the soil.

Around me, the woods quiver with sound. Birds singing and a soft breeze whispering through the remaining leaves on the trees create calming music to my ears. It's a pleasant sort of sound; I feel a little less alone and a little safer when I am outside. An hour passes by quickly when nature's music suddenly ends.

Tension coats the air as I pull up a weed. Unnatural stillness settles over the trees, and I know without a doubt I am being watched. My body goes still. Is this what deer feel like when they pause in the presence of a predator? My skin feels tingly. I expect it now. The shadow shows up in my vision in the corner. It's darker this time and has a shape. I also think if I look up, it won't be gone. It will be there waiting for my interaction. I slowly suck in a deep breath and decide to be brave.

Without looking up, I clear my throat and speak in the steadiest voice I can manage. "What do you want?"

I'm not sure I expect an answer, but I want one nonetheless.

"What do you want with me?" The shadow shifts. Is it thinking?

"I don't enjoy being stalked. If you're going to kill me, can you...get it over with?" I face the monster now. It watches me from mere feet away, or I think it does. It doesn't reflect any of the shapes around it. It is not the shadow from the trees or the broken polls around my garden. It doesn't look like a person and has no eyes or face. It is tall and narrow with black wisps floating around it in various directions. It moves as if the wind blows through it; like coal black hair, silky and smooth and fluttery in a breeze.

I suddenly don't feel afraid. I don't know why, but it doesn't seem to be a threat to me. If it is, it doesn't want to be. Is this real? Am I seeing this?

I swallow, "Well if you're going to, uh, *be* there, can you at least be where I can't see you? You're very distracting." The shadow shifts again. This time, I realize the darkness is creeping along the ground from the base of the shadow towards me. The relief I was feeling might have been misplaced.

I stand up quickly trying to step back on the soft turned earth of my garden. Of course, now is the time I trip over my spade and fall on my butt with a grunt. I roll over quickly to my hands and knees and go to stand when I realize the darkness has surrounded me and settled on the soil in front of my fingers. I freeze.

"Okay," I whisper. "You can stay." I can't breathe. There is a strange longing swelling inside of me. Something familiar and safe. I want to touch the shadow like it is an old, familiar friend. I want to know what it is. Without realizing it, I rock back onto my heels and reach forward slowly with my right hand. My fingers are shaking and tingling. I can't stop it though. My heart pounds in my chest; maybe it will burst and I'll die from fear right now.

My fingers feel cold. The tips are an inch away from the darkness. I know at this moment I'm not going to stop. As they pass into the shadow, I feel a spark of pain and power. A current rushes up my arm into my core, and I gasp. It feels cold and warm like plunging into a pool of cool water on a hot summer day. It is strangely good, almost comforting. My heart calms and my breath evens out. I twist my hand side to side through the dark. The shadows are tangible. They are soft and velvety—cold but alive. These are not shadows from the trees or any other being. They belong to a sentient being I had no idea existed.

My mouth turns up slowly into a smile and for the first time in two years, I am not alone. The shadows respond like a cat, curving and arching up around me. I giggle–I actually giggle–and turn to face the origin of this darkness. The figure has shifted and molded looking more like water shimmering as it pours over a ledge in a creek. It doesn't seem any different. It doesn't look afraid or mad (as if I could tell the difference in this creature). Its liquid-like appearance melts into the ground and spreads out to fully encompass where my knees press into the earth. It is all around me, within me, and on me. I hold my hand up to my face and see little flames of shadow lick from finger to finger.

Suddenly a bird caws in the treetops and the spell is broken. The shadows disperse from my vision, and I am left gasping for breath on the ground with my basket of vegetables knocked over. For some reason, I don't think it left me. I look at the woods and my house. I don't see the full-fledged form of darkness standing anywhere, but suddenly all the shadows around me seem less ominous.

I'm not alone in this world. The relief is intoxicating, and I'm pretty sure I touched magic.

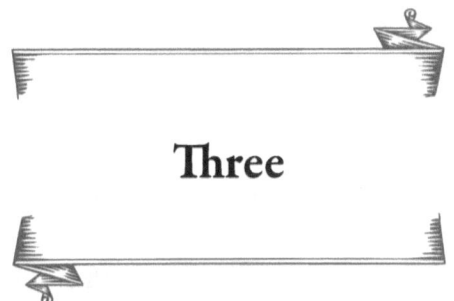

Three

Two Months Later

Shadows flicker on the wall as the fire warms the living room of my house. Occasionally, they slide across the floor and mingle with my shadow. When they do, I feel them. Every day, I wake up to them on the walls and in corners they shouldn't be. I know them now though, and I am not afraid. Maybe I've completely lost it, but I speak to the shadows like they are people occupying my rooms, my home, my heart. They don't speak back. I kind of wish they would. Whatever this creature is, it seems to understand me. Sometimes, it takes a more solid form like a man's silhouette; but other times, it remains as scattered splashes of dark around me. When it comes close enough to touch, it feels like soft blankets.

Tonight, I'm working to keep the house warm as fall gives way to our first winter storm. The coming storm will likely drop a lot of snow. The skies look grumpy and heavy with precipitation, and the sun appears fainter than usual because of the darker cloud cover. It's nothing I'm not used to. I put the extra wood on the back deck next to the door within easy reach so I can feed the fire all night. I'll sleep in the living room on a mat near the hearth. The room will stay warmer than my bedroom and I'll be able to avoid shivering all night.

Shadows trickle off the walls and twine around my fingers.

"Hi there, how are you this evening?" I smile softly. It responds by wrapping a little tighter around my right thumb.

"Maybe someday you'll tell me your secrets, hmm?"

It's nice having company, but I long for real conversation. Since the shadows revealed themselves to be friendly, I have not noticed nor heard any other sounds in my house. Yet, unease seeps into my chest at the thought because I start to wonder if maybe the shadows weren't the ones who made those sounds in the first place. Maybe the shadows are keeping me safe.

I crawl under the covers and stare at the fire. If I dwell too long on the state of this broken world I live in, I'll find myself worked up over things I can't change. Fire still burns within me, even in my reticence. I hate the destruction of what was once good and beautiful. Monsters come for us all eventually, though. Don't they?

I went hunting with Mr. McClane a month and a half ago. We spent a mere four days in the woods or on the edges of it. They didn't scare me like before. Ever since my encounter with the shadow creature, I have felt a lot braver in the world of trees. Between the two of us, we brought home six deer. The plus side of fewer people living here means the deer are multiplying faster than ever. Mr. McClane was gracious enough to help me with cleaning my portion and hauling them back to my home. I enjoyed working with him. He is a man who speaks little, but whose company is steadfast. When I got home, I worked on smoking most of the meat and saving a small amount to cook fresh for a few days.

Tonight, I'm lying here with a belly full of potatoes and smoked deer. A welcome feast to keep me warm with the plummeting temperatures. Two and half years of solitude leaves me rough around the edges. I miss the life I lived with my sons and my husband. It's better this way though. Fewer people to feed means surviving isn't as difficult, and I don't have to watch anyone else starve.

I sigh, and the shadows sweep over me again–velvety and warm. I can't resist the pull of slumber any longer.

SCREAMING AND EXPLOSIONS echo all around me. I'm running as fast as I can, feeling the crunch of nuts under my feet. I trip down the hill towards the woods, towards the danger. My voice is raw as I scream their names. I can hear them in the woods. He's right behind me. His voice is raw too. We breach the wood line and plunge over the edge of a small ravine into rocks and branches and blood. I see them moving up ahead, dragging them off. My boys fight, clawing and screaming. They're too small! Tiny and frail next to the monsters leading them farther away. Monsters looking like men, but shrouded in darkness and evil.

My lungs are on fire, and my heart is pounding. He surges ahead of me leaping over fallen logs and into the fray of smoke and weapons and more explosions. I hear other screams and other children being stolen. He's almost there. He's almost to them now. I know this feeling. The smell of ash and burnt flesh and the metallic taste of blood in my mouth—it feels like war.

I want to scream, but my lungs have no air to spare for sounds. I might vomit, but I swallow down the bile and force myself to continue. This is terror. This is death staring me in the face. The shadows on the trees swell and move. They're stealing my boys.

I trip and fall head-first into a branch I didn't see ahead of me. Bright pain wraps its claws around my head and stars flash in my vision before spots of black spread out. I can't get up. The only things existing are blood, pain, and darkness.

Gasping I sit up. Sweat makes my clothes cling to my skin. My heart pounds like I've been running through the woods. I can taste blood on my tongue. I may have bitten it in my sleep.

"It was a dream. It was just a dream." I whisper. But it wasn't just a dream. It was real, and it was my life. It was everything I had locked away in my mind months ago. After months of being numb, all the shock and trauma is raging to the surface, my ability to hold them at bay waning. I take a deep breath trying to calm the adrenaline and sorrow pulsing through me. I feel a sob deep in my throat, and I swallow it back down. I will not cry tonight.

I glance around the room noticing the fire has died down more than I would like it to. I stand up flexing my fingers and walking towards the back door. I throw a couple more logs on the fire and then poke it for a few minutes to encourage the flames. The wind howls outside. It is colder than it was earlier, and the pings of icy precipitation pelting the window rivals my meager fire's crackles. Once I'm sure the fire is happy and roaring, I make my way to the front window and pull the makeshift curtain–an old blanket–to the side. Snow. Lots and lots of snow. Exactly what I thought might come. Winter is here.

As I walk back to the living room with the fireplace, I get the strange sensation I'm not alone in this room. There is nowhere to hide or disappear, but something feels off. I've grown used to the presence of the shadow creature, but I can't figure out why I sense another person here. My skin tingles, and I force myself to open my senses to any sounds or smells that seem out of place. I instinctively look to the walls seeking out my shadows. Scanning the room, my eyes linger on the door to my boys' bedroom, but only for a moment. What I see or don't see around me makes my blood run cold.

Instead of shadows, I see nothing but faded paint and old wood. The fire dances now with the influx of fuel I gave it. Its shadows should be on the walls, but they aren't. *My* shadows aren't there either. It's like someone sucked all the darkness out of the room and replaced it with...nothing, not even light. This makes no sense, but it is unnatural–wrong. It's the only way I can describe it.

The shadow creature has fled or hidden itself, and I don't know why. If I focus on listening, I would almost say I can hear someone breathing in the room and the shuffle of feet on the floor. Fear swells in my chest.

"Hello?" I wish I sounded braver, but I don't. Soft thumping grows more distinct. Footsteps. How did they get in? Did they slip in while I slept and hid in another room? I glance at both doors to confirm they're locked.

"Whoever you are, show yourself." I have nothing to protect myself with. There isn't anything within reach. I could return to the front room and get into the closet to grab my bow, but I'm afraid to turn my back on this room. No neighbors have visited me since death knocked on my door all those years ago, but I wish I had prepared more for the possibility of intruders.

"Mr. McClane?" It's the only name I can think of to whisper, which is completely illogical. The footsteps stop; my heart pounds.

A scraping sound comes from the side room. I don't see anyone. How is this possible? No one answers me. *Because no one is there. Not really.*

The scratching continues, and I decide stepping closer to the fireplace feels safer than standing here with my back to a dark front door. I tip-toe towards the fire. I reach shaky fingers toward the thick stick I've used to poke the fire, wrapping my fingers around the warm wood. I hear the rush of blood in my ears, and it is taking everything within me to keep from panicking. I turn around quickly with my back to the warm fire now and look toward the room I heard the sound come from. The firelight quivers across the door, and I notice something in the paint. My skin tingles. The air is heavy with anticipation.

"Are you still there?" No answer. The scratching has stopped; there are no more footsteps. I stand frozen for several minutes waiting for someone to show their face–waiting for someone to open the door to *the* room and announce their presence. It feels like I'm waiting for them to attack me, but nothing happens. Then, as if someone flipped a switch, the walls are covered in shadows again. Normal shadows created by the firelight, in addition to the shadows of my strange companion coating the walls and the floors with their presence.

I breathe out, feeling my heart slow and the cool comfort of relief coursing through my veins instead.

"There you are. Where were you?" The shadows glide over the floor to my feet and slide around my legs like they did the first time I met them. I feel a tug as they push against my calves toward the closed door.

"I don't think going in there is a good idea." It's my sons' room. I *don't* go in there. The shadows flick across the couch and kitchen chairs hopping across the surfaces and making their way to the door. I get the distinct feeling they want me to follow them. I take a deep breath and walk forward.

All of a sudden, the scratching sound makes sense. The closer I get to the door the more my eyes adjust to the jumping light, and I see what caused the noise in the first place. There, on the door, scratched into the old paint are two words. My breath hitches, and the adrenaline that had finally abated comes back in full force. Someone wrote on my door. A person I couldn't see. I reach up slowly to touch the scars. I hiss and pull back my hand. They burn with the deep cold only frostbite can generate. I bring my fingertips to my quivering lips and whisper the written words.

"Hello, Shadow."

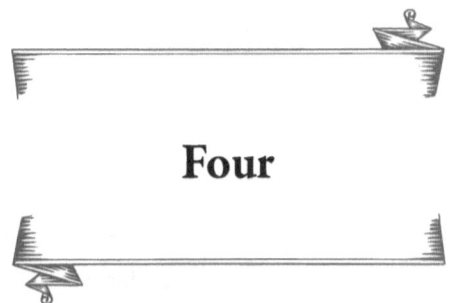

Four

The storm died out this morning. From what I can see, the world is covered in several inches of snow. It's still windy making it feel even colder, but I'm used to it. What I'm not used to is having ghosts draw words on my doors...in my presence. Was it a ghost? It didn't feel ghostly. It felt like someone was there. The shadows knew it too because they directed me towards the words. They wanted me to see. Did they do it? I shake my head. I don't think they did. It wouldn't make sense for them to have simply vanished and then returned when whatever it was had finished writing on the door. The words were directed to the shadows, weren't they?

"'Hello, shadow. Hello, shadow.'" I murmur as I sit holding a cup of warm water. I didn't bother with brewing tea. The warmth feels good in my belly on a cold morning, and it is easy to make. I've been sitting here staring at the words for the past hour. A thought stirs in my mind—something strangely familiar. *Magic.* Was I wrong when I questioned how a kingdom like Khatum could take over an entire continent? Perhaps they have access to something more like magic that gave them the power to do the unthinkable.

I'm not sure why I was chosen to be tormented here. Part of me thinks I deserve it. I wish I'd been spared the nightmare at least. I hadn't thought about the invasion in a long time, yet my memories flooded my mind in such detail I felt like I was there again. Running through the forest, blood coating the bottom of my bare feet.

These thoughts drive me to make what is probably an irrational decision.

"I'm going to the woods today." I breathe deeply. "I need to see where my family was taken." I'm lying to myself about the fact that I feel like something is calling me toward the trees. Regardless, I declare my intentions knowing the shadows are the only ones listening. Voicing my plans might ensure I have company on my walk as well.

I set my cup down and walk to the wardrobe by the front door. The air is frigid. I pull on a heavy cloak and worn boots desperately in need of replacing. Flames from the fire barely crackle at this point, and I plan on letting it die entirely. There is no sense risking a house fire by throwing more logs on now. My heavily mended leggings must suffice. I pull on gloves and raise my hood. To be safe, I bring a couple of knives. I don't want to weigh myself down more than necessary so I leave my bow and arrows here.

Properly bundled, I walk out the front door onto the porch, step down the creaky frozen steps, and turn to make my way around the back of the house toward the woods. For a moment, I hear a creak behind me that sounds a lot like my porch when someone stands on it, but glancing over my shoulder reveals nothing. My house sits on a hill with the woods surrounding it on the east and south sides. Images from my nightmare flash in my mind, but now is not the time to dwell on the past. I move through the crunchy snow towards the tree line, taking my time so I don't slip and fall down the slope.

The trees are wild and close together. I use the branches to keep my balance pushing through the brush. If this place didn't remind me so much of death, I'd find it beautiful. The snow blankets the ground and the trees. Birds are singing and squirrels are hopping on the forest floor no doubt searching for their stores of hickory nuts and walnuts for breakfast. My stomach growls. Unlike the squirrels, I forgot to eat.

I move in a straight line down the hill. The ravine is only a little farther. I say ravine because it dips down so abruptly, an unexpecting ankle can easily sprain going into it. It formed over years of water runoff down the hillside. When I reach the steep drop, I squat low to the ground and scooch down inch by inch until I'm in the middle of it. The other side has roots from trees along its bank making the climb out a lot easier.

Several minutes into my walk, I notice movement in the corner of my eye and smile. My shadow creature.

"It's about time you showed up." Shadows slither across the forest floor far more noticeable than usual because of the white canvas provided for them today.

"I need to give you a name since you seem to be here to stay." Who would have thought the darkness could be so comforting? "I could call you Shadow." The sudden disappearance of the shadow creature makes it clear it does not approve. It appears peeking out from around a tree as I hold in a laugh.

"Okay. Well, what about Umbra? I think that means shadow, right? It's not bad." The shadows flee to the top of the nearest tree and vanish from sight again. "I guess that's a no." I chuckle, shaking my head; and the distraction causes me to slip on a covered tree root. I flop backwards sinking into the snow. Laughter bubbles out of me now, and I lie there a minute staring up at the gray sky and the branches streaking it with black.

My shadows appear beside me and curl around my arms. I sit up slowly and roll over onto my knees to stand. Smiling, I pause as a name comes to mind that fits perfectly. Kneeling in the snow, I look down at the shadows wrapped around my arms.

"What do you think about the name Meiora?" The shadows hug my arms, at least that's the sensation I experience. After, they slowly spread out around me blanketing the white ground with their darkness in a perfect circle around my body. "I take that as a yes. I feel better having a name to call you. I still wish you could talk to me."

Meiora was the name we were going to give a daughter. I might be a little crazy naming my friendly dark magic creature...whatever it is...a name I would use for family; but at this point in my life, it is family. Granted, I don't think this shadow has a gender, but the name suits it and it suits me too.

"Okay, Meiora. I think you know where I'm trying to go. I need you to help me get there, and I hope I don't hesitate once I do."

I rise to my feet and dust my cloak and pants off. The wind sweeps through the treetops, but down here I don't feel the full bite of it. Thankfully, I'm not too cold even after lying in the snow.

Meiora follows me as I continue walking through the trees. Branches claw and scratch at me, but I press on. I will not be dissuaded from this venture. When I chased after my boys through these same woods, I was stopped abruptly by branches and pain. Today, I'm walking slowly, absorbing all my surroundings and noticing the details in the world around me. Deer prints, stalked by paw prints close behind, zig-zag across the snowy ground. Some branches are twisted and broken, left dangling by invading soldiers. Black, scarred bark stands in stark contrast to the white of the snow. Entire trees are gone, blown apart by power that tore through these woods mercilessly. Even after two years, the damage is still here–still evident. Scars that never quite healed. New growth pops up alongside the broken remnants, but it doesn't cover up the horrors of those armies coming out of the darkness.

The farther I walk, the less familiar things become. I pause and look around. I know I have passed the area where I fell in my pursuit. I'm deeper in this time. Meiora lingers on the edge of my vision, but it doesn't move forward anymore. Ahead of me, a discrepancy disturbs the otherwise tranquil setting. The trees should extend for miles outward only giving way to wide open meadows and fields.

Instead, I notice a small clearing twenty feet ahead of me. In the fullness of summer, you could probably miss it easily. Yet, here I am looking at the unnatural break in trees, the untainted ground, and in the center, a dark pit.

I push aside the branches in front of my face stepping through a tangle of dead weeds, thorny and angry at my invasion. Everything is so dense around this clearing like a wall erected around the space; it makes me feel odd. Like I'm not where I'm supposed to be–an invader in this space, seeing something I shouldn't.

I feel the prick of a thorn breaching the protection of my garments, but I don't stop. I'm within a foot of the break in the trees now when I notice something oozing out of the hole. Dark and liquid-like blood from a wound. Meiora isn't in my peripheral vision anymore. I think it doesn't want to go near this darkness. I know I shouldn't cross the border into the clearing. My gut twists at the sight of it, but it draws me to itself. A stirring deep in my soul recognizes this place, but I can't place it in my memories.

Looking around, I notice the clearing is a perfect circle. There is no evidence of trees or brush having been removed. No uneven soil or stumps. Nothing broken. Simply a perfect hole in the middle of a forest.

The clearing existed, and the trees grew around it, skirting an invisible barrier. In the center of it, a perfect, dark circle quivers with life–or death. I don't know which yet. It's only now that I notice a heavy silence in the air. The forest life has stilled around me, and the ground is perfectly undisturbed. There are no footprints in the snow covering the clearing. No disturbances anywhere near it. The whole scene feels a bit ominous. I find part of myself repulsed by the idea of crossing the border into the clearing, but another, darker part of me hears the call of an unknown essence hidden there. My warring emotions leave me frozen in place. I stare at it. The darkness shifting around it and within it feels very much alive. The surface is shiny and metallic. Honestly, if I wasn't terrified by it, it would be beautiful.

But Meiora isn't coming near it. My shadows aren't beside me or inside the untouched circle of snow on the outskirts of the clearing and that terrifies me more than I care to admit. My boys were taken in this direction. Is this where they died or where the soldiers brought them? It could be a portal of some sort. A thought niggles at the back of my mind that this is very close to the truth. The oppressive weight of its presence wears on my resolve to resist the call.

My mind races. How am I supposed to sleep at night knowing this is out here so close to my home? I have to get away from here. My instincts scream to run.

As I turn to leave, I hear something all around me, washing over my skin like ice. Whispers. Voices softly drift over the snow and through the trees around me. My stomach drops, and I look back again at the pit. I can't tell if the voices are coming from there or if they are coming from the outside being drawn towards the hole. I don't know what they're saying. There are too many voices in a language I can't understand.

I press my hands over my ears and close my eyes trying to block them out, but they are still present inside my head. Adrenaline surges through my veins, and I open my eyes to find the darkness from the pit seeping outward toward me. I'm not safe here. It's coming this way. Whatever it is, it senses me. I crossed some imaginary border between what is safe and what might be deadly.

I never experienced the sensation of being frozen when I've faced dangerous situations. When my family was being taken from me, I never hesitated. I'd heard stories of people being terrified to the point of indecision, unable to run, and unable to fight; but I never was. But now, I am a deer facing a predator and their inevitable doom.

I watch as the darkness gets closer when I am abruptly dragged backward. It takes me a minute to realize I'm not moving myself on my own– someone has their hand wrapped tightly around my right forearm. Their interference is enough to wake me from my stupor. My feet are fumbling as I turn to run with the person who is pulling me. The slippery snow slows me down, and panic controls my movements making them even more haphazard. My brain is trying to log all the information. Meiora is in the corner of my eye. I conclude this isn't my shadow grabbing me. It is very much a firm hand made of flesh. A man's hand. He is cloaked in shadows, but I can tell he isn't looking directly at me. His focus is away from the pit in the ground and the darkness seeping out of it toward us.

I should be afraid, but the darkness behind me is scarier than the stranger in front of me. He is tall, though I'm rather short so that's not saying much, with short black hair. He wears dark clothes covered by a black cloak. All this information floods my brain while I stumble after him through the woods back towards my house. It seems too far away. I peek over my shoulder. The oily black is still coming for us, slithering like a snake across the pure snow.

His grip is strong, but he loosens his hand enough to let my forearm go free. My hand slips into his, and he tightens his grip again. My legs feel sluggish trying to plow through the snow as the terrain begins to incline. I'm not paying attention when the ground gives out, and I fall down the side of the ravine. I lose the stranger's hand and feel my ankle twinge with pain as it rolls to the side. Thank goodness for snow to cushion my fall. Meiora sweeps around me giving me a boost back to my feet. As I try to get my bearings, hands reach down and pull me to my feet again. I glance up and catch a brief glimpse of his face. The only thing my mind registers are his eyes–such a deep brown color they're almost black. He pushes me in front of him up the other side of the ravine. Adrenaline helps me ignore the pain in my ankle, and I start to run again without looking back. All I can think of is one word...*home.*

I can see the tree line ahead of me, ending at the edge of my land. I hear his breathing behind me. He's still coming which is concerning, but burning lungs and lead-filled legs dominate my thoughts. I crash through the last branches and make it about ten feet from the tree line before my legs give out. Still, I crawl a few more feet before I give up. Meiora returns to me. Covering me with shadow and warmth and weight. I look over my shoulder towards the trees expecting him to come through the brush any moment.

But no one comes. I look carefully and see no one in the woods at all. The darkness chasing me is retreating slowly back down the hill. I gasp for breath and begin frantically searching for any sign of the man, but there is nothing. I can't even remember what his face looked like. I only see those dark eyes staring into mine with wonder and fear.

"Where did he go?" I wheeze. Meiora doesn't answer of course. "He was there, right?" Meiora remains still around my body not giving away anything.

"Meiora, next time I think I should do something brave, tell me to sit down." The shadows wisp over my hands and neck. My heartbeat is slowing, and I can finally get a deep breath in. As the adrenaline lets up, I feel, quite deeply, the pain in my quickly swelling ankle.

I crawl the rest of the way up the hill. When I get to the top, I gingerly get to my feet and try to put weight on my foot. Wincing, I hobble the rest of the way to the front porch leaning far too much on the rickety railing to make it up the few steps and into my home.

With the chase over, my mind is flooded with questions, fears, and worries. What on earth was the dark pit? Who whispered and what were they saying? Magic seems to be a logical answer to a lot of this, but it still leaves a nasty taste in my mouth with the uncertainty of it.

While I welcome answers to those questions, I'm most curious about who the stranger was and where he disappeared to.

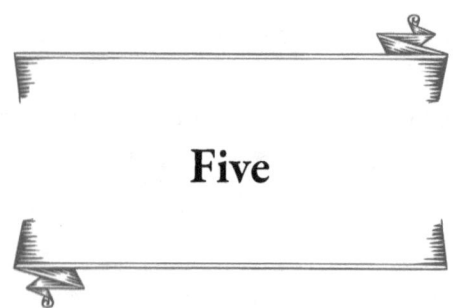

Five

I pull the pot out of the fire and carefully set it on the table in my kitchen. Taking an old rag, I dip it into the water and wring it out gingerly over the pot. My arms and legs were mostly spared from the branches and thorns during my run through the woods, but my face took the brunt of it. A gash above my left eyebrow looks especially ragged, and I cringe as I gently wipe it clean with the rag.

When I stumbled into my house, I was still trembling from the leftover adrenaline and terror of the ordeal. The fire had burned down to embers, but they were still hot enough it didn't take a lot of encouragement to get it roaring again. Once my hands stopped shaking, I took an inventory of my injuries. My reflection in the mirror wasn't terrible, but I needed to make sure these wounds healed well.

I gently rub the remaining bark pieces loose from my skin and then limp over to the couch. Wincing, I lower myself to the cushion and carefully pull my pant leg up on my injured ankle. It's not broken; it's just a severe sprain. Not great news, but it could be worse.

I peel my sock down and grit my teeth. It's already swelling, and a deep purple bruise is starting to form along the outside of my ankle. Taking a deep breath, I try to flex my ankle but shudder at the pain. I give up for now and adjust myself on the couch, positioning myself to lay flat with my ankle elevated on the armrest. Once I've taken care of my pressing needs, my mind has a chance to start racing around the information overload I'm experiencing.

Meiora appears on the floor next to the couch. It slithers up on the side and spreads out like warm water across my body. I don't think I'll ever get used to the sensation, but it is comforting and cozy.

"What in all of Oria was that, Meiora? Did the man get taken by it?" Meiora vibrates around me. If it knows anything, it can't share.

"You knew, didn't you? You knew to stay back from whatever it was. You didn't cross the perimeter to get too close. But where did *he* come from, and where did he go?"

My mind paints a picture of the man. I'm trying to piece together what I saw into one cohesive image. He was taller than me by several inches, maybe a foot. It was hard to tell when we were running. The clothes he wore were dark and similar to mine, but what I remember of him is fuzzy. He appeared blurry or enclosed in actual shadows. I couldn't see him well enough. It was like looking at someone through a misty fog, obscured but not invisible.

His eyes were so dark like coal. Fear and confusion were reflected in them. I'm sure they were a mirror image of my own. My fear was because of the black oily wound in the ground pursuing us; he looked like he couldn't believe he was seeing *me*. He saved me anyway. His skin, shrouded in shadows, appeared brown–a warm tone making his eyes deeper and seemingly endless. He might be the same age as me. Even in the middle of all the confusion, he was oddly familiar. As quickly as he had appeared, he vanished; and I was left on the hillside alone with Meiora. Did he see the shadows? The possibility worries me. Is Meiora safe? It has become my friend these past two months. I can't lose it; I can't be alone again.

My eyes drift to the bedroom door still shut with the words scratched into its surface. Did the writer of those words want to harm me? Maybe they came from the dark hole or used magic of some sort to reach me. Magic must be in this world. Excitement stirs in me at the potential power. It is quickly suppressed by dread. With Meiora draped across me like a blanket, a thought develops in my mind. Was it the stranger? He *did* appear without warning and was gone abruptly. Is he the writer?

I can't figure it out, and I'm too tired to think anymore. I hope this sleep is dreamless because resisting the weight of slumber is futile as I absorb the warmth Meiora gives me. The last sound I remember hearing is the fire crackling in the stone hearth.

Adrian

SHE WAS RIGHT THERE—RIGHT in front of me, and I grabbed her arm because it was the only thing I could think to do. She was so close to getting swept away by it, and I couldn't understand why she just stood there transfixed by it. I had to get her away from avgrunn. It wanted her, and she had been frozen with fear at the sight of it. Did she not realize how dangerous it was to be in the presence of this darkness?

I blow out a breath and run a hand over my head as I pace back and forth before the fire. When I had been walking through the forest earlier, I thought I'd heard laughter. It's not often I venture into the trees, but the urge to walk under the canopy was too strong to resist today. I wondered who would be out here this time of night. Following the sounds of laughter and a whisper on the breeze, I was startled to find a woman traipsing through the trees towards the avgrunn. Her dark hair had been braided but wisps of it framed her face. Her skin was pale, and it seemed to glow in the light of the moon. Her beauty made my throat tighten. The magic in my veins came alive at the sight of her, and I followed her through the trees silently. She was shrouded in a gray mist, and I'm almost certain I saw an even darker shadow playfully surrounding her feet as she walked. A dark creature feared by everyone in this kingdom. My stomach tightened at the sight of the monster, but the woman wasn't afraid. Her mouth moved as she spoke to it like she was speaking to a person.

When I realized that she wasn't going to run away from the avgrunn, I had to step in. It felt surreal, and for a moment, I wondered if I was dreaming. If I hadn't felt her arm in my hand, I would have thought she was an illusion. She had gotten hurt though, hadn't she? I heard the gasp of pain escape her mouth when she fell into the ravine. She was limping when she worked her way out and up the hill. Illusions don't limp, do they?

I glance at the wall to my right where words are carved into wood. Something has haunted me for the past few months. I feel like someone is watching me. Even in my room, I don't feel completely alone. I pause and take a deep breath. Collapsing into the large armchair next to the fire, I stew over what all of this could mean. I don't know how long I sit here, head propped up on my fist, lost in my thoughts. I may have even fallen asleep, but a sound reaches my ears making my skin crawl.

Scratching. Someone or something is scratching on the wall behind me. Lifting my head and rising from the chair, I face the wall carved with words. Below the words I carved into the wood one more appears.

Hello.

Darci

I AM CRAZY. IT'S OFFICIAL; I have lost my mind. But when I woke up from a restless sleep on the couch, I knew I had to write back to the phantom in my house. I sat up and forgot for one brief moment about my swollen ankle until I stood and stumbled to the side. Catching the arm of the couch, I righted myself and hopped carefully to the island picking up a knife along the way. Now, I stand in front of the door carving one word into the paint.

I can't stop thinking about the whole encounter—about him and the hole in the ground and everything I have lost. I can't help but wonder if it all means something. If there is more here than meets the eye. I decide the best thing to do first is say hello.

The sun is starting to set now, and I am famished since eating wasn't a priority when I first got home safely. I get to the kitchen and begin to gather some food for dinner. I don't feel like cooking eggs; instead, I grab smoked deer and three carrots along with a piece of bread. I set the food on the couch and then toss a few more logs onto the fire. It will be another cold night, but at least there isn't a storm dumping snow all over us again.

Settling onto the couch and lifting my injured ankle to the side to keep it somewhat elevated, I pick up the food and take a bite of the bread first. I'll need to make some more soon. Although getting to town or the McClanes to do any sort of trading is not going to happen on this ankle. At least I'll have a good warm loaf to enjoy. Meiora is flitting around the room, and I smile at the memory of my boys jumping around on furniture and rolling on the floor. Meiora reminds me of them. Maybe shadows can be young and old. Seems like a weird concept, but not far-fetched considering I have these thoughts concerning a shadow creature I didn't know existed two months ago.

I sigh and nestle into the couch some more, taking a bite of the smoked deer meat. I wonder if I'll get a message back—if whoever is visiting my home will continue to write to me. Will I meet them in person eventually or are they phantoms separated from me by worlds? The idea of worlds feels familiar. Like a thought resting on the tip of my tongue waiting to be voiced, but I can't quite get it out into the open.

I finish off my cold dinner and reach for the cup of water on the floor next to the couch. Meiora ventured off somewhere. I still see it in the corner of my eye, but it seems to control its visibility making it more or less noticeable when it wants to.

There's not much else to do, and I'm still feeling sore from the morning. I decide it's better to go ahead and call it a night. Looking up at the door, nothing has changed. No new message. Just the strange greeting and my response marking the paint. I reach up for a blanket off the back of the couch and make myself cozy. Watching the fire crackle and dance, before I know it, my eyelids grow heavy and sleep comes.

SCREAMING AND EXPLOSIONS. My world is shaking, and I can't breathe. I hear them calling for me. I fly out of the house not stopping for anything, not even shoes. I plunge down the hillside feeling the broken nuts and branches cut into the soles of my feet. There! Up ahead, they are being pulled farther into the woods. Monsters dragging them away from me. My boys! They keep screaming, calling for me and their dad. He is right behind me.

I plow into the tree line; branches grabbing me and holding me back. I know I am getting cut, but I can't stop. I chase after them. I want to scream, but my lungs are full of lead. I push past the pain in my legs and keep running down the hill. Every step I take seems to make no progress at all. I can't get to them. My chest aches and throbs.

Shadows and darkness are swirling in the air. The soldiers don't stop. They move effortlessly while my husband and I are beaten back by the forest around us. We have no allies here.

He surges ahead of me. I see his back as he races past and tries to reach them before they are gone. There is nothing but screaming and bursts of power all around me. And shadows. Were there always these many shadows?

I stumble forward, unable to catch myself before my head cracks hard against a tree branch. I hit the forest floor and stars flash before my eyes, followed by black spots melting together into solid darkness.

I jerk awake, damp with sweat. My eyes notice the darkness of the room and the waning glow of the fire. It's getting colder. I push myself up, moving on unsteady feet to the back door to grab more wood. It was another nightmare. I feel the tears burning the backs of my eyes, but I don't want to cry. I don't want to cry about them when tears won't bring them back. I shuffle towards the fireplace and set two more logs within it to bring the flame back up to its full strength.

I realize Meiora is not here.

The thought makes me pause. I cannot feel its presence. I used to be fine without it, but ever since we were introduced, I always feel it close by like another appendage. It is a part of me and belongs with me always. Except—I pause—except the last time words appeared on my door and all shadows disappeared–sucked from the air itself.

A chill trickles down my spine, and I look towards the bedroom door. It's hard to tell in the orange of the firelight, but there is something more there. Something etched into the paint that wasn't there before.

I wipe my hands clean on my pants and limp over for a better look. I see it. Three words etched into the paint. The writing looks the same as the first two words written.

Who are you?

"Well, how presumptuous of you to ask. I would like to know who you are, strange writer." I touch the letters. They burn like the deepest cold of midwinter. I anticipate the sting this time and trace my fingers over them regardless. I didn't hear anything–no footsteps or scraping sounds.

My dream masked it. The dream felt different this time as well. A darker, more malevolent presence hid there.

"Meiora? Where are you?" Just like that, the shadow of a man appears on the wall beside the door. It took this form the first time it greeted me, but I haven't seen it this way since then. It feels important.

"Something is going on, Meiora. I don't know how, but I will find out what it is." Meiora spreads out across the wall and down to the floor. I smile and turn back to the couch. As I'm about to walk away, all the shadows in the room vanish, and I hear scratching. I know what this means. Meiora is gone again, and I'm getting another message on the door.

Turning to face the door, my blood runs cold as I watch another message form letter by letter. The words make my heart plummet to my stomach.

Why are you in my house?

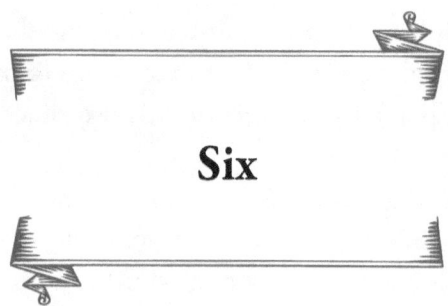

Six

My heart is a weight in my chest suffocating me for the next few minutes. I feel sick and violated. *This is* my *house. It belongs to me; I created it.* Anger builds in my core before I catch my train of thought. Shaking my head, I release the strange essence boiling inside of me.

With the disappearance of the writer, Meiora returns to me washing over the door and the words haunting me now. I feel the urge to open the door to this room. I haven't opened it since they died, but what if there is something there? What if there is something to these words being written and the room my sons called their own? A sense of foreboding fills the room.

I reach a shaky hand to the doorknob, but I hesitate. I cannot make myself open the door. Clenching my fists, I withdraw my hand and take a deep breath. I resolve not to respond to the question the mystery writer wrote. Besides, it didn't sound like they were too thrilled with my presence in their home. Perhaps, like me, they are seeing writing on a wall with no person there to do the work. Maybe I'm the ghost in their story.

My thoughts drift back to yesterday to the strange man who saved my life. None of this feels like a coincidence. I can't deal with this right now and my body knows it. Exhaustion comes over me as I limp back to the couch and curl up under a blanket. I hope there are no more nightmares and no more messages to read when morning comes. Mostly, I hope I don't open my eyes to an actual stranger in my house.

Adrian

I'VE STOOD HERE STARING at the wall for longer than I probably should. I wasn't sure what would happen if I wrote back-to-back messages, but this mystery is driving me crazy. I can't sleep with all these questions haunting me. To add to my distress, the encounter between the avgrunn and the woman makes me feel even more uneasy. She seemed familiar, but I am certain I have never seen her before. Someone is tampering with forces in the world that shouldn't be messed with. The question is whether they intend to use them for evil or good. Experience suggests evil is usually the way these things go. I worry my bottom lip with my teeth as I make mental preparations for our defense.

If the woman is the one talking to me, is she also the one using magic this way? I haven't told anyone of this. I'm half afraid they'll think I'm crazy, that the pressure I'm facing is getting to me. They're wrong though, and too many people are counting on me. I won't let harm come to them.

I'm relieved Marcus is out on scouting trips. Searching and finding any threats to the establishment of a new throne takes priority for now. We are strong, but not where I prefer us to be in light of the increased activity around the avgrunn. I can't keep this from him forever though. He'll know something is bothering me the moment he walks through the doors.

Darci

MORNING CAME FAR TOO quickly for my preference. I tossed and turned, as much as one can toss and turn on a couch, for most of the night. Lying still, I stare up at the ceiling wondering, what in Oria, today can bring. I can't stay here all day, but I don't want to get up either.

Unfortunately, the fire is dying down and outside's frigid temperatures require me to attend to it. Groaning, I set my feet on the floor and feel every sore muscle from my run through the forest yesterday. I should stay more fit with dark monsters lurking in the trees' shadows, but that is tomorrow's problem.

Today, I plan to stay next to the fire and rest. I realize after several minutes I haven't seen Meiora yet. Odd. I move at a torturously slow pace to stand and limp toward the fire. I set a few logs on it and make a decent breakfast. I finish the last of the McClane's eggs I had picked up earlier this week before the snow and force myself to drink some cold water before putting some in the pot next to the fire.

I peek at the door with the words and am relieved to see no new phrases etched into the paint. At first, I thought it would be nice when Meiora appeared– I wouldn't be so alone anymore. However, after yesterday's events, I feel uneasy. The idea of discovering more about this person leaves me unsettled.

The week passes slowly; my efforts to keep my scratches clean and resting as much as I can manage prove fruitful. I'm able to walk with only a slight limp. The bruises and scratches have faded, and I think I'm ready to stretch my legs and get outside more today. There is still plenty of snow, but the sun is shining and fresh air would do me good. As I'm about to walk out the door, someone knocks.

My adrenaline spikes in instinct. People don't visit me. Not out here. I haven't had someone come to my house since Mr. McClane helped me bring the deer home a couple of months ago.

I walk to the door and brace myself. "Who is it?" I call out.

"Just me, Darci." My shoulders sag. It's Mr. McClane. I unlock the door and swing it open.

"Come inside, Mr. McClane." I step back holding the door wide. "What brings you here today?"

Stomping his feet, he enters. "Well, you know how my wife is. She worries about everything. This snow has her thinking you're up here freezing to death all alone." He smiles lightly at me. The thought that someone remembered me floods me with warmth.

"I know. I wish I could have made the trek yesterday, but I sprained my ankle a few days back when I went out for a walk in the snow. Didn't see a hidden rock." I don't know why I tell the lie. I feel a bit uneasy about his sudden appearance. His face looks concerned. I have a feeling he wants to ask more but doesn't.

"I hope it's not too bad. Not good to be hurt and alone out here nowadays." He glances over my shoulder into the house and then turns his gaze back to me.

"Very true, but I'm feeling a lot better now. I was getting ready to go out for a walk." I'm a terrible liar. My husband always said you could read my face like a book. A tight feeling balls up in my stomach at the memory.

"I suppose that's good then." He pauses. "You should be careful though. I've been hearing rumors of a predator roaming the woods. Getting a little too close and friendly with some of the other farmers' livestock. I also brought you some more eggs. Now," he holds up a hand, "before you put up a fight about it if I return with these eggs, I'll be the one getting in trouble." He gives me a knowing look and I can't help my smile. I catch a brief glimmer of a white in his eyes I hadn't noticed before. Odd.

"Okay. I owe you a loaf of bread though once I'm back to normal." I take the basket of eggs from his hands and go back into the kitchen. He doesn't follow me, and I'm glad because I don't know how I will explain the words on my door. After transferring the eggs to the bowl on my counter, I return the empty basket to him. "Thank you for the eggs."

He takes it and shrugs. "Just being neighborly. Remember what I said, okay?" Mr. McClane is normally a man of few words. He is quiet and gentle and more comfortable in nature and around his cows than he is in my presence, yet he's spoken more to me now than he did when we spent days in the woods hunting deer this fall. Another odd occurrence. He nods his head at me and turns to go out the door. I watch him go down the steps and head over to his horse. I stay there in the doorway watching as he rides down the hill and back to his farm.

I snatch my cloak off the stand by the door and slip my feet into my boots. My ankle is still tender, but bearable. I don't plan on going all the way into the woods, but I have to explore a little bit. Meiora hasn't come back yet. It disappeared when the last message came through. I have come to rely on it quite a bit when it comes to companionship; its absence makes my heart ache.

My mind circles back to what Mr. McClane said about the animal coming through the woods. It could be wolves. We've had them in the area before, and I remember seeing paw prints stalking the deer when I walked through the forest not long ago. The cold may have drawn them out in their search for food. My mind drifts to the dark void I encountered—-a creature in its own right, an evil awoken from a deep slumber. Could it be the danger in the woods he speaks of?

I walk down the hillside, slowly making my way to the tree line. My heart beats a little faster, and memories flash in my mind of my encounters here before. My memories from a few days ago are bleeding into other, darker ones. The ones drenched in blood and death and loss. I'm not sure I can separate them as easily anymore.

I stop several feet from the start of the first trees. My stomach clenches. I remind myself to breathe. Scanning the trees for any signs of shadows more alive than others, I secretly hope I'll catch a glimpse of someone or something.

"Meiora?" I whisper. I know I don't need to call loudly. It can hear me if it is somewhere nearby. However, it could be held up from coming to me by another more powerful force. I don't want to think about it. I'd rather not lose another friend.

I stand there for several minutes waiting. I'm not exactly sure of what I'm looking for or hoping to find, but there is something in the woods. This is certain. Nothing happens though. Nature is awake and active, with birds and squirrels flitting about and darting around. No deadly silence or ominous noises come my way.

After a few more minutes, when I'm about to turn around, I feel a prickling on the back of my neck. I used to feel this when I first started seeing the shadows in my vision. The feeling of being watched.

Adrian

A DOOR CLICKS SHUT behind me making me jump. I know exactly who came into the room before they even speak.

"What are you doing?" Marcus sounds only slightly annoyed at me for acting strange.

I pivot and attempt to keep my back to the writing on the wall. I haven't shown Marcus it yet. I know he'll overreact when he sees it.

I clear my throat. "What do you need, Marcus?" He narrows his eyes at me.

"Adrian, I know you well enough to know something is bothering you. Your presence reeks of worry. Also, it's dinner; and we had plans. At least we did when I checked with you yesterday. But I guess something more important came along."

I forgot. It shows how distracted I've been lately. I casually walk to the windows facing the forest. I do my best to not draw attention to the words. I've checked for a response every day, multiple times a day, hoping I would receive one. Still, nothing appears on the wall.

"I hadn't forgotten. I've been a bit busy." Busy losing my mind. It's a terrible excuse. Marcus is my commander. He knows my schedule as well as I do.

"You've been—busy?" Marcus says it like he doesn't believe me. He is too perceptive for his own good.

"Yes. I have." I swallow and force myself to gaze out the window again. Dusk is beginning to fall across the forest. The tree line is covered in snow; the sky is a deeper shade of gray than earlier in the day.

"You want to know how many times I've walked in on you staring and lost to the world? Doesn't seem like you've been very busy. What are you looking for?"

My heart skips a beat when I realize I haven't covered the words on the wall with the tapestry. I'd placed the tapestry there after the words appeared and usually, I remember to keep it covered when people come, but I had been too deep in thought just now. Distracted. It takes everything in me not to look at the words.

"Well, I've had a lot on my mind." I swallow.

Marcus stares at me. He doesn't believe me. There isn't much I can do about it at this point.

"Where were we going for dinner tonight?" I attempt to change the subject as I face my friend. My attempts at nonchalance fall short. As soon as the words leave my mouth, I catch sight of shadows in the corner of my eye near the window. Just like I had seen three days ago and had been seeing ever since. I want to look toward it. Instead, I keep my eyes focused on Marcus. The shadow in the corner of my eye pulses and moves. It's alive. Something or someone is here. Fear spikes momentarily in my chest because I know what this creature is.

Marcus raises a brow and then flicks his gaze toward the wall I had been facing when he walked in. I know the moment my friend's brain registers what is out of place because his eyes widen briefly. My efforts to intercept him fail. Marcus strides to the wall and stops himself in front of it. I can do nothing other than take up the space beside him and cross my arms.

"Adrian? What is this?" The words are slow and halting.

"Just words." As if stating the obvious helps the situation. My fear of having a guard placed on constant surveillance near me trumps reason and makes my words sound foolish.

"Why do you have random words carved into the wood of your ancestor's five-hundred-year-old house?"

When you put it like that, it does sound a bit crazy.

"And don't try to say you don't know. That is your handwriting." He pointed at the first words and the other phrases I had carved. "But this word isn't." He pointed at the one word belonging to someone else. *Hello.*

I drop my arms to my side in defeat. "I honestly don't know. I think something has been living in my house with me."

"Living. In your house. With you."

"Yes, I...I see them. Well, not them. I see shadows moving around and sometimes I hear footsteps. The shadows kept moving around the room, and I don't know. I thought maybe I was losing my mind a bit. So, I decided to say hello first. I feel magic. It is strong."

"Why on earth did you carve it into the wood? And you called it Shadow? Really creative there." He smirks.

"Thanks." I roll my eyes. "I don't know. I had a gut feeling. I didn't expect..." I wave my hand toward the wall.

"A response? Yeah, it's a little unexpected, to say the least. Some sort of phantom magic? You should have told me about it. I'm your friend and your commander. I need to be aware of breaches in our wards."

I shift away from the wall and walk back towards the window. "That's not all." I notice the widening of his eyes quickly turning to irritation in his reflection. "I have been having weird visions or something. I get this feeling something or someone is...waking up. I saw a person in the woods."

I pause and face my friend leaning a hip against the window sill. He says nothing and waits for me to continue. "I followed her one day, and she came across an avgrunn." Marcus whips his head towards me. I don't miss the terror splashing across his face for a moment or how the color drains slightly from his skin.

"Wait a second, you said *she*." It isn't a question.

"Yes. I saw a woman. I felt this pull to go walking through the forest one night, and it seemed like fate to find her. I pulled her away and ran back to get out of the forest. She was there, Marcus. I felt her hand in mine, and then she disappeared. She had a cryarsh following her. It seemed to help her when she fell. Like it belonged to her."

Marcus stares at me open-mouthed, unable to comment. The rest of the words spill out of me at this point.

"I thought maybe she was *the* shadow. She might be the one who had written on my wall in response. She wasn't clear when I saw her in the woods. I think she came from somewhere else?" I sigh. "My mistake was getting forceful with my questions, and now whoever was writing them has stopped."

Marcus looks ready to rip my head off when I feel my breath hitch. He moves to join me and looks out the window as well. "What is it?"

I barely hear him though. My mind must be deceiving me. My heart pounds. There she is. She is standing a stone's throw from the edge of the tree line watching the forest. I'm stunned to see her so close to my home.

"Adrian, what is it?" Marcus repeats, searching out the window and the trees for whatever I see.

"Can you not see her? She's right there! At the tree line!" I sound frantic, but I can't seem to control my response.

I move before I even think about it, ignoring Marcus' questions. I snatch my cloak off the hook by the door and tug it on as I step outside. It is cold but not uncomfortable, and the snow crunches under my feet as I hurry toward the trees. I should call out and confront her and tell her to get away from the forest. Nothing comes out of my mouth though. Only the sound of my boots on the snow reaches my ears. I halt several feet away from her. She didn't hear me coming. She should have. I wasn't trying to be quiet.

A shadow appears in the corner of my eye. I want to look toward it, but I can't tear my eyes away from her.

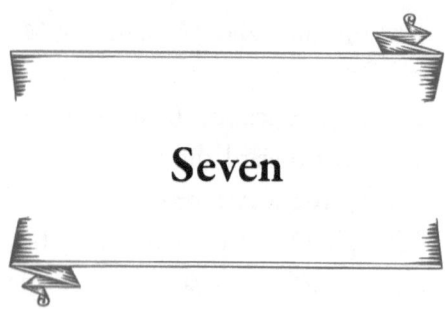

Seven

Darci

I know who it is before I even turn around. The feeling of him watching me, being near me, presses into my back. It's the man from the woods. If I turn around, he'll be there. When I saw him before, I needed to only think about getting to safety. I'm not sure I'm ready to encounter him again though. I'd feel better if Meiora was here, but it's not. Instead, I inhale; hold my breath, then exhale slowly as I turn around.

He stands completely still, staring at me with as much fear and wonder as I feel. The image of him isn't clear. It's fuzzy and shimmering. Shadows swirl around him and sparkle like the night sky. I wonder if I look strange to him. He almost seems translucent. If I reach out to touch him, will he even be there? Is he a ghost or the writer of my mysterious messages?

We stand there staring at each other for several moments. The spell is broken when he suddenly turns his head to look behind him. I don't know what he's looking at. He seems to say something or gesture to someone. I can't see anyone. A chill runs up my spine. The idea of other strangers lurking nearby bothers me. I am also starting to wonder if the shadows hiding him from me are Meiora. They seem to be alive, or they are being influenced by a wind I can't feel.

He turns back to face me, and I see his eyes flick over my shoulder behind me. I didn't think about the woods. I didn't think about what hides behind the line of trees. I swallow and shift my weight to turn. He takes several quick steps toward me, gesturing that I continue looking toward him. I see him say something, but no sound reaches me. This is becoming even more bizarre. I shake my head slightly and instinctively shift a foot backward.

Then, I hear something coming from the woods. Dread creeps along my spine, and I turn my head to see exactly what I was afraid would be there. Darkness trickles along the snowy floor in my direction. It is still in the confines of the forest, but I don't think it will stay there for long.

I don't hesitate and spin quickly to run back up the hillside to my house. It may not stay locked away in the trees; I can't stand here and let it touch me. Of course, in the process of trying to run up the hill, I slam into *him*. What happens next leaves me stunned and even more confused. The most intense pain surges through my body, and everything burns. It's like lightning strikes me, and I'm on fire. I am nothing but shadows and pain. I close my eyes to this torture. I can't tell if the darkness in the woods has seized me or not. When I think I'm going to break entirely, it stops. I open my eyes to the stranger no longer shrouded in darkness.

He steadies me with his hands on my upper arms. I look up into his eyes, seeing shock painted there. Then, he lets go of me and turns quickly, grabbing one of my hands in the process. It's deja vu. We've been here before, but not *here*. I'm gasping in part from the pain and in part from the shock. It is getting dark outside and nothing around me looks like my hillside with my home. There is a house he pulls me toward, but it isn't mine. I struggle to keep pace with his long legs. My mind races, and it takes me a minute to see someone else coming towards us. Fear bursts in my chest; there may be other dangers here besides the evil in the woods.

He wastes no time as he hands me off to the other man. "Go with him." To him, "Get her out of here." He speaks with authority, and the other man obeys. A commander speaking to a soldier.

I'm still stunned at the sound of his voice. He is real. This is real. His friend or companion doesn't wait for my cooperation. He grabs ahold of my arms. Reflexively, I start to fight. I pull back away from him, yanking my wrist free of his grip. He reaches out faster than I thought possible though and grips my forearm so tightly I'm certain it's going to bruise. This man towers over me and his piercing blue eyes flash with anger. His light brown skin is marked by pale scars on his wrists and hands with a single scar crossing his right temple. This is a warrior, and he towers over me, standing at least a couple of inches taller than his leader.

"Let me go!" I know I sound ridiculous. Danger comes for me from the shadows, and they are trying to protect me. I fight nevertheless. The stranger who saved me before handed me off to someone and disappeared behind me to confront whatever was back there. I'm about to turn around and run when I feel a sharp pain slide up my arm where this man holds me tightly and the most intense headache explodes behind my eyes. Everything goes dark as my body goes limp. I think I've been abducted.

Adrian

"WHAT DID YOU DO?!" I had been running towards the woods to stop the darkness in its path. It hadn't taken much to discourage it this time–a flash of blue magic exploded along the perimeter, and I watched it slither away back to where it belonged. When I turn around though, Marcus is holding the woman's limp body in his arms with wide eyes. She looks tiny in his grasp; the hood of her black cloak has fallen back revealing long, dark brown hair and pale skin.

"I had to get her to stop. She was about to run towards the woods like a idiot."

I jog up the hill quickly and gently take her from his grasp. A spark of magic passes from her to me when we make contact. My magic unintentionally swells from my hands in response. She does have power, even if it's only a small kernel.

"So, you knocked her out?!" My voice is louder than I intend it to be. I need to control myself. One minute she was a shadowy phantom on the edge of the woods; the next moment she was in my arms. When I spoke to her, I knew she didn't hear me. How did she bridge the plane between us? "We can't stand out here. Let's get her inside."

"What do you want me to tell the servants? It's going to be hard to hide a whole *person*." Marcus jogs to catch up to me.

"I don't know. Clear the path for me to get her to the study. I'll explain everything to them later."

Marcus runs up ahead of me. I look down into her face. She is thin but strong, a woman close to my age. She knows something about surviving. But why does she keep showing up here? Her pale skin is marked by light scratches and the remnants of a bruise. She probably acquired them a few days ago when I first encountered her in the woods. Her hair is pulled half up and half down with a few strands lying across her face. Her eyes are green. At least I think that's the color I saw when she ran straight into me and looked up with equal parts terror and awe.

Something stirs inside me when I look at her. She's beautiful, and my magic vibrates when my skin touches hers. I know her. A sliver of my soul recognizes hers.

I'm coming up the back steps to enter the house when Marcus opens the door. "All's clear. I made sure the servants got to work preparing dinner here since we obviously aren't going to the pub tonight." He raises an eyebrow at me as I walk in, careful to not bang her head into the doorframe. "Is she who you keep looking for out the window? Is she the woman you saw in the woods the other day?"

I gently lay her down on the cushioned bench against the back wall and step back. I'm silent for a moment, lost in my thoughts. Then, instead of answering my friend's questions, I ask one instead. "What did you see now?"

Marcus' body stills, but he doesn't look away. "Do you want me to be honest?" I nod before he continues. "Because if I'm being honest, I thought you'd completely lost your mind. I didn't see anything until there was a woman pressed against you and you were holding her arms. Everything was black, and then she was there."

Neither of us speak for a moment. Then I whisper, "She's the one I saw, and I think she's the shadow I've been seeing in my house." I pause noticing the other shadow in the corner of my eye still there.

Marcus stares at me. "She doesn't look like a shadow now." We both look at her, neither of us saying a word.

"I think you should leave the room. If she wakes up with you in here—" I pause.

"She might panic thinking we kidnapped her?" Marcus finishes for me. Eyebrows raised, he shrugs and walks out the door closing it behind him.

I observe her for a few more minutes before she begins to stir. Stepping away from the bench, I move to the window to at least give her the chance to get her bearings first without seeing a stranger staring at her. Gazing out at the woods I don't notice the shadow in my vision anymore. Darkness coats the room instead.

Darci

MY HEAD POUNDS. IT smells different here. I keep my eyes closed for a minute trying to reconcile the previous events. Two men. Darkness. Pain. Even now, my body aches with the residual effects of whatever I experienced. I feel the firmness of wood beneath me and hear the crackling of a fire. The skin on my arm tingles and burns, reminding me of where the other man had gripped me.

I blink my eyes open and realize I haven't been dreaming. Adrenaline floods my veins, and my weary body fights to muster up the energy to escape. They took me. *He* took me. This is not good.

I sit up faster than I should and try to jump to my feet, my ankle protesting—all of me protesting—-a lot. My knees give a little, and black dots swell in my vision. When I think I might fall, I'm enveloped in warm black velvet. The room dims, and I know this feeling. My voice cracks, "Meiora."

It is all around me, comforting and safe. It's then I realize I'm not the only person in this room. At the sound of my voice, the man whirls around and then pauses, shocked. He looks carefully at me and at the shadows now winding their way down my arms to my fingers, pooling at my feet and rubbing against my legs like a cat.

"Impossible." He whispers.

His eyes drift upward from Meiora to meet my gaze. I feel safe with my shadows though. Then, he says two words that make my heart stop and my stomach tighten.

"Hello, Shadow."

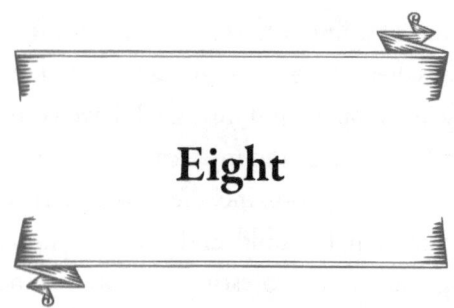

Eight

"**W**hat did you call me?" My voice sounds weak, and I hate it. I don't take my eyes off him, but I need to start looking for a way out of this house. I need to get back home.

"You're the shadow that's been here the past few months, aren't you?" His eyes spark with amusement.

"I don't know what you are talking about. I haven't left my home to go anywhere nearly this extravagant in years." I take this moment to look around me. The room is large but still has a cozy feel. Its tall ceilings, with wood beams crossing above, are stunning. The stone fireplace has a giant beam of black wood as a mantel and is carved with strange designs and creatures. Is that a dragon or a snake across the front?

"For the past few months, I have heard footsteps and seen a shadow moving around these rooms. I thought I was being haunted, but something told me to write a greeting to whoever my intruder happened to be." As he spoke, he walked towards a wall opposite the window he had been standing at. A tapestry woven with red and violet strands has been intentionally pulled to the side. He points to something on the wall I can't quite decipher because the only light in the room is provided for by the fire and a couple of flickering wall sconces.

He waits, and I don't know if he expects me to move closer. I'm not taking any chances.

I lock eyes with him and wait. I have no plans to move anywhere near him. His movement across the room gave me a chance to spot a door leading outside, and no one is blocking my exit now. Surely Meiora will scare him enough to keep him from interfering, but he notices my eyes shifting and casually walks to stand in my path.

"You can't go out there. It isn't safe, and you don't seem to know where you are."

"Well, how do I know I am safe here?" I cross my arms. Meiora slides away from me across the floor to the wall. I drop my arms and instinctively feel naked without it.

"How did you tame a cryarsh?"

"A what?" I've managed to follow Meiora to the wall. I plan on keeping my back to the wall and my eyes on him, but I notice Meiora hovering around something. Words...etched into wood. Everything fades around me as I stare dumbfounded at them. *Hello, Shadow. Why are you in my house?* He's talking again, but I hear only muffled sounds. His words are on the wood, but my response of hello is also there. I've been talking to this stranger. I jump when I realize he has walked across the space and is standing shoulder-to-shoulder with me. I step to the side away from him, gaining space again.

"It was you? That's—that's impossible." I can't wrap my mind around this. Impossible is exactly the appropriate response to this situation. He nods knowingly.

"My name is Adrian. I thought you were a ghost. I didn't realize you were real."

I stare at him without speaking. Then, Meiora nudges me, and I know it is annoyed by my reticence. He says "ghost" like it is a perfectly sane response to everything happening.

"Darci. My name is Darci." I say softly.

He smiles but only one corner of his mouth turns up. "What did you call it? The cryarsh I mean," he clarifies.

"I have no idea what you are talking about. What *is* a cryarsh?"

He gestures behind me toward Meiora. "*That* is a cryarsh. It's a dark daemon. They usually leave everyone alone for the most part, but they can kill easily if provoked." He tilts his head as he notices the confusion no doubt evident on my face. "They are the lords of shadows and a creation of the God of Death himself. I've never heard of one allowing itself to be captured or tamed." Meiora responds by covering my shoulders like a blanket and cascading down my back like I belong to it more than it belongs to me. The thought unsettles me. A slight tingling sensation in my skin sparks to life at the mention of the God of Death. I don't want to know more about him.

"I, uh, I didn't know. I didn't know what it was, I mean. I've never heard of a cryarsh." I'm rambling now. I force my mouth to close so I don't look any more foolish than I already do.

"You didn't know." He says slowly thinking. "What do you call it?"

"I call it Meiora. It has saved me more than once if I'm honest. One of those times was the day you were there. I've had it as my companion every day for over two months. Every day, at least, until I got the last message from you."

"Meiora, or at least I'm pretty sure it's the cryarsh I've been seeing, has been present with me for the past few days."

"It knew you were there. It made me aware of the messages being sent. It's like it wanted me to get here." I pause, "Um..where exactly is here?" I survey the room we are in and pause a moment on the window facing the woods I had run from.

Adrian watches me carefully. I can tell he is conflicted about how much he should share with me. But he takes a deep breath. "You are in Myzonia."

I have never heard of this place. "How did I get here? I mean, I was standing outside my home one moment, and the next I ran into you. I thought I was running towards my house." My mind races through the past events. It occurs to me he isn't a fuzzy picture anymore. He is crystal clear. Before, it was like looking through fog.

"You somehow crossed the border into our world." He speaks slowly, uncertainly, like he's speaking to a frightened animal and doesn't want me to bolt.

"I didn't see any border. I wasn't far from my house." My mind stutters when I realize he mentioned *world* as if there is more than one.

"I don't know exactly what happened, but I have a feeling you're not even from this realm."

At this, I hold my hand up forcing him to stop. I can't digest any more information. I'm starting to get the feeling I'm trapped here. It's dark outside. It wasn't dark before when I had walked to the tree line.

He ignores my forced pause, "I know you must be confused, but I can't let you leave while it's dark. Especially if you don't even know where you are. You need to stay here. At least until the sun comes up."

I'm about to protest, but we're interrupted by a knock at the door. The doorknob starts to turn. I move towards the bench again trying to put as much distance between the door and myself. Another man walks into the room and stops abruptly. The one Adrian had passed me off to when I was running from the darkness in the woods. The one who knocked me out somehow.

He looks at Adrian and then back at me. "You're awake." He turns to Adrian, "The servants are saying the food is ready. I told them to bring it in here." The look he gives Adrian makes me think he wants to keep me confined to one room in this house—preferably a dungeon. He is suspicious of me.

Meiora, who was still wrapped around me when he entered, slips away towards the back wall and seems to melt into the wood. The new man notices it.

"Was that cryarsh touching her?"

Adrian responds quickly. "Yes. Apparently, she has become friends with it. Marcus, this is Darci. Darci, Marcus."

"Darci," Marcus says only my name. He looks at Adrian. I almost missed it, but I'm pretty sure Adrian shook his head very subtly.

I nod in greeting and can't help but wonder why Meiora left.

Marcus smiles like he's putting on a show to look friendly. "Well, Darci, we have food coming. I hope you don't mind if we eat because I'm starving." He walks over to a small table and pulls out two chairs sitting down unceremoniously into one. Shortly after, another knock on the door precedes dinner; carried in by three servants. If they are surprised to see me, they don't show it. They don't even look my way, though their movements are stiff. They place the food on a small buffet next to the table and walk out as quickly as they come in. Neither Adrian nor Marcus say anything to them, not even thank you.

Adrian walks to me slowly with his hands open like he wants to herd me towards the table. "You can have the other seat. I can sit in the armchair."

I feel nervous about this because I don't want to sit at all. Especially not next to this Marcus who somehow knocked me out earlier. I know they seem to think I'm better off sealed up here for the night, but my body aches to be home in familiar surroundings.

Warm, spicy smells waft in the air, and my stomach rudely announces to them how hungry I am. I step gingerly feeling every sore muscle and achy bone in my body and sit down stiffly in the chair. Adrian moves to get a plate for me, and I stare at my table companion with distrust. I'm still dressed in my cloak and boots. I realize I look ready to run for the door. My arm feels hot where Marcus grabbed it earlier. I loosen my cloak and gently pull it off; I'm about to set it on the back of my chair when Adrian sets a plate of food down and takes it from me.

"I'll set it on the hook by the door." It's like he knows what I'm nervous about without me saying a word. I nod and carefully roll up my sleeve to see a handprint branded on my skin. It's so cold it burns a little. When I touch it with my fingertips, it aches more. It reminds me of the icy hot letters carved into paint on my door.

"Marcus! What, in the name of Araina, did you do that for?" Adrian sounds angry, but Marcus is quick to defend himself.

"I did what I had to do. I may have used a little more than I should have, but she wasn't stopping." Magic. Magic had to cause this. Three months ago, I would have said it was impossible. Now, I can't deny something strange is going on, and I am trapped in the middle.

"You're saying he did this to me?" I direct my question to Adrian because for some reason he seems more trustworthy than Marcus. Granted, he has saved me twice from the dark creature in the woods.

Adrian sighs and then drops to one knee next to my chair. He holds his hand out palm up, and I slowly let him take my arm. I wince as he traces his fingers over it. "I can't explain everything right now. But yes, Marcus caused that when restraining you. I'm sorry."

He casts a disapproving look at his friend who simply shrugs. "I can help with this if you will let me. But it won't be completely better. It's too deep unfortunately."

I have no idea what he is talking about, but I nod my head, "Okay. Yes, go ahead."

He gently presses his hand over top of the imprint. It hurts, but I stay still. Warmth seems to pulse from his hand, and I get a tingly sensation in my arm. The same feeling you get when your arm has fallen asleep and you move it, and it hurts like needles along your skin.

I stare at where we touch. A soft violet light peeks out along the edges of his fingers. Then, the feeling is gone, and he lets go.

The handprint fades and no longer burns. It aches a little like an old bruise, but the improvement is incredible.

I move my eyes to meet his gaze, and he stays there staring at me. Marcus clears his throat and gestures to the plates.

"Shall we eat now?"

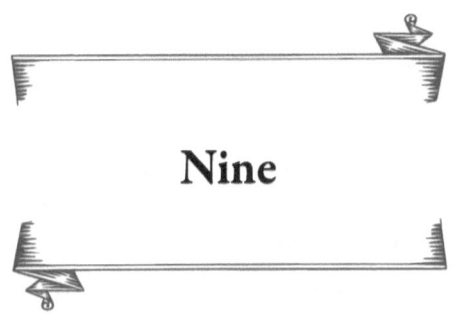

Nine

The meal is simple yet delicious. The chicken is perfectly seasoned with a flavor I don't recognize. Spices warm my belly, and I close my eyes sighing softly and basking in the satisfying first bite. I haven't had anything besides deer and eggs for so long. No matter what happens the rest of this night I am certain I can die a happy woman. I open my eyes to get another bite when I notice Adrian and Marcus staring at me.

Marcus' eyes glint with annoyance and Adrian looks perplexed. I'm not sure which it is. I feel my face redden and quickly look back down at my plate cutting into what looks like a root vegetable of some sort.

"Sorry," I mumble. "It's been a long time since I had something that tasted interesting." I don't look up while I continue to cut and take bites of the food. They both remain silent, and the only sound to continue for the next few minutes is the scraping of silverware on plates. I reach for the glass of water in front of me and take a quiet sip. The water is a little bitter. It tastes different from mine. Nowhere near as good as the food.

"What do you normally eat?" Adrian asks.

I'm not expecting the question, and I jerk slightly. "What?" My response is about as mundane as my brain at the moment. I feel a little foggy.

"You said you hadn't had anything that tasted interesting in a long time. What do you normally eat?" Adrian looks at me intently.

"I don't have these seasonings, whatever they are, and I can't afford salt. I mostly eat eggs from my neighbor's chickens and deer I've hunted. It's all plain and gets old rather fast."

"You don't eat the chickens?" Marcus questions.

"They're not my chickens." I deadpan, "Why would I eat something that doesn't belong to me?"

Marcus stares at me for a minute, then grunts in response before returning his attention to his plate. Adrian gives him a pointed look.

"I didn't realize you didn't have access to livestock of your own." Adrian studies me for a minute. I can see the calculations he's making in his mind. The realization I'm poor and hungry flashes through his eyes. Based on the beauty of this room and the servants at his disposal, he is neither of those things. I know there is no hiding it. I'm not emaciated, but I don't carry a lot of extra weight, and my clothes appear worn, bordering on threadbare.

Marcus examines me, his eyes trailing over me, cold and calculating. "Hard to see how you survive with so little meat in your diet."

"I live off the land entirely. There isn't much to buy from others, and besides, getting into town requires me to walk miles. Not worth it to be honest. I also don't want to have to care for another living thing other than me. So, I barter with the neighbors, and I manage." I don't know why I said all of that. I gave away too much information about my living situation. I cringe and turn back to my plate. I think the time in solitude is finally causing me to break. Before, I had nothing to say; but now everything feels different–dangerous even.

Marcus turns his attention back to Adrian. "We need to talk. Alone." Adrian tenses but nods and stands from his seat.

"Excuse us for a moment." He turns stiffly towards the door with Marcus following close behind. It shuts with a click, then silence. I wait for a moment before I hear the soft sound of metal sliding into place. I'm pretty sure they locked me in here. Or locked me out of the rest of the house. The door to the outside is accessible now. I wonder if that was intentional.

I stand and tiptoe carefully towards the door. I can hear faint murmuring, but they are speaking low enough that discerning words is impossible without pressing my ear to the seam. I'm not going to waste this opportunity on eavesdropping. I look for Meiora. It's tucked into the corner of the room. I nod my head in the direction of the outside door. Knowing what I want without explanation, it glides across the floor quickly and cloaks me as I walk toward my potential escape. I reach for the knob and pause. I don't know if this is actually a good idea. It's dark outside now. The creature was out there not long ago, and I don't think I'll be able to escape it if it finds me again. If Adrian is being truthful, I'm also not in my own world now, and I have no clue how to get back to mine.

I listen for any sounds indicating the two men are returning. Only the heavy weight of solitude and the crackling fire acknowledge me. My heart beats faster. What if I can't get back home?

I reach to pull my hood up when my hand meets with nothing. In my haste to leave, I forgot to grab my cloak. Maybe I can leave it. I should try. I start to grab the doorknob again when Meiora tightens around me painfully and then flees to the corner again. It hurt enough to knock the breath out of me. I turn to summon it back when I hear the metal sliding back again. I can't get back to my chair, but I'm only a few feet away from the wall with the carved words. I turn quickly to stand in front of the messages and try to look like I wasn't about to make a run for the dark woods, where dark creatures lurk.

The door swings open, and Marcus halts in the opening, noticing I'm not at the table with the food. He is tense, and his distrust of me radiates from him like heat. The feeling is mutual. Adrian isn't with him. With only him standing there, I take a closer look at his features. His skin is a light brown, fairer than Adrian's, and his eyes are a deep blue. His brown hair is braided and held back with a leather strap, reaching down to his shoulders. He is taller than Adrian, which is saying something; and he carries himself like a soldier. Or maybe a commander. He holds authority but obviously submits to Adrian. He scowls...a lot.

"What are you doing?" He definitely doesn't like me.

I take a deep breath to steady my nerves. "Nothing. Just..." *Come on...think of something.* "Just trying to figure out what all of this means."

He observes me critically. His eyes flick toward my chair and then to my cloak by the door. Probably a good thing I hadn't grabbed it now.

"Adrian had business to attend to. You can stay the night; and in the morning, we'll take you home. The couch is comfortable enough. There are plenty of blankets, and you're not tall." I can almost taste the disdain he has for me on my tongue. Are they going to allow me to sleep in a room with a door to the outside so easy to access?

He reads my mind, "The outside doors are secured with wards that will trigger should they be opened without the proper..." He hesitates like he doesn't quite know which word to use for me. "The proper means."

"So, you don't trust me to be in any other room in this house? Only this room?" I reply cooly. I wouldn't trust a stranger in my home either, but we're not discussing my home.

He crosses his arms. "If it were up to me, you wouldn't be here at all. I would much rather he left you outside or in your own world. But this isn't my house. Not my call."

"I didn't ask to be here either, you know. I don't even know where *here* is." I cross my arms in a mirror to his stance.

Marcus scowls, "Well, I guess we'll have to make due. But you can't stay here. You have to leave and not come back. He can't have you here."

Now I'm confused. "What do you mean? We've only just met."

Marcus doesn't speak. His gaze makes me feel vulnerable and alone. Like he has secrets I will never be privy to. I want to go back to my lonely existence before I found a hole in the world bleeding out into the woods. We remain in this stand off for a few minutes, neither of us engaging the other.

Finally, he sighs, stomps towards the door, and leaves. I hear the lock click again.

I look around the room at the furniture and blankets. This can't be too awful, right? I walk over towards the sofa. It's green velvet with black woodwork. More serpents and elongated dragons are carved into the wood. I shudder.

I suddenly feel bone tired as the high from the adrenaline wanes. I grab a blanket out of a basket next to the sofa and lay down draping the blanket over me. Meiora returns from the corners and adds itself on top. I don't want to sleep, but before I can stop myself, I start to drift away to the sounds of fire and scratching.

SILENCE. COMPLETE AND utter silence. I don't know where they are. I'm standing in the middle of a dark forest. Someone watches me from the shadows. I try to call out, to ask who is there, but when I open my mouth, nothing comes out. The vacuum of sound around me is deepening. I feel my ears start to pop and my head hurts. This is wrong.

They are still watching me. I can't see them, but I feel them. I begin to panic. Where did my boys go? Where is my husband? I spin around searching the trees, the shadows, anywhere for a sign of them. My feet are bare and aching. I look down and see blood pooling out from underneath my soles. Seeing the blood triggers my brain to feel the pain that should be there and a burst of it slices through my body. I collapse to the ground, crying out silently. I look up again to where I think someone is standing.

They stand a few feet from me. Black and soulless eyes pierce into my very center. I feel something inside of me pull back and retreat. Pure terror swells within and I try to scramble away. They come closer, and as they do, I become transfixed. My mouth is open in silent screams no one will hear. No one will know. I'll be lost forever, and my boys will be gone, and I'll be nothing. I look up into their eyes and see only shadows pouring into me.

Someone is shaking my arm and saying my name urgently. I jolt awake to the sound of my screams and the realization I'm not home. My brain switches to fight mode, and I start to jerk and kick, doing anything I can to escape my captor.

"Darci! Darci, stop! You're okay. You're safe!" I blink my eyes a few times and look up into coal black eyes full of concern. Adrian.

"It's fine, Darci. You're safe." He is holding my face between his hands and forcing my eyes to focus on his. My racing heart slows slightly, and I take a shuddering breath closing my eyes.

When I open them, I realize he's not the only one standing in the doorway to the room. Marcus is there and other eyes peek out around him into the room. Servants. I've woken the whole household.

My face reddens, and I turn my eyes back to Adrian where he still holds my face so gently, I feel like a small child. I pull back enough to make his hands fall away.

"I'm sorry. I...I had a nightmare." I pull the blanket up tighter around me though I'm hot and sweaty from fighting in my sleep. Meiora slithers across the top of the sofa and curls up around my feet making itself small. Adrian looks towards it and appears baffled at the display of affection.

"Do you want to talk about it?"

I shake my head quickly. I glance again at Marcus. Adrian follows my eyes and tilts his head towards the door suggesting Marcus leave with the servants. Marcus turns around reluctantly, shaking his head and herding them away.

Before they disperse entirely, Adrian calls out, "Gennet, will you bring a warm drink for her, please?"

I see the stiffness in Marcus at the request. I can tell he doesn't want any of them around me. I'm not sure whether he's protecting Adrian from me or me from the rest of them.

"I don't need anything, really." Adrian looks at me and lightly brushes his fingers across my head.

"You feel a little feverish. Maybe the transition here was harder on your body than we initially suspected. Something warm to drink will help you settle."

"What time is it?" I ask this like I knew what time it was earlier when I fell asleep. The only indication time has passed by swiftly is the dying fire in the hearth.

"It's just after midnight." He's kneeling next to the sofa and still observing me, waiting for some indication I will open up about what I dreamt.

"You don't have to stay with me. I'm okay." I look pointedly at Meiora to show I'm not alone.

"Your screams were...chilling to say the least. It must have been an awful dream." I'm not taking the bait though. I stay silent this time as he stares at me. "I can stay here with you if you'd like. If you don't want to be alone."

It's like he sees straight into my mind. He sees my fears and loneliness, but I'm more afraid of him and all the questions I have surrounding this whole situation.

"No, I don't think it's a good idea." He looks a little disappointed which I find odd. We don't know each other. We've never met. Why would he want me to still be here? Unless he's as curious as I am about this strange connection we seem to have forged across...worlds.

He stands and walks over to the fire picking up a poker to stoke the flames back to life. He grabs another log from next to the fireplace and carefully sets it on the weak flames. Within a couple of minutes, it is warm and vibrant again. Someone knocks at the door and proceeds to enter cautiously. She's a lovely woman. Short and round and grandmotherly. Her skin is so similar to Adrian's, I wonder if they are related. Hers is maybe a shade darker, but both possess vibrant dark brown eyes. Pieces of gray hair peek out from under a nightcap. She is cautious but not unfriendly.

"Thank you, Gennet." He takes a steaming mug of something from her hands and carries it to me. Holding it out, he waits as I reluctantly take the mug from his hands and bring it to my nose to sniff. It smells like chocolate. I take a tentative sip, well aware Gennet hasn't left yet. My belly warms instantly, and my mouth is flooded with the deepest, richest dark chocolate drink I've ever tasted. It's luxury in liquid form. I would never experience or afford it at home.

I look at the woman and smile. "Thank you." I say softly, "It's delicious." She smiles in return and then walks out the door. If I'm not mistaken, a knowing glint sparks in her eye as she leaves.

I take another sip and look up at Adrian. "You're hovering, you know?" He shakes his head slightly like he forgot where he was.

"I'm not meaning to. There is so much I want to know about you. About where you come from and why you might be here."

"I don't think talking about it now would be very helpful. My life is quite boring, and I have no idea how or why I'm here. I simply want to go home when morning comes." I'm a little afraid he doesn't want to let me go. I'm not sure what to think about Marcus.

"I will do everything I can to get you back to your home. I promise." He seems so genuinely concerned for me and my welfare.

All I can think to say is okay. I finish my drink, and he takes the empty cup from me and walks to the door. He looks back one more time and then walks out the door and shuts it quietly. I hear the familiar slide of metal into place as the door locks.

I reposition myself and tuck the blanket up around me. It takes less time than I thought it would after my nightmare, but I feel the heaviness of sleep envelop me again. I close my eyes and let the darkness come.

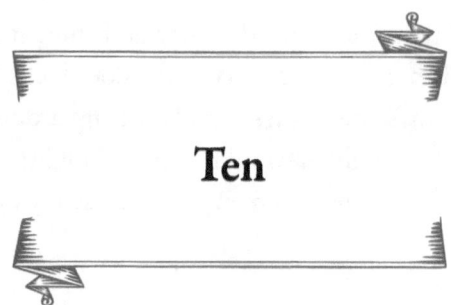

Ten

Searing pain rips into my body. I feel like I'm being torn apart from the inside. I'm dying; it's the only explanation. I think I was sleeping; and the sudden influx of pain disorients me. Behind my eyelids, I see flashes of light like stars, and my teeth clench so hard I feel my jaw pop. As quickly as the pain hits me, it recedes. My jaw loosens and tension seeps out of my body like sweat from pores.

I squint in the brightness of the morning sun. My arms and legs are heavy and aching, but I force myself to reach up and rub my eyes. As the fog of sleep lifts and my mind clears, I notice very quickly something has changed. I scramble back through the previous day making sure I could still pull up memories of yesterday and last night with Adrian and Marcus and time in his house. I can still see all the details of his ornate home in my mind.

This reassures me since I no longer see any of those details now with my eyes. Even the air smells different. I'm lying on the worn couch in my living room surrounded by dull walls and an empty fireplace with nothing but ashes from previous fires. The room is freezing, but it's my room—in my home.

Which makes no sense at all.

"Meiora? Meiora, where are you? I need you!" My words slur slightly like I've been hit on the head. Maybe Marcus had enough last night and decided to do something about my presence.

I sit up on the edge of the couch taking stock of the room. Nothing is out of place. No evidence shows someone has been in here with me. The pain waking me up is familiar when I think about it. It reminds me of the sharp pain I felt when I ran into Adrian last night and ended up in his backyard. But I wasn't moving in my sleep. So how did I end up back home?

I know I should be relieved, but a part of me feels more concerned about being transported against my will at any moment. I also didn't get the chance to ask any questions or find out any answers. I lean forward resting my elbows on my knees and cover my face with my hands. I know without looking Meiora is gone too. I don't feel its presence. I'm alone. Again.

Adrian

SHE'S GONE. WHEN I arrived outside the door to my study where Darci had slept the night before and knocked, she didn't respond. I even opened the door quietly thinking she might still be asleep. Instead, when I stepped into the room, the study was empty. Absolutely no sign of where she went either.

I pace at the window staring intently at the tree line. I don't know if she left or slipped out in the night, but I can't believe she's actually gone.

Then, I notice her cloak. It rests on the hook by the door where I placed it last night. Why would she leave without it? If she is poor or at least doesn't have extra money to spend on clothes and such, why would she risk running away without it?

I stand here frozen in the room staring at the couch, frowning and thinking. Marcus bumps into me on his way into the room, looking up from the parchment he's reading.

"Wha..wait...where is she?" Marcus' voice pitches upward. Everything about his body language declares how much he doesn't like this whole situation. Darci worries him, and her presence, and lack thereof, pose a dilemma.

"I don't know. She wasn't here when I got here."

"That doesn't make sense. Why aren't we hunting her down in the woods? She couldn't have gotten far."

"Her cloak is still here, Marcus. It's like she completely vanished." My gaze shifts towards the words etched into the wall. *What if...* I stop myself. This is impossible.

I walk over and trace the letters. Marcus says something, but I can't hear anything over the humming building up inside my head. I move to a desk and pull a dagger out of a secret compartment hidden on the underside.

"What are you doing, Adrian?" Marcus steps up next to me now.

I don't answer though; I start to carve into the wood, slowly and deliberately, right beneath the last line. Three words. *Are you home?*

Marcus protests, "It's not possible. There's no way she was able to transport back without assistance. And why? If she did, she must know more than she was letting on. I knew we should have taken her to Rizyrk interrogate her properly."

Ignoring my friend, I stare intently at the words willing new ones to appear. A response. Anything. But nothing happens. Finally, I turn around to grab her cloak off the chair. The faint smell of berries and forest linger on it. It smells like her. Holding her in my arms last night, I remember her scent so fervently. There is something else there beneath the surface, but I can't place it.

Marcus' voice is louder than he intends it to be. "You can't possibly think I'm going to let you wander through the woods alone again, looking for danger? What if she's been sent here by *him*?"

I want to protest. It doesn't feel that way. *She* feels different. Magic and shadows. A sound at the door startles me out of my thoughts. Gennet watches us carefully. Marcus stops himself from further protests. The presence of the High Mother silences him.

"Gennet, what do you know? I can see it in your eyes." I wait and resist the urge to prod her incessantly.

"You are mistaken if you think she escaped out the door." The woman's voice is soft and tender as a summer breeze. When she speaks, you want to do whatever it is she tells you. She has that effect on everyone.

"Did she go back?"

Marcus lets out a derisive snort. "It's not possible, Adrian. She couldn't possibly have gone back without the token."

There are two ways to travel quickly between worlds here. A token one carries on their body but also requires you to know the ancient language of spells to activate it. Or another way involving runes and blood performed by a high priestess or high mother.

Gennet silences Marcus with her eyes alone. Then she turns her focus back to me. "She has gone back." The next words she speaks are to Marcus. "And she doesn't need the token."

Neither of us speak. We exchange a confused look. It can't be possible. Can it?

Locking eyes with Gennet again, I whisper, "I'm going to need you to tell me everything you know."

In the corner of my eye, I notice a shadow lingering.

Darci

I BUSY MYSELF WITH chores around my house. The fire burns happily, warming the house once again. I get ingredients together to make bread, warming my leaven by the fire. I do anything I can to keep myself occupied—hands working flour and water and leaven together into a ball of malleable dough. I try to think about all the chores to be done around here. Maybe I can chop more firewood. My ankle is still sore, especially after last night, but it isn't terrible.

It's all pointless really. I can't help it. My mind replays everything. The transition to his house and back. Was it a completely different realm or simply a different location in this world? I'm getting a headache, and the temperature outside drops even more. Clouds gather, and I dread the next snowstorm coming for us.

The room across the kitchen with the closed-door calls to me. Their room; their refuge. It waits for me to confront the memory of them. Words mar the door, reminding me the world is more complex than I thought it was. They stir up dread for the coming night. I wish I understood what all of this means. But a part of me doesn't want to know.

As I place the dough into my pot to bake by the fire, I hear the familiar scratching on the door. I cover the pot with its lid and set it on the stones next to the hearth. Taking a deep breath, I face the door.

There, scraped into the paint, are three words. *Are you home?*

I walk closer to the words and trace my fingers over the marks. Still freezing cold. I feel a vibration coming through the door. I place my palm flat against the wood and my heart speeds up automatically. The call grows stronger; the urge to open the door builds within my soul. I don't want any of this. I don't want mysteries. I don't want magic. I don't want death and suffering. I don't want to be alone.

The last thought startles me. I have grown so used to my life of solitude it wasn't until Meiora showed up that I realized I miss companionship and belonging. If I'm being truly honest, I might even have enjoyed having other humans to eat with last night, despite one of those humans barely tolerating me. I shared a meal in mostly silence with them, but it was more than I had had as far as companionship goes in a long time. I imagine I have spent all my life on the outskirts. Unwanted and feared. Forgotten and misplaced. Too much for most and not enough for others. Grief speaks over rational thoughts now, and I know it. But sometimes, grief is too difficult to push away.

I wonder if I should write back. If I do, will I find a place to belong alongside another person? I know the words have to be coming from Adrian. We figured this much out last night, and deep in my gut, a piece of my soul recognizes him. I long for human contact and to speak with someone who can speak in return. But the pull of this door—it is too strong, and I don't need to remember the bloodshed to know only pain and sorrow waits on the other side.

I step back and leave the question unanswered.

The day proceeds as usual without any more words. It is late afternoon when I decide to chop some more firewood. The sky has turned a deep gray, and big white flakes of snow are falling now. It won't be long before another few inches coat the ground and the frigid air bites even harder.

I reach for my cloak by the front door and pause. It's not here. I had it last night. But... I sigh. I had it at Adrian's and I took it off when we ate.

I don't remember grabbing it when I went to sleep. My best guess is the cloak didn't come with me when I came back home somehow. I close my eyes and rub my forehead. I don't have another cloak to wear. Not one meant for this sort of weather at least. I don't have a choice though. I grab the thin gray cloak I use in the spring and fall months. It won't help much, but I guess it's better than nothing.

Thirty minutes in the cold and snow has me shivering even with the work of chopping wood. I take what I can inside and leave the rest for later. Or for tomorrow. My arms are full and starting to ache as I shuffle into the living room going towards the fireplace. I set down the wood log by log. Dusting my hands off on my pants, I turn and feel the heaviness of another presence in the room with me. The hair on the back of my neck stands up and my fingertips tingle with fear. My eyes slowly scan the room and stop on the bedroom door.

Every fear in my body rushes to the surface of my skin. Ice slides down my spine, and I stop breathing. *The* door is open. Not all the way. Only a crack letting in nothing but shadows and dark. Nausea sweeps through me at the sight. For the longest moment, I don't think I can move.

My adrenaline kicks in, however, and I surge forward grasping the doorknob and slamming the door shut. The door is blank with no sign of the words anywhere on the old paint. I'm transfixed, and I can't look away until I hear the soft tread of footsteps behind me. I whirl around and find rich brown eyes–so dark they're almost black–drinking me in.

"Hello, Darci."

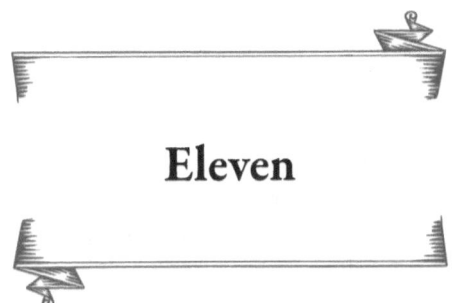

Eleven

"Adrian." My voice comes out breathy. Am I awake or is this another dream? He stands in front of me unimpeded. No shadows or mist obscuring him from my sight.

"I'm sorry I came here. I had an idea of where you might live from when I helped you the last time. I had some help getting here. But I thought you might want this." He holds out my cloak. "It's freezing here, and you look like you could use this."

A chill grows in the pit of my belly. This is wrong. I don't know if I should be afraid or if the sliver of relief I feel at the sight of him is trustworthy.

"How did you get here?" I step sideways away from the bedroom door.

"I don't think I can explain it. I'm not sure you would believe me. It took some unusual methods to accomplish." He's still holding my cloak, and I still can't step toward him to take it. He's closer to the fire, and the cold seeping deep into my bones makes me want to be brave enough to step closer to it. I suppose the longing is written plainly on my face because Adrian stretches his hand to me holding the cloak out as an offering.

"Please take this." He takes two smooth steps farther from the hearth. An invitation.

I carefully approach him and take the cloak making sure I don't touch any part of him in the process. I never drop eye contact until

I have the cloak in my hands and I'm able to step over to the fire, feeling the heat penetrate my clothes and skin.

"Thank you?"

He smiles softly. "You're welcome. You didn't respond to me. Did you not get my message?" I see his eyes search the walls for anything similar to the words in his home. He won't find them, all of it is gone.

"I did. This is all a bit much. I thought I'd pretend none of it happened." I feel a little embarrassed now. I'm not the only one experiencing weird things. Adrian's life has been impacted as much as mine.

He stiffens a little. A slight huff of air escapes his lungs. "I'm sorry I showed up here. I had a feeling you would need a cloak of this quality, and apparently, I was right. It's freezing here. Your winter seems far more hostile than mine."

For some reason, this makes me smile and his eyes light up a little at the sight of my face. "Yes, it's awful and it's cold; and I am over it, though it's only the beginning." I feel suddenly embarrassed I haven't offered him anything to eat or drink. I'm out of practice. "I'm afraid I don't have much to offer you."

I remember the bread in a pot behind me next to the fire. Turning quickly, I use my cloak to protect my hands and pick the pot up. Carrying it into the kitchen, I steal a glance towards Adrian. He's smiling. Do I look as frazzled as I feel? Probably more so.

"Well, I guess I have more to offer you than I thought." I gesture towards the pot. "Care for some bread?" I lift the lid, and steam carrying the smell farther into the room wafts up towards me.

"I'd like that." He moves to stand near me. I work hard to keep my body relaxed. Lifting the loaf up with my fingertips, I set it down on the table. Adrian moves behind me at the same time and comes back over with a knife in his hand. I flinch.

"I'm sorry. I thought you might need a knife for the bread?" He's holding it out towards me.

"Oh. Oh yes. Thank you. I'm not used to having someone here after all this time." I take the knife from his hand and notice the questions he wants to ask in his eyes, but he resists.

I feel strangely self-conscious about my home. I only saw one room in his, but it was grand and beautiful and intricate. He had servants for goodness' sake. This must look like a hovel to him.

I hand him the slice I just cut and then cut one more for myself. He takes a bite, and I see him close his eyes at the warmth and flavor. I know exactly how he feels. I may not have the complicated spices and herbs he is used to enjoying with his meals, but my bread reminds you of warm moments from your childhood.

"This is amazing. You actually made this yourself?"

"Of course I did. No one else lives here but me." He surveys the room and then walks away from me and sits on the chair next to the fire. He seems more at ease now. Leaning back and crossing one leg over the other, he raises his eyebrows as if to say aren't you going to sit down.

"You didn't bring your friend with you. Marcus?"

He sighs, "Marcus is not thrilled I am here at all. He thinks you're dangerous or working for..." He stops himself and redirects. "For someone we know. But I think there's more to what's going on than those things. And you don't seem very dangerous to me."

"I don't have the desire nor the energy to be dangerous. I prefer to live quietly away from the world rather than seek out trouble." At least it's what I tell myself. I'm curious to know who Marcus thinks I'm working for.

"How far is your home from the town?"

"A few miles. But I don't go to town unless I need supplies that I can't grow or hunt or make here. Or get from my neighbors." I let out a breathy laugh.

"Don't you get lonely? Sitting here by yourself every day?"

I swallow another piece of bread painfully over the lump in my throat forming at his words. "Yes," I say softly. "I do get lonely. But I don't feel like leaving either. Everyone else fled to the city. I stayed." I stop myself from saying the next sentence on my tongue. *No one would miss me because I'm the only one left.*

Sadness fills his eyes. "I'm sorry. It must be hard."

"Yeah. It is. But enough about my life." I need to change the subject. "Why exactly are we communicating? I mean, are we somehow connected? It feels like that, right?"

"I'm not entirely sure. But I find this whole situation peculiar. I don't think I'll be able to fully let it go even if you ask me to." A flash of something dark passes through his eyes. Or maybe it's the firelight.

He continues, "I feel something towards you. Like maybe I've met you before? You seem—familiar."

"Well, I have a feeling we won't be able to avoid each other for long. How did you get here, exactly? The first time I saw you it was like seeing you through mist. Same with the second time, until I ran into you. Oh, and do you know what on earth the thing is in the forest?"

I have definitely not been around enough people in recent years.

He chuckles, "I can at least answer your last question. The darkness you saw is called an avgrunn. There are several spread amongst the worlds. The ancient gods and goddesses established them as a means of traveling between the realms. After the Thousand Years War, their purpose was corrupted, and no one can safely be in their proximity without the evil within them destroying any in its path. Only one of the divine can move one, and I'm not sure any being can destroy them. They are a form of magic, archaic and dark."

"Magic. Like real magic," I say incredulously. Something inside me sparks. Gods and goddesses. My head is spinning with the information.

"How else did you think you traveled to my world?" His eyes widen as realization spreads over his face.

"There are other worlds!?" I think my mouth might be hanging open. I snap my lips together.

"You actually didn't know?" He shakes his head like this is more outlandish than the possibility of worlds and divine beings ruling them.

I shake my head firmly. It feels familiar. Like something I've read about before or known in the past.

"There are six realms. Your world and mine are only two of those six." He holds up two fingers and smiles.

I hold a hand up to stop him. "Wait, this is confusing and strange. Let's start with one thing. Magic. Is it real? It's real. It has to be." I answer myself.

"Yes, it is real. I think your world has been without outward magic for a long time based on your reaction alone. But in all worlds, magic is the life force by which all things exist. Without it, we would be rather hopeless. Your world has it, but it must be suppressed for some reason. Magic pulls you into our realm, and I imagine it is what brings you back."

"But how is it possible here? Wouldn't I feel magic? Or wouldn't other people know about it?" My mind is racing through the possibilities and implications. Did the new sovereign use magic to ruin our world with war? All those theories I have about powers behind the scenes impacting us in catastrophic ways seem more plausible by the minute.

I have more questions, but I don't get the chance to voice them when I hear a hissing sound in the room. Like air sliding through cracks. I look to the back door and jolt when I see the shadow of a man standing there watching us. Adrian is looking right at it too. The shadow melts and slides across the floor towards me.

"Meiora! You're back." I'm pretty sure my shadow creature is from Adrian's world.

"I still can't believe you've befriended one of these." At those words, Meiora forms a wall around me blocking Adrian's access and swelling up like flood waters behind a dam.

"Meiora, it's okay." It never seems to like Adrian. I can't tell if it's protective or if I should look more into its response. For now, I'd rather prevent unnecessary chaos in my home.

Adrian lifts his hands in surrender. "I apologize. I don't mean to offend. Your kind are rather elusive." He looks me in the eyes, "It seems to claim you as its own though." I think I hear him whisper *very interesting* under his breath, but I can't be sure.

"Are you needing a place to stay?" I hope he says no.

"No, I appreciate the offer, but I'm pretty sure Marcus would have half of my people hunting me down if I don't return soon. Actually, I should probably go now."

I feel a little disappointed, but I also know this is for the best. "Okay, well...thank you for bringing my cloak back." The darkness outside grows thicker as the sun sets. "Are you sure it's safe for you to leave? In case it comes back?"

He smiles grimly at me. "I'm sure it is. Don't worry. If you don't mind, I would like to see you again."

I have far too many questions. It's the only reason I say what I do. "Of course."

Without another word, he leaves out the front door. I wait a moment and then walk quickly to the front window to watch him walk away. But he's already gone. Vanished like a ghost into the deepening night.

I open the front door to peer through the twilight and falling snow and notice the lack of footprints on the front porch other than mine. I shut the door before I have time to dwell on it any longer.

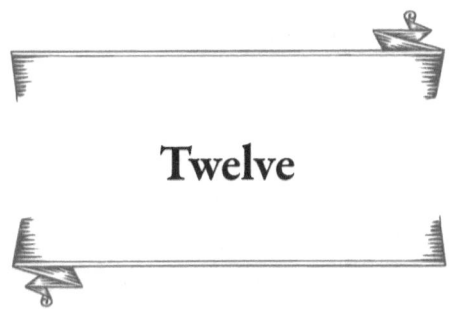

Twelve

The next few days are spent with no one other than Meiora. The snow finally ended two days ago, and now I spend my days keeping wood in the fire and eating smoked deer and bread. I'm working through the produce of my garden slowly, but at some point, I'll need to make a journey into town for more flour and minor things. No new words appear on the door. Nothing and no one open the door again including me.

I'm finishing up the last of my flour in three loaves of bread. I'll keep one for myself. I'll take the other two into town along with some deer meat and potatoes to trade. As much as I don't want to walk to town in snow, I don't have a choice. I'm packing my supplies into a basket when a knock sounds on my front door.

Fear stirs in my chest. I'm not expecting anyone. I tiptoe toward the door and raise my voice to be heard through the wood.

"Who is it?" I brace myself until I hear a familiar voice.

"It's me. Just checking in on you."

Mr. McClane. My gut tightens. A sense of wrongness settles in my chest. Why is he here again, so soon after the other time? Once was out of character enough; this second visit has my senses on high alert. I see Meiora glide into the corner of the room as if it, too, doesn't trust the situation.

I open the door a few inches, using my body to shield the rest of the room from him. He's standing there bundled up from the cold watching me intently. There's an air of concern about him. When

I look into his eyes, something that doesn't belong there meets my gaze. His eyes are hard and empty.

"Mr. McClane, why are you here today?" I want to close the door, to leave and get on the road to town; but my survival instincts rise to the surface.

His vacant smile unnerves me. "Peace to Novundo." Ice runs in my veins. He offers no other response to my question, waiting for the mandatory response on my end.

I drop my eyes briefly before answering. "Peace to Novundo."

A glimmer of darkness passes across his face. "Well, when I checked in a few days ago you had a limp with a sore ankle. I thought I'd make sure you were managing in this nasty cold weather." He rubs his gloved hands together.

"Oh well, I'm doing fine. Mostly staying in and staying warm." I force my voice to steady though I feel nothing but shaken by this encounter. "The most I do is chop wood." I try to chuckle lightly, but it sounds off. Meiora moves to surround my back—-out of sight of Mr. McClane, but its presence is felt. His eyes flick over my shoulder.

"We've heard more news of attacks happening along the woods. If you want, I can take a look and make sure your house is secure enough. The missus doesn't like you living so close to the woods as it is." His eyes look over my shoulder into the house.

"I hate to hear that. It's hard enough trying to survive the elements, let alone monsters. I haven't heard anything suspicious. Of course, I don't have any livestock so maybe I'm being left alone. I'm sure I'm safe for now." *Please leave.*

I glance back into the house and debate whether I should let him go ahead and enter. There is nothing suspicious on the door; but something holds me back. When I look back into his eyes though, it takes everything in my power to resist recoiling. His eyes are solid black now, empty and lifeless. Before I can react, they look normal once again. Did I imagine it?

"Darci? Darci? Are you sure you're okay?" He obviously noticed the terror pass across my face.

"Uhh, yes, sorry. I'm feeling a little under the weather today. I'll probably stay by the fire for a bit." I move to shut the door and feel his foot stop it. I look up again. He doesn't say anything for a moment, but he looks closely into my eyes, peering into the depths of me.

After what feels like forever, he blinks and pulls his foot back. "Well, you be careful, and have a good day. I'll let my wife know you're doing okay right now." He nods his head and turns to walk down the front steps.

"Thank you," I murmur. The crunch of snow beneath his boots lingers in my ears. I close the door and lock it. I don't leave it unattended until I see Mr. McClane walk out of sight down the road. Where is his horse this time? My hands are shaking when I turn to go back to the fire.

I'm not going to town today. I don't think I could make it that far with my mind as distracted as it is. Mr. McClane has never shown this much interest in me. Or at least I think the person standing there was Mr. McClane. What if it wasn't? He seemed different, a man possessed. I can't stop thinking about Adrian's world. A part of me longs for the place that smells and feels more alive than mine. I'm drawn to the magic there. I shake off the feeling and go about the rest of my day.

I throw three more logs on the fire to make the flames burn brighter. The day passes at a snail's pace, but as night falls my nerves push me to my feet to pace the house. My anxious energy spills out of me. I check and recheck every door and window except for the ones in their room. But they were boarded up two years ago.

I keep peeking out the back windows toward the woods expecting some monster or darkness to be working its way up the hillside to come for me. I wonder if I offended some great creature that requires my blood in exchange for my insolence. Nothing hides in the shadows outside though; nothing I can see. The sky turns black, and the white of the snow lights up the night in a soft, blue glow.

I annoy myself with all the pacing and finally make myself sit down on the couch and lose myself in the mesmerizing dance of the fire. My stillness prompts Meiora to slip around my shoulders like a shawl. Warm velvet brushes my neck, and I close my eyes.

But I don't sleep at all tonight.

MY EYES ARE BURNING; my back is aching; and my body feels like it's going to crash and burn soon. The coming of dawn brings a small breath of relief to my frayed mind. I sigh and rub my face. Meiora never left my side all night. Every time I dozed a little, it tightened around me or moved, and I woke up again.

I stretch my stiff body and walk to the window. The woods stand tranquil and quiet in the back. Nothing is out of place. Nothing is wrong yet. I know what I need to do though. Denying the strange happenings around me is not going to keep me safe or prevent bad things from occurring.

Adrian is the only person who might have answers for me. At the very least, he knows a lot more than I do about worlds and magic. I need to find him. Going into the woods might somehow transport me back to his home. A tingle reaches my fingers, and I want to answer the call growing within me.

"Meiora, we have to go back, don't we?" Of course, Meiora says nothing. It doesn't ever speak, though I wish it did. I walk to *the* door. I gently touch the unmarred paint, and then I step back to the kitchen to grab a small knife. I move with purpose before I can change my mind.

I carve two words carefully into the paint. If there is a delay for magical transport of messages, I don't know about it, but I'm hoping whatever magic connected us before will work again.

I look at my handiwork and then grab my things. Pulling my cloak on and slipping my feet into my boots, I notice the tingling sensation swells. I hope this works.

Walking out the door, I move around the house crunching through snow that reaches midway up my calves. I hesitate at the tree line. Noting Meiora in my peripheral vision, I cross over into the shadowy realm of the trees.

Adrian

I TAKE A SIP OF MY hot tea as I watch the woods behind my house. Nothing has changed since I managed to get to Darci's house a few days before. I've heard nothing else from her, and I have made no effort to get to her again. I can't force the situation. It doesn't stop me from thinking about her constantly. Her land was plunged into a frost and snow so deep and cold, it has left me constantly worrying about her survival in such temperatures. I wonder if she lives a lot farther north in her world than we are here.

Marcus was livid when he found out I had taken Gennet up on her offer of help to get back to Darci. I can't understand why Marcus hates her so much. He has always been protective though; it's how he was raised and trained. A warrior in every sense of the word, but he isn't seeing the big picture here. He doesn't see the value in learning more about Darci and her role in all that is coming.

The significance of her relationship with the cryarsh also intrigues me. I sigh and close my eyes, picturing Darci and her cautious green gaze. If I am completely honest, I might even say I miss her which makes no sense because I don't know her. No, she might be dangerous; but I won't find out by keeping her at arm's length.

My daydream of Darci is interrupted by a sound I don't expect to hear ever again. Scratching and scraping.

Words being etched into wood.

I set my mug down quickly and walk over to the tapestry pulling it back gently. The other words had vanished the night I arrived at Darci's home. Now, two new words appear on the wall.

I'm coming.

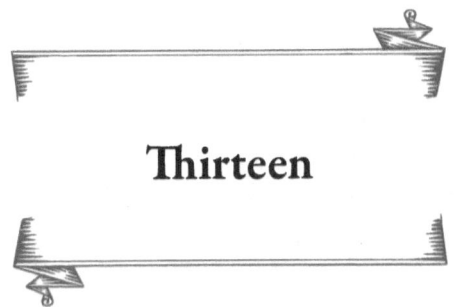

Thirteen

The cold bites into my skin, and my toes are beginning to feel a bit numb. My mind is made up, and for the first time in years, I feel alive and full of purpose. Fear mixes with curiosity but resisting the desire for more proves futile. Meiora slips around trees and winds its way around my feet from time to time, reassuring me I am not alone on this trek. I pull my cloak tighter around my body and make sure the hood is pulled as far forward as possible. It doesn't stop the wind from assaulting my nose and cheeks, and the chill makes my eyes water.

I know the general direction I took to find the hole before; I don't want to follow the same path entirely. If I get closer to it, I wonder if I'll somehow make Adrian aware of my presence. Our connection might call him to me. I need to discover all I can about his world and mine; and how I am meant to exist in this strange reality. Because that's what it feels like—it feels like I'm drawn to him. It might even bring some excitement to my mundane life. The emptiness I'm so familiar with might be soothed as well.

A mouthful of icy snow interrupts my thoughts. I somehow slipped into a drift a few feet deep and managed to plummet face first before I could react. I quickly get to my feet again, dusting myself off and spluttering snow. Meiora sweeps around me quickly, spinning off into the sky and vanishing for a moment before forming its bodily shadow a few feet away from me.

"Are you laughing at me?" Meiora swells in size in response. "Of course you are," I mutter. I *feel* the emotion from the shadow. It's becoming easier for me to understand it as time goes on. I throw a handful of snow that was wedged in my hood at the cryarsh. This does nothing, but it makes me feel better. Meiora disintegrates only to reappear in a tree above my head and somehow knocks more snow off the branches onto my head.

"Are you kidding me? Since when did you become a playful shadow?" Meiora resumes a casual demeanor, and knowing I can decipher this strange language between us eases an ache in my stomach. It drifts ahead on the breeze, leaving me behind.

"The least you could do is help me find the way to Adrian!" I shout at the air. Thankfully, only the squirrels and birds know I talk to myself. I resume walking, keeping an eye out for the avgrunn and making sure I don't lose sight of Meiora completely. Maybe it will lead me to where I want to go.

An hour later, I have no idea where I am, and a hill stands guard in front me looking vaguely familiar. I stop long enough to catch my breath and look around for any other signs of life. At the top of the hill, the trees thin out into a grassy meadow. No sign of the black hole; and all the creatures here are still whispering and chattering with one another. It feels safe until I hear the crunch of footsteps in the snow not belonging to me.

"Do you hear that, Meiora?" I glance up at the trees, but there is no cryarsh amidst the shadows. "Meiora?" I whisper. It's gone. Goosebumps prickle my skin. The sound of footsteps is drawing closer and I'm in the middle of a snowy wood with no way of disappearing into nonexistent brush.

I search for any tree large enough to step behind even for a moment. When I spot one a few paces away, I scurry as quietly as possible to stand behind it. I chance a quick look around the tree to see if I notice anyone else walking through the woods.

Two people dressed in all black with swords strapped to their backs stroll between trees, checking the ground for something every so often. *Me.* They're following the trail I made through the snow. I can barely make out an emblem on the front of their cloaks. It looks a little like snakes. *Novundo's guards!* I press my back to the tree and do my best to quiet my breathing.

Novundo's guards are never here. There must be a reason they were sent to this region so far from the capital. I don't trust the new sovereign, and now I worry the disturbance in the woods near the avgrunn is drawing unnecessary attention. All I know is I don't want to get caught, but I don't see a way out of this situation. I squeeze my eyes shut, desperate to find a solution.

When I open them again, movement catches my eye to the right. I turn to face it and see the shadowy form of *him* walking towards me. Adrian. Something loosens in my body at the sight.

He speaks, but no sound reaches my ears. It's the same mirage-like appearance when I'm seeing him through the veil between worlds instead of standing in the same one with him.

He stops in front of me, tall and handsome, and smiles. I stare back like the suspicious person I am, but there's no turning back. I peek over my shoulder again, feeling fear growing in my chest. His brow scrunches in concern, but he holds his hand out waiting. I take a deep breath and reach with mine in return, hoping this will work.

The grip of his fingers on mine grows heavy—more tangible—and my skin burns a little. The way your skin burns when you are so cold and just warming up. He gently pulls me towards himself as he steps back. The burning sensation worsens and pain creeps up my arm. I don't let go though. I hang on and allow him to pull me towards his chest.

I think I cry out. I'm not sure. I closed my eyes for a moment, attempting to regulate my breathing, but I still feel myself gasping when the pain subsides.

"I got you. Are you okay? Was someone following you?" His voice is soft and low. He's still holding my hand. I swallow and pull away, tugging free.

"Yes. I'm okay." This feels awkward. Our last encounter wasn't much better. I suddenly feel foolish coming here. He waits for me to say something else, but I keep the answer to his second question to myself. He nods his head and walks farther up the hill toward the clearing. It's daylight here. When I came before, night kept most details of my surroundings hidden from me.

I follow him carefully absorbing all the sights and sounds here. The air smells fresh and alive. I never noticed how stale the air felt at home until I came here. It's chilly, cold but not bitter. A faint dusting of snow covers the ground, but it's more winter wonderland than northern wastes. There is life—a humming reaches my ears and sinks into my bones. So faint, you can barely hear it, but I feel it.

"What's that sound?" I ask him.

He looks over his shoulder, "What sound?"

"The humming." He looks at me puzzled. "I hear humming. It's faint. Like a low buzz you feel more than anything." I must sound crazy at this point. He stops walking and looks around going still, waiting to experience what I am.

"I'm sorry, I don't hear or feel anything different. Maybe it's an effect of the transition to our world?"

I sigh. "Maybe. Did my world feel different to you?"

His head tilts as he thinks before speaking. "Now that you say that, it did. It felt..." He looks down and then away from me.

"It felt like what?" I prod.

"Empty."

I blink at him for a minute and then break eye contact.

"I don't mean to be offensive, but it's the feeling I got when I was there. Like it was empty or abandoned." Those words feel appropriate; I can't deny that. What bothers me more is I notice how alive this world feels compared to mine. Maybe mine doesn't feel empty. Dead might be a better word for it.

"You didn't offend me. I notice the difference between our worlds quite strongly." I wait for him to begin walking again, but he doesn't. He looks at me.

"What differences do you notice?"

"You say mine feels empty. Yours feels alive. The air smells different here. Fresh and new. Maybe mine is empty because there is no magic there."

"Well, there must be some magic. There is an avgrunn there; and you exist, crossing between worlds. Maybe you're the magical one in your world."

I hadn't thought about the possibility. My soul seems to vibrate with expectation when I'm here. It's a strange calling I feel deep inside of me.

We stand there still and quiet for a moment before I finally ask if we'll continue our walk up the hill. He smiles and turns again.

As we crest the hill and step into the clearing, I gasp at the beauty before me. A house stands before me in all its grand splendor. It's like the most beautiful and ornate cabin I have ever seen but on a far grander scale. Multiple chimneys and deep cherry wood stand in contrast to the sparkling white of the snow around me. The big picture windows on the back of the house are familiar. The view toward us and the woods is what I remembered from my last visit.

I catch him smiling at me. Then he looks back at the house and offers me his hand as we step over a fallen log onto a stone path. I take it cautiously to get over the log but let go again quickly.

"So... Where is your friend?" I secretly hope his friend is gone on a mission somewhere far away. Warriors do that sort of thing, don't they?

"My friend? You mean Marcus?" I nod my head. "He is up at the house." My heart sinks a little. My face must show it too because he comments. "Don't worry about him."

"Well since he doesn't like me and doesn't want me here..."

"Why *did* you come here again?"

I feel my cheeks flush. "Well, I... uh... I don't know how to explain it." He waits for me to go on. "It will sound ridiculous. But...I needed to get away."

"And did something inspire this sudden desire to escape? Tired of the bitter cold?" I smile at his jest.

"I had a visit from my neighbor. He seemed...off. I needed to go to town to get supplies, but I didn't feel safe going after he dropped in." He raises one brow at this. "He doesn't normally drop in. I live far enough away from him it isn't easy to stop by suddenly. And he seems to be showing up more than normal. Also, I feel unsettled. Like something is calling me to this place." I feel my face heat. It sounds more ridiculous when I say it out loud. His eyes are perceptive and thoughtful though.

"I understand. What about your neighbor is bothering you?" Concern edges his voice.

"I've known him and his wife for a few years now. He has come to my house unexpectedly twice during this time frame. Both times happened in the past week. I feel like he's watching me, but I don't know why."

Adrian doesn't say anything. His brow furrows and he turns his gaze toward the house. I wait for some sort of response, but the opportunity never comes. Marcus appears at the top of the hill, arms crossed and abounding with joy. Not really, but I can pretend.

Adrian takes a deep breath and then picks up the pace to greet his friend. I find myself slowing instead and crossing my arms myself. Out of the corner of my eye, a shadow appears. The weight building in my chest melts. Meiora is here now.

"Adrian, why in Araina's name have you brought her back here?" Marcus gestures angrily in my direction.

Adrian opens his mouth to respond, but I interrupt instead. "Who's that?"

They both look at me quizzically and then look around to see who I noticed nearby. Adrian finally asks, "Who are you referring to?"

"Araina. I've heard you both say her or his name. Who exactly is Araina?"

They blink in surprise.

Marcus clarifies, "Araina is the Goddess of Light." Something wicked coils inside of me. I'm momentarily startled by the sensation. A goddess. There is a goddess here.

"Is she the only deity in this world?" I feel my stomach tighten in anxiety which feels a little unfounded.

"She is one of six here. She is the most powerful one though," Adrian answers. "I assume you have different deities in your world?"

I fidget a little. "No. Ours is a godless realm. The capital is our god, and it is heresy to worship anything else." At least, as far as I know, this is true. Empty. Dead. My world is both of those things. No god or goddess would want to be there.

Adrian and Marcus exchange a look. Marcus' eyes narrow as he looks back at me. I break the silence with another question.

"Will I be welcome here? Will she allow me to stay here?" It seems like an odd question, but it popped into my head and spilled out of my mouth regardless.

"I don't see why you wouldn't be." Adrian's response barely beats Marcus' muttered words. I am pretty sure he said something about that being uncertain. Adrian gives him a reprimanding look before continuing. "Something is drawing you here. Maybe it's the magic. Maybe it's something we haven't figured out yet. But we won't know unless we have you here."

He offers me his hand which I accept, and he leads me toward the house again. This time we walk around it toward the front. I guess I get to use the main door this time. Marcus shakes his head and follows close behind. My skin tingles with anticipation and a little bit of fear.

Something tells me Araina is not as forgiving a goddess as they believe. I don't think I will be as welcome here as I would hope to be.

Fourteen

We walk up the steps to the front door. Lanterns and sconces with flickering flames light the outside of the house. He leads me through the door with Marcus close behind me. This alone is bothersome, but I don't think anything will happen with Adrian right here. The woman from before greets us and offers me a warm smile. I think her name is Gennet. Adrian releases my hand and gestures to the woman.

"Gennet, I know you met Darci before, but I don't think you were properly introduced."

She reaches for my hand and takes it gently covering it with her other hand. Her presence is a balm to my restless soul. I think she sees me in more ways than one. Her warm eyes lock onto mine and never waver.

I murmur, "It's nice to meet you. You make delicious hot chocolate."

At this she laughs, free and unabashed. "I knew I would like you." Her gaze turns towards Adrian. "Why did you wait so long to bring her back? Did you scare the poor creature away?" My skin grows cold in her hands. I've never been referred to as a creature before.

"I didn't intentionally try to scare her. Marcus did."

Marcus' lips pull down into an even deeper frown if that's possible, and he crosses his arms again. Adrian claps him on the shoulder and laughs.

Gennet releases me and turns a scolding finger towards Marcus. "You should not be so quick to judge young *faolan*." He drops his arms and looks slightly embarrassed but doesn't defend himself.

I keep my eyes down for a moment until Adrian gestures for me to follow him. I stay a few feet behind him while I take in the rooms. It's beautiful. Simple yet lovely. The details in the wood display craftsmanship I haven't seen in a long time, and the sconces cast a warm glow across the space. A staircase is to the right, but he leads me down the hall towards the back of the house. We pass a few servants who nod discreetly toward Adrian, then do a double take when they notice me following behind. A few look as displeased as Marcus to see me.

No one outright scoffs at me—not like Marcus—-but they definitely were not expecting a stranger who looks very different from them to be here. I notice the varying shades of beautiful brown and olive skin tones. Some are darker; some are quite fair. My pale skin doesn't even carry a slight tan from sunshine since the snow and cold have kept me hidden away mostly. I imagine I must look sickly compared to everyone else. My fingers twist the fabric of my cloak as unease adds tension to the air.

A small child scampers across the hall from one room to the next and then gawks at me going so far as to point her finger at me and whisper shout to someone behind them about the dead woman walking through the hall. I see a woman I suspect is her mother grabbing the little girl and tugging her farther into the room, scolding her about being rude.

The dead woman. I drop my eyes to my feet but not before I notice Adrian's back stiffen. Marcus releases a derisive snort like all his worst opinions about me were finally confirmed. My face reddens, and I know everyone can see it plain as day.

Adrian steps through a doorway into a large room with a cozy fireplace, and I immediately recognize the space as the room I was in the last time I was here. Part of my instinct tells me to run. The other part demands I stay to learn all I can. I choose the latter. I wouldn't get far anyway with Marcus standing behind me.

"I'm sorry. She is not the most tactful child." He smiles apologetically.

I wave it off. "No need to apologize. I'm well aware I look a bit sickly compared to everyone else here."

Marcus mumbles not very discreetly. Adrian shakes his head subtly, but I don't let him speak.

"It's okay. I understand children. I'm sure she didn't mean any harm." I turn away and study the paintings on the walls, hoping to put an end to the conversation.

Adrian doesn't say anything else, but Marcus has no issue continuing the conversation. "And how do you know about children?"

I turn towards him and take in his presence. Strong and immovable. Unimpressed and always on guard. Maybe knowing a little more about me would be helpful.

"I had two sons. They were as crass and free with their words as any child is." I don't look away. For once, I boldly stare at him. His features soften slightly, but he says nothing else.

"You *had* two sons?" Adrian's voice is soft. Knowing the past tense makes the words painful to breathe out.

Facing him, I meet his eyes and feel tears burning. I won't let them fall. I

won't let them see this weakness in me. "Yes, I had two sons. I wasn't strong enough to be worthy of them."

Vivid images of my last memories of my family flash in my mind. Painful and stabbing. I don't remember the exact details of how we got to where we were then, but I can see them. I can see their deaths and their bodies destroyed by darkness I didn't know could ravish my world. I bite my tongue hard enough to draw blood in an effort to divert my mind.

"I'm sorry. I didn't know you had any family." He pauses. "Your home seemed quite..."

"Empty?" I offer.

He nods not missing my use of his words to describe my world. Marcus uncrosses his arms but doesn't move.

I turn back to face the paintings, locking eyes with Marcus for only a breath. I don't hide the death in mine. I don't shutter the windows to my soul for even a second. His demeanor softens more and something like pity appears for a moment before we both harden ourselves to each other.

"Are you someone important?" I ask Adrian. He chuckles, and Marcus narrows his eyes.

"I'm not important." A lie. I sense the shift in his position. They're hiding something because I am a stranger and pose a potential threat.

"But you live in this grand house, with a lot of servants. People follow your orders." I eye Marcus. "Who are you?" A vibration pulses between us. Connection. Knowing. I wait for his response.

His eyes widen; I know he feels the tether between us. He opens his mouth, but I see the inward struggle in his eyes. Marcus moves to stand between us, but he's too late. Adrian breathes. "I'm the Sovereign of Myzonia." A flash of fear and surprise passes through his eyes. Marcus freezes before zeroing in on me again. The distrust deepens.

I startle momentarily at the news, but Adrian attempts to shrug off the strange exchange between us and treats the news he revealed as uninteresting.

"So, is this your only home? It seems a little small. For a sovereign." They both laugh at this.

"This is my primary residence where I prefer to stay. But I also have a house within the city limits. I enjoy fresh air and space more often than not." He turns towards the large picture window. "I love the woods and the nature of things out here."

"He *loves* to avoid work whenever he can." Marcus scolds. Adrian smirks.

"No, I prefer to keep an eye on the borders in person."

"You have commanders for those things. And armies." This is obviously a sore spot.

"Doesn't change the fact I owe the people here in this house some of my attention part of the time." This volley back and forth is making me dizzy. I interrupt with another question.

"Are your borders in danger often?" They both look at me before exchanging a meaningful glance. I continue before they can explain. "You both have magic. Do all people have magic here? Or is it only important people?"

"You remembered all of it then?" Marcus inquires. His guard goes up again as if I have broken some unspoken rule. His hard eyes cause a restlessness inside of me. This uncertainty makes me notice Meiora's absence. Although given the nature of the response from the servants we passed, I have a feeling a cryarsh following me through the house might have been even more disconcerting.

"I do. I wasn't completely incapacitated when I was here last time. You subdued me with magic." I gesture towards Marcus before turning back to Adrian. "And you healed me with it."

"Magic is available to all who live here. But to varying degrees. Some have basic forms. Like being able to make tinctures to aid your health or growth. Some use magic for growing things or making fabrics. Some are stronger and have magic that can be useful in combat. The more powerful magic tends to remain with those in places of leadership. Like Marcus and me. He is my commander of the armies." That explains a lot. I'm an unknown. No wonder he doesn't like me.

Adrian walks over to a chair and gestures to the one across from him. I move toward the chair passing Marcus on the way. His body is tense, ready to attack if needed. He waits until I'm seated before moving toward the doorway.

"I'll check back in later. I have to patrol the perimeter." Without waiting for a response, he leaves.

"Any other questions, Darci?" Adrian inquires with a bemused expression on his face.

"Well, is there a reason why the child thought I looked like death? I'm not denying I am quite a sight to see at the moment."

He grimaces. "Her name is Risa. I'm not entirely sure why other than an overactive imagination. You look fine, by the way. Maybe a little malnourished. Maybe she noticed. She is the youngest child here at the moment. They are safer staying here than in the capital."

I tilt my head at him. "Safer?"

He clears his throat. "Yes, Risa's parents were being pursued by guardian hunters—mercenaries paid to kidnap anyone from other kingdoms who display a natural tendency toward seer magic. I offered them refuge here because this house has a way of healing people's souls. They are well taken care of and free to live however they like in exchange for helping to maintain the house. Myzonia is newly under my rule. The previous ruler was quite ruthless. He did not see the benefit of mercy and compassion when creating an empire. Other kingdoms in this world followed his example unfortunately. I'm left with the cleanup of trying to make a better kingdom for my people and my own children someday. One without violence and war."

It's a nice idea. I understand the desire for peace in a war infested world.

"It sounds...beautiful. What is so special about seer magic?"

"Seers are given access to the thoughts and movements of the divine. Very few people have that magic. It is highly coveted, and people are often kidnapped and sold for a high price."

"You mean, they can see what the gods and goddesses here are doing and want to do? Like the future?"

He shakes his head. "Not quite the future. More like the intentions of the gods and goddesses. Risa has the gift, but it is barely developed. She only sees tiny glimpses of their thoughts. Her whole family is at risk because of it though. Anyway, I know she didn't mean any insult by the statement."

I laugh. "I won't take any then. Children say what they want to. They usually mean no ill will by it. One needs to have thick skin."

He smiles, and my heart warms at the sight now.

"Okay, what would you like to know about my world?"

"I feel like there are too many questions and not enough time." I pause and look out the window again. "I don't want to impose on you. If I need to leave, tell me to."

I turn and lock eyes with him. He says nothing for a few heartbeats. "You don't need to leave. You're welcome to stay here as long as you want."

I nod and then blink away. "Okay." We both sit silently for a moment. He breaks the silence with a question of his own.

"Where's your shadow?" I scrunch my brow.

"I actually don't know. It always disappears when I draw near to you in my realm. But I thought it would be here by now."

We both survey the room, letting our eyes linger on each dark corner. I decide to whisper its name instead in the hopes it will reappear. "Meiora?"

Within seconds, a shadow slides under the door that leads outside and creates the shape of a man. Adrian stiffens and watches warily as Meiora floats across the room towards my chair passing him in the process.

I reach my hand out and let the tendrils of shadow tickle and tease along my fingers and knuckles. "There you are." It shifts into a wispy blanket of darkness as it rests its form across my shoulders and down onto the floor like a cloak. It feels safer here with Meiora. Hopefully it doesn't scare everyone else.

Adrian stares amazed for a bit longer.

"I still don't know if I can get used to that. Do you want to see the room you can stay in? Maybe a tour of the rest of the house?" He stands and extends his hand. Meiora puts a shield up quickly in front of me. I let my fingers coax the shadowy wall to drop.

"It's fine, Meiora. I'm safe now." I stand and take his hand. The coldness in my hands melts into the warmth of his. "I'd like that."

He leads me from the room, and Meiora slips away into the corner.

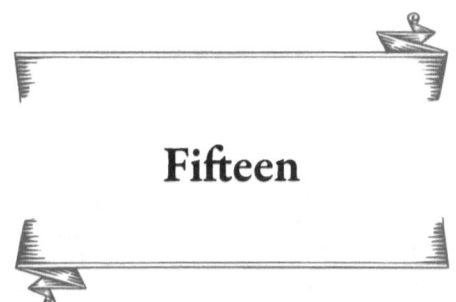

Fifteen

Adrian

Her hand is soft in mine, cold and strong. There are calluses along her palms from the work I'm sure she does to simply stay alive in her harsh world. Despite the cold of her fingers, I feel a warmth spreading up my arm, a hum of power pulsing from our point of contact. It makes my heart speed up unnecessarily. She feels familiar and foreign all at once.

I understand what she meant about something calling her here. I feel it when she's around me. Like the magic in me calls out to something deep inside of her. I suspect she has magic herself, but it doesn't explain the strange connection I feel to this woman. She's becoming a problem for me and my ability to focus. I think about her and her striking green eyes more than I should. During a meeting with Marcus and the commanders of the varying regiments of our army, I completely missed a question sent my way. Marcus had to repeat it for me much to my embarrassment. Darci was there instead in my mind's eye. The tug in my gut was becoming unbearable.

Now, she's here, and I feel lighter, and all I want to do is show her and her shadow the rooms of this house, my home. I was going to lead her to the room where she would stay, but instead, find myself taking her to the kitchens first. I don't have Marcus here to scowl and stomp behind me; I take my time letting her see everything. Gennet was right; I shouldn't have scared her off last time. I should have made her feel safer. I glance back and see her eyes scanning every wall and doorway as we walk toward the stairs leading to the kitchen below.

She's beautiful, and I'm in trouble. I clear my throat and let her walk in front of me into the warm kitchen bustling with life. Risa is there laughing behind her mother's legs. I see a smile ghosting Darci's lips, but pain subdues the reaction. Everyone notices our presence and the activity comes to a halt.

"I want to introduce you all to Darci. She'll be staying with us for a while. I thought she might enjoy getting a tour and proper introductions to everyone while she is here."

Aster, Risa's mother, steps forward nudging her daughter towards us with firm but gentle hands. "Risa, you have something to say to Miss Darci?"

Risa's eyes drop and her whole demeanor turns bashful. Darci surprises me by kneeling on one knee in front of her and gently taking her small hands into her own.

"Hello, Risa, you have such a beautiful name." Her voice is soft and gentle. Risa shifts her eyes to meet Darci's and smiles widely.

"Do you think so?"

"I absolutely do." Darci smiles and Risa wiggles. Aster nudges her in the back as a reminder of what she wanted her daughter to do.

Risa gets a serious look on her face trying to look remorseful. "Momma, says it is not nice to say that people look dead."

"Risa!"

I stifle a laugh and catch Darci doing the same. She manages to nod very seriously in encouragement.

"I'm sorry I called you dead. You are not dead. You are beautiful." Pink flushes Darci's cheeks, and I find it endearing.

"Well, Risa, I accept your apology." Darci lowers her voice conspiratorially, "But between you and me, I have not seen much sunshine lately; and I do look rather sickly." Risa's eyes widen and she turns to her mother as if to say, *see? I told you so.*

Aster extends her hand to Darci, "You are too kind, Miss."

Darci stands and shakes her hand. "Your daughter is beautiful. Honesty is always a lovely quality."

"My name is Aster."

"It's nice to meet you."

I finish introducing her to the rest of the kitchen staff including Aster's husband, Hoku, who walks in from hunting with a large deer across his shoulders.

Darci's demeanor softens the longer we walk the halls. I show her the library and sitting rooms letting her meet anyone who happens to be passing by. Finally, I lead her upstairs to her bedroom. I know Gennet will have had someone prepare it for her in the time it has taken me to show her around. I open the door and let her step into the room. There is a large four poster bed, a desk, and a wardrobe. The window faces to the back of the house displaying the forest and the life within it.

She stands in the middle and turns slowly taking in the details of the space. She is always observant. Always soaking up all the information presented before her.

I want to speak, but I wait for her response.

"It's...very big." Her eyes spark with amusement when she meets my gaze.

"Well, yes. There's a lot of space in here. You are welcome to explore as much as you like. I wish I could stay, but I have business to attend to. Unfortunately." I smile.

"It's fine. I will find some way to make myself useful, I'm sure."

"I'll see you later for dinner?" Part of me wonders if she will vanish like she did before when I came to find the room empty and only her cloak left behind. I hope it's not the case. Something strange flashes behind her eyes, and a hum buzzes under my skin. There's more to her than meets the eye.

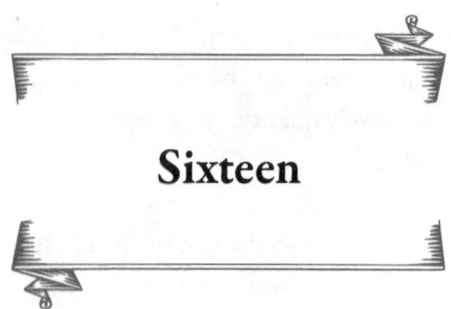

Sixteen

Darci

Adrian closes the door behind him as he leaves. Instantly, Meiora mingles with my own shadow at my feet. I feel a spark of something deep inside of me. It's warm and alive—strong. I walk around the room taking in the earthy green of the walls, the ornate carvings along the window and door frames. A large rug is spread across the floor near the bed, and a fireplace with a small crackling flame sits directly across from the bed itself.

"What do you think, Meiora? Are we safe here?" Meiora remains aloof around my feet. Offering no evidence of its opinion whatsoever. I walk toward the desk and open a drawer. There are some writing materials, but nothing of interest. Looking out the window, I can see two men walking along the tree line to the woods. They are dressed in tunics of dark green and black and have swords strapped to their backs. What looks to be a leather breastplate bears a symbol of some serpentine creature. The distance is too great to make it easily decipherable. Guards?

I wonder if Marcus is among them or if he is farther out in other areas. I can't see much else out the window. The view looks out on the stone path we walked on to get to the house from the woods. There are a lot of evergreens around the edge. Perhaps intentional. They create a tighter barricade than the leafless trees blanketing the hill farther down.

I don't want to sit here and do nothing. The best place to start might be the kitchens. Surely, there is a place for me to help amongst them. I do know how to make bread after all.

The door opens with a soft creak, and I poke my head out looking for any sign of servants or children. Finding nothing, I slip through the opening. Meiora starts to follow me, but I stop it.

"I don't think it's a good idea. You might scare everyone. Find something else to do that is less...ominous." Meiora stiffens (if it's even possible for a shadow to be stiff) but reluctantly obeys slinking back toward the window.

I step into the hall and trace our steps back to the first floor. It takes a few moments for me to remember which hall leads to the staircase that goes to the kitchens. A few servants nod their heads in greeting as I pass by, but I'm not quite brave enough to ask for directions.

When I finally find the stairs leading down, I take them quickly and am greeted by the warm smells of bread and the sounds of work. Pots clanging, water splashing in a cleaning tub, the rhythmic beating of spoons and whisks. All mingling together with chatter and giggles from a little Risa.

I step through the doorway and am pleased to find the activity doesn't diminish much. A few servants cast their eyes my way, but otherwise, they remain focused on the tasks at hand. No one really appears happy to see me, but they don't send me out either. Aster is kneading dough on the counter when she looks up and notices me. Risa follows her mother's eyes and bursts into a smile that could light a thousand cities. At least someone is happy to see me.

"Miss Darci!" She bounds off her stool and grabs my hand, yanking me towards the counter. "What are you doing? Are you here to play?"

I laugh, "Well, I actually came to see if I can be of use somewhere." I catch Aster's eyes. "If you will have me, that is. I feel a little useless sitting in a room all alone." My heart aches for a moment. Alone. I've been alone for so long, the sound of life all around me is almost overwhelming, yet it soothes the wounds in my heart.

I think my eyes reveal more than I intend because Aster nods before pointing to a large bowl holding more fluffy dough waiting to be worked.

"You are welcome to knead dough if you like. There are a lot of mouths to feed in this house, and everyone loves warm bread on a chilly night."

I wash my hands at the sink before stepping over to grab the bowl, dumping the dough out onto the already floured surface. "I do have some experience with making bread." I work the dough, getting it stretchy and smooth.

"Where exactly are you from, Darci?" I pause and look at Aster. Her eyes are sharp. She is kind, but not a fool.

"Umm, I don't know how to answer." I look back down and continue my work. "Far, but not far if that makes sense." Do these people understand the realms existing outside of their own? I didn't until recently.

She nods and continues her work in silence. I can't resist making conversation though. "How long have you lived here? How long have you known Adrian?" Her eyes meet mine again, and the fierceness there makes me nervous. I think I offended her.

"His Sovereignty has been in power for six years. His father was a ruthless man, and we are fortunate he is nothing like that man. His mother's kindness is what molded him into the leader we know. Myzonia would be doomed without his goodness."

Yes, I have definitely offended her in some way. It doesn't escape me she didn't use Adrian's first name, and she revealed the previous ruler of Myzonia as his father. I wonder where his mother is.

"I'm sorry. I didn't mean to be irreverent."

"He is a good man, and he deserves to be treated with respect. He sometimes cares too much, if you ask me." Another voice hums their agreement behind me.

"I don't want to impose on him. I have a lot of questions I can't find answers to by myself; and for some reason, I keep ending up back here...near him." Risa pinches a piece of dough from my loaf and shoves it into her mouth before Aster can snatch her hand back. Her giggling breaks some of the tension as she scampers away.

Aster shakes her head and smiles softly. She's guarded though. She reminds me of the way Marcus treats me. Careful and suspicious. Waiting for something evil to come out of me and destroy their beloved leader. I don't think Adrian is foolish or blinded though. I think he is drawn to me as much as I am to him. Which might be terrifying if I think about it too much. Another question I need to find answers to.

My mind drifts back to the door in my house where all of this started. The words being etched into the paint. It was open when he appeared at my home in my realm for the first time. I don't go into the room or open that door. Too much sorrow and darkness and death await me there. Yet it keeps calling me back to it.

"I don't want to hurt anyone. I only need help." It's as truthful as I can be at the moment.

She purses her lips and watches me for a minute before shaping her dough and placing it in a pan to bake. I do the same with mine. We continue like this for the next hour. Preparing loaf after loaf of bread and rolls and then starting on desserts and savory side dishes. She is not the main cook, but she maintains a place of authority in the kitchen—maybe even the house. Everyone around chats and laughs at jokes. Speaking about what the latest gossip is from the nearby village. No one else speaks with me, though. There is a wall between me and the others that I'm not sure I can tear down.

In the time I've been here, I've learned the main city of Myzonia is at least two hours away by foot, but I don't think Adrian and the others travel that way. I'm not entirely sure how they get around this kingdom, but I'm sure magic plays a role. My stomach grumbles angrily as we finish up the last of the meal preparations. Everything is now either baking or simmering and all the scents flood my senses and remind me I haven't eaten much of anything lately.

Risa happens to be standing next to me when my stomach protests its neglect and giggles as she declares I must be starving or about to turn into a *myrukim* (not that I know what a myrukim is).

Aster hands me an apple and a wedge of cheese in response. "Here, this should hold you over for another hour or so. You can go clean up now." She gestures to the door, and I decide not to overstay my welcome. A couple of other servants wave goodbye as I head up the stairs. Most do not.

I take a big bite of my apple and sigh softly at the sweet juices flooding my mouth. My eyes close for the briefest moment as I step through the doorway into the hall savoring the flavors that are both familiar and yet different from my world. I walk straight into a solid wall dropping my apple as a grunt comes out of the solid surface. I open my eyes quickly, looking down at the sad state of my apple, and find black boots touching the toes of my worn brown boots. At least I still have my cheese.

"Sorry," I mumble around the apple in my mouth and look up into the face of Marcus. He furrows his brow and doesn't look happy to see me. Nothing new there.

"What are you doing?" He doesn't step back so I'm forced to retreat from him which I hate. His presence triggers my fight or flight response every time.

I swallow the rest of my bite. "I was helping in the kitchen." He quirks an eyebrow and looks down at my half-eaten apple at his feet. "I didn't want to hide in my bedroom all day doing nothing." He flexes his hands at his side, and I notice a spark of blue light dancing across his fingertips.

A phantom burning sensation swells in my arm where he last used his magic on me. It's enough to make me drop my gaze slightly and squat to grab the apple. The evidence of my kitchen work is there where flour coats the front of my shirt and small Risa sized handprints of flour dot my pants.

"Well, don't let me stop you from making yourself at home." His words carry a venom that makes my skin crawl. His magic flares again before he forms fists and steps to the side to give me room to pass.

My cheeks burn, but I force myself to look him in the eye again. The fire inside my belly grows, and though I feel shame at his rebuke, I also want to fight back. I'm not quite that brave; and he is the one holding magic in his fingers, not me. The reminder of the pain he caused is enough to make me scoot around him and down the hall towards the staircase leading to my room.

When I walk into the room, I explore the two other doors within. One leads to an empty closet except for a stool and a dress so flowy and beautiful my breath catches for a moment. The other door opens to a private washroom. Meiora appears at my shoulder as we both take in the beautiful ivory tub and silver lined sinks.

"I guess it's time to get cleaned up, huh?" Meiora slides into the room, and I realize I can take a hot bath without the use of a bucket. It sounds wonderful right now.

The warm water on my dirty skin makes me sigh. I scrub my skin and hair trying not to notice how the bath water changes color. It doesn't occur to me I have no clean clothes to get into until I am finished and grabbing a towel to wrap around my body.

My damp feet leave footprints on the wood floors as I walk across the room to the closet door. Opening it, I realize the only clothing I have at my disposal is a dress that looks far too extravagant for a regular dinner, but I don't have any other choice. I sigh and loosen the towel to dry my hair. I reach in and pull the dress out into the light. The top is crisscrossed and two-toned with lilac and pink and a small cutout in the middle on the front and the back. Gauzy sleeves of turquoise end in white beaded cuffs. The bottom flows down to the floor with a fading of pink to purple on the bottom. It looks impractical for the weather and the occasion, but I won't have anything else to wear until I can get my clothes cleaned.

I drop my towel on the floor and pull the dress onto my body. I step into the washroom and look at myself in the mirror. I blush as I take in the sight of myself and too much skin showing through the cutout in the center of the dress. I can't go to dinner dressed like this. I turn to grab my dirty clothes off the floor, but they're gone. My pulse spikes as I wonder who came in here. Is it possible no one did— the magic here has taken my clothes somewhere?

A knock at the bedroom door makes me jump. I peek out, "Who is it?"

"It's Adrian. I was coming to bring you down for dinner."

"Oh, umm..I think I'll stay up here for now." I bite my bottom lip clinging to the washroom door like it will keep me anchored.

"Are you okay? Did something happen?" He sounds concerned, but I need him to leave. Maybe he can send food up to me.

"I am...not feeling well."

"Are you sick? I might be able to help." I hit my forehead with the palm of my hand. Of course, he would offer to help. He has magic. He can heal me of something minor like sickness surely.

My mind is racing with ideas for how to get him to leave. The resulting pause must cause him to become more concerned because he starts to open the door. I shut the washroom door with more force than I intended. I can hear his footsteps as he walks quickly to where I'm hiding.

"Darci, let me help you. Maybe your body is overwhelmed from traveling. I might be able to ease the symptoms."

"I, uh, I think I'm just tired. I'm going to lie down for a while." *Please leave* is what I don't say.

He pauses before whispering. "Please let me help you."

"It's embarrassing actually."

He chuckles, "Being sick is nothing to be embarrassed about."

Silence follows.

"I'm not actually sick."

More silence.

"Darci, can you open the door please." He says it like he knows he can easily force the door open, but he is willing to give me the chance to do it myself.

Taking a deep breath, I turn the doorknob and let it swing open. His eyes lock with mine before traveling down my body to take in the full sight of me in this ridiculous dress.

"I'm sorry, I didn't have any clean clothes. Then my old clothes disappeared, and I didn't have anything else to wear other than a towel. I kind of thought that would be a bit more scandalous." *Why are you rambling?!*

He stares.

"If there are some other clothes I might wear..." I wait to give him the chance to respond. Before he does though, heavy footsteps echo down the hall and stop in the doorway of the room.

Frowning as usual, Marcus lifts his hands up in frustration. "What is taking so long?" Adrian currently blocks me from his view. But not for long as he turns to face him and to give me room to step out of the washroom. Marcus looks even more disgusted at the sight of me. "Where did you get that? Seems a bit impractical don't you think?"

"It was in the closet." I grit out through clenched teeth, feeling a bit irritated by the entire situation.

"That's weird. But the house is magical. Maybe it put it in there. No idea why though." His scrutiny makes me feel even more awkward. "It looks familiar though."

He examines me again, but this time with a furrowed brow trying to place where he might have seen this dress before. It seems odd to me a dress of this beauty could appear out of nothing. But maybe the magical house has a flair for the dramatic.

Adrian takes my hand and leads me to the door. "It's okay. You look fine." He glances down at my bare feet and the cutout in the center before quickly averting his gaze. "Although, you might get a little cold." He looks to Marcus whose eyes widen. Only Marcus has a cloak draped over his shoulders still.

He grumbles something and unclasps the cloak, shoving it into my hands. His fingers brush against mine and the sensation of electricity pulses into my body reminding me how dangerous he could be. I swallow and softly thank him draping the cloak around my shoulders. It holds the scent of mint and earth and a lighter note of smoke and sweat. I refrain from grimacing at the strange combination.

I gather my damp hair, untuck it from the cloak and follow them both down the hall and to dinner.

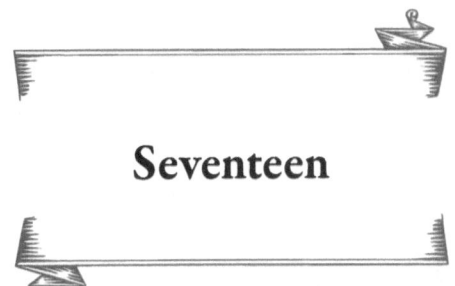

Seventeen

I have reached the point of being uncomfortably hungry. The few bites of apple and the wedge of cheese I enjoyed didn't last me long; and as I sit here across from an intrigued Adrian and an irritated Marcus, I hope my stomach can stay quiet for a few moments more. To my relief, three servants walk in, setting platters of food and bread on the table and then walking out after a quick bow towards Adrian.

Marcus doesn't hesitate as he begins to fill his plate with the delicious-smelling food. Adrian nods his head toward the food encouraging me to do the same. I unclasp Marcus' cloak and shift to lay it across the back of the chair. The fire has made this room warmer than the halls of the house; I think I can manage to eat without being bundled. Though my skin still prickles from the cooler air, I don't want to risk getting any food on his cloak either. Another reason for him to dislike me, I'm sure.

I catch Adrian watching me when I turn back and reach for a spoonful of potatoes. We lock eyes for a moment before Marcus grunts or maybe it's a growl. I turn my focus back to the task of filling my plate with the varying vegetables and meats and a slice of bread.

Adrian clears his throat. "I heard you helped in the kitchen this afternoon? Making bread?" I feel a little embarrassed though I don't know why.

"I hope it's okay. I wanted to do something useful." I didn't want to be all alone. He smiles and I return the gesture.

"You're telling me *you* made this bread?" Marcus holds a piece of it in the air. I'm beginning to feel annoyed at his attitude toward me.

I lock eyes with him and respond, "Well, I'm not sure if I made that exact loaf, but I did help with preparing several." I shift my eyes to Adrian. "This house must be full of people for how many loaves of bread I saw being prepared."

"There are several families staying here along with soldiers for security. We have a barracks on the eastern side of the house. It allows them to keep an eye on the borders easier."

"And what exactly do you watch for here? What is in the forest?" The border he seems to always refer to is the woods, I think. Is the avgrunn here too?

"There are some things you have no business knowing, woman." Marcus snaps at me. Adrian lifts a hand to calm his friend.

"Marcus, it's okay. She already knows more than others do." He meets my eyes with a wariness and maybe fear. "You know of the avgrunn. There is a connection here with it. It appeared a couple of years ago. So yes, darkness and evil live within the woods. We guard against the black fire that would consume us if we did not work to keep it at bay."

Black fire. Those shadows seemed to ooze from the avgrunn the day I encountered it. My skin grows colder and my appetite wanes. I stare at my plate moving food around it casually trying to force myself to take a bite.

"Is it alive? The fire?"

Adrian stills. "Yes. Yes, it is. It is aware and makes choices like a calculated being. There is nothing but death in its wake if it chooses to destroy. It can turn anything to ash in an instant."

I set my fork down and reach for the glass of water to my right. My hand shakes, but I force myself to control the movements. To control the fear. Something feels familiar about this. But I can't quite place my finger on it.

"And the cryarsh are not a part of the darkness. That black fire?" Meiora has always felt safe to me. But what if it isn't? What if it simply wants me to feel safe?

Marcus interrupts as Adrian tries to respond, "The cryarsh are as old as time. They have existed before the dark fire. They will exist after. They might be ancient, but they aren't evil. Well, unless they choose to be." He shrugs. "Better to stay out of their way than to regret it."

I swallow. This is good news. At least I should feel like it's good news. I force myself to take a bite of bread, but the warmth of it doesn't touch the coldness in my bones now. My stomach feels leaden, and I can't eat much more of this food. Without thinking, I grab the cloak and wrap it around my shoulders again. Marcus stills as he watches me use his belongings. My cheeks warm, but I make sure to keep looking at my plate and try to force down a couple more bites.

We eat in silence for a few minutes. Thankfully, the door opening breaks the awkwardness. Marcus and Adrian both stand abruptly as Gennet walks in carrying a tray with a teapot and cups. I don't have a chance to stand as well before she sits down next to me, setting the tray in the middle of the table and waving the men back to their seats. Within moments, a servant walks in briskly carrying an additional plate and silverware and setting them down in front of the matriarch. She smiles at me and reaches over to squeeze my forearm.

"You look absolutely lovely tonight, Darci." I blush, but she isn't discouraged. "Why on earth are you covered up by Marcus' cloak?" How does she know so much?

"I was a little cold. I didn't have any clean clothes, and this was just sitting in the closet." I shrug, acting nonchalant.

"Aww, she knew it would look lovely on you then." Gennet prepares a plate for herself as she hums. Marcus and Adrian both look up at Gennet then.

"She?"

"Luna of course."

Marcus covers his face with his hand. I look between him and Adrian before turning back to Gennet.

"Who is Luna?"

Marcus waves his hands. "Don't say anything else to her! We don't know if she can be trusted."

"*Faolàn*, peace." Gennet scolds. Her eyes soften as she turns to me. "Luna is the Goddess of Wind and Space. This house was built originally as a shrine to her, and her presence fills this space often. Her magic is imbued in the very wood of the walls. It makes the house more alive than others. It's interesting she has shown such interest in you already."

"Araina helps us." Marcus mumbles.

Gennet laughs. "Araina and Luna do what they wish regardless of what you want, Marcus. You must learn to let go of what you cannot control." Marcus softens in a way I've yet to see under the gentle gaze of Gennet. She turns her attention to Adrian now. "You did not think to offer her some form of clothing, Adrian?"

I'm surprised when I see Adrian fidget in embarrassment, and he looks anywhere but at me. Who is Gennet to him that she so freely scolds the Sovereign of their kingdom?

He stumbles over his response. "Well, I.. I, uh, didn't really think about it."

"Obviously." She smiles. "That dress reminds me of the one Araina wears in the painting in my study." She tilts her head. I feel the heat of Marcus' gaze on me, and Adrian looks like he finally realized why the dress was familiar to Marcus. Before any of us can ask a question, Gennet continues speaking. "Darci, tell me more about your world, child."

Now it's my turn to fumble with my words. Of course, she knows I am not from here. I'm sure most of the people here realize this.

"Well, it's cold." Adrian chuckles drawing my attention toward him for a moment before I continue. "My world is nothing special. It has been broken ever since the war."

Gennet peers at me—-deep into my soul. I squirm under her attention.

"You do not seem to think it can be made whole again."

I drop my gaze to my plate. "I don't know how it can be. We were broken by war and more deaths than I thought possible. I thought we were safe far from the major cities. But we weren't." I meet Adrian's eyes. "They came through the woods to invade every small settlement that didn't stand a chance." His eyes are filled with understanding and grief. We both know the dangers of forests and shadows.

"Hmm, this is the way of evil sometimes. The way of darkness. Your family is not with you anymore, are they?" Again, her ability to know more than she should is unsettling.

I swallow over the lump in my throat at the images conjured up by the word family. "No. They aren't. I couldn't save them."

She nods knowingly. "Saving people is hard. Who were they?"

Adrian intercedes to my relief. "Gennet, she may not want to talk about them. It could be too painful." I smile softly in gratitude at him. Marcus has stopped eating and stares intently at my face now. I shift my eyes to meet his gaze and feel only sorrow and fear there. He knows this pain as well. The normal disdain for me isn't there. I'm surprised by his response.

Gennet shifts in her seat to face me more. "Child, death is painful. But to never speak of those we have lost is more painful still. We speak of them to keep them close to our hearts. You have carried your sorrow and loneliness for long enough."

As she speaks, she makes a cup of tea for me and sets it down next to my plate. I can't stop the deep ache swelling in my chest and throat. If I don't breathe out, I won't cry; but I also might suffocate too. A sob slips from my lips and tears escape my eyes.

"Oh, child, it is okay. Sorrow held at bay too long will eat you alive." I can't look away from her. I can't break eye contact. She sees straight to my soul and the darkness within it. In the corner of my eye, I see Adrian shift in his seat and drop his gaze to his plate trying to give me the privacy I so desire. But it is Marcus who surprises me.

He steps into my field of vision and kneels on one knee between my and Gennet's chairs. His hand reaches for my clenched fists tucked tightly in my lap and the warmth and electricity that seems to always live beneath the surface of his skin stings and slips between my own fingers. It isn't overtly painful. I look at our hands and the blue light that glimmers there before looking up at his deep blue eyes. I see all the same feelings reflected there. He knows loss and death. He knows it intimately. A bridge between two souls joined together by our collective tragedies expands between us.

I take a shuddering breath and close my eyes. As the pain subsides enough for me to breathe, Marcus releases me and moves back around the table to his seat. His absence is deeply felt; but I steady myself and open my mouth to speak.

"My husband and sons were lost in the war. There is only me left. Anyone I knew and loved is gone, but their deaths were the most painful. My husband and I. We tried to save them."

I pause to draw a tight breath. No one speaks though. Not even Gennet. "I wasn't strong enough to get to them in time. The enemy took them and spilled their blood; and they didn't even hesitate. They came out of the shadows and the trees; and all I hear now when I sleep and when I am alone are their screams."

Gennet nudges the teacup towards me again. I reach forward and lift it to my lips smelling warm spices and honey as I take a sip. It is like a warm blanket on a cold winter's night. An image of Meiora flashes into my mind.

"Death is painful. But we cannot escape it forever. May Khitaen guide their souls." She pauses and smiles knowingly towards me. "He is the God of War and Peace." I smile and take another sip of tea.

It's my turn to break the silence. "Gennet, why am I here? Why is there this connection to our worlds?"

She looks thoughtful for a moment and sips her own cup of tea. Marcus and Adrian each fill cups, the latter taking sugar and milk while the other takes it black.

"I'm not entirely sure. I don't know what something like you is doing somewhere like this. I think you are lost with your family gone. Your world is broken by war and violence, but maybe it can be fixed too."

I ponder this for a moment. Sighing, I reply. "I don't know what I could possibly do to help. I'm too tired to keep fighting. Waiting to live or waiting to die. I'm tired of being alone." "You can stay here as long as you want." Adrian offers. Marcus eyes him skeptically.

"I appreciate that. But I know at some point I have to return, don't I?"

Gennet tilts her head and squints her eyes, deep in thought. "You could return. But I think there is more to know here. I think there is more for you to do."

"That is kind of what I'm afraid of."

My mind drifts for a few minutes, and we all work silently through the fragrant food. The meal reminds me of the smells in the kitchen, and I smile to myself when I think of Risa bounding around amongst the adults working. When I think of Risa, I remember the word she called me. Curiosity opens my mouth.

"What is a myrukim?"

Adrian chokes on the sip of water he was taking; Marcus glares at me with such intensity, I imagine I will burst into flames soon. Before Marcus can burn me, Gennet chuckles.

"Who told you about myrukim?" She doesn't seem angry.

"Well, my stomach growled in the kitchen earlier, and Risa said she was afraid I was going to eat her or turn into a myrukim." I glance around at each of them. "Is that a bad thing?"

Adrian mumbles under his breath as he wipes his chin. I think he says something like *that child,* but I can't be certain.

Marcus lifts a finger to speak, but Gennet holds a hand up to silence him yet again. If it's possible, his scowl deepens.

"Myrukim are ancient and sacred creatures of Myzonia. They are the serpent dragons who guard the temples. It is a wonderful thing to see them, but they are very secretive. Moving by magic, appearing only when they want to be seen. We revere them, but we also know they can be deadly as much as they can be gracious in their dealings. Araina created them as a symbol of beauty and life and protectors against the darkness, but this doesn't mean they will not condemn you if you are found wanting."

My skin crawls, but I'm too afraid to ask how one of these creatures finds you lacking. With nothing else to add, Gennet takes a sip of wine. Adrian smiles at me, and I return the gesture even though I don't feel like smiling. There are so many things I don't understand about this world. Mysteries and magical creatures I could never imagine. All of them remind me of stories passed around campfires from years ago. But the familiarity of them ends there. Like my dream, I recognize them, but a door is closed against the truth of the matter. Perhaps, I'll open that door one day. I'm afraid of what I might find.

I remain quiet the rest of the meal, letting Gennet question Adrian on the comings and goings of commanders and leaders. They discuss happenings in the house and stories of what one of the children did to his sister during their lessons. It is lighthearted and comforting. It feels like home and community. I desperately want to be a part of it, but I know I can't be. I don't really belong here.

Later, Adrian walks me to my room, stopping next to the door. I unclasp the cloak again and hand it to him to give back to Marcus.

"Tell Marcus I said thank you. I know it was probably painful for him." Adrian chuckles.

"I'm sure he'll get over it. Though I might have to hear him complain about it smelling like you now."

"Goodness, I hope I don't stink." A joke. I'm making jokes now.

"I don't think you do." There is tense silence where neither of us knows what to say to the other.

Meiora eases out from under the door and rubs against my bare ankles.

Shaking his head, Adrian points down the hall. My room is the one at the very end. If you need anything, please don't hesitate to ask."

"Thank you, I think I'll be okay though. Have a good night."

"Darci." I pause with my hand on the doorknob and look over my shoulder at him. "Please don't disappear again through the night."

"I'll try not to."

I step into the room and close the door. I use the washroom and then collapse onto the bed feeling every muscle release its weary aches and pains into the soft fabric. At least the flowy dress is comfortable enough to sleep in. My clothes haven't returned to me yet, and I'm not sure if I should be worried about this or not. I'm too tired to care right now. Meiora drapes itself across my body letting warm and velvety softness soak into my skin.

My heavy eyes close, and I drift into unconsciousness.

Eighteen

Someone is screaming. It might be me. This feels familiar like somewhere I've been before. Only now, there is only darkness. No light or life other than the pounding of my heart. An explosion happens somewhere. I hold my hands in front of my face, but I see nothing. Humming fills my ears and my veins. My skin is on fire.

I'm looking around for someone. Is it my family? A breeze carries whispers to me, words spoken with menace. Venom drips from every syllable. It's in a language I can't place. Familiar but not quite second nature.

Death is here. Death is all I will find in the shadows.

I yell their names. The moment the words slip from my lips, silence reaches me instead. I feel half awake and trapped in this nightmare. Someone is watching me. Someone is coming.

I feel their presence though I still see nothing. The air feels heavier. The sound of great wings beating the air echoes in the distance. What is that?

A tearing sensation doubles me over as I clutch my stomach. My hands are sticky with blood. My blood. I've been stabbed. I taste copper as I sink into the nothingness around me.

"DARCI!"

I jerk awake to someone shaking my shoulders. Angry, amber eyes lock with mine. Aster.

"Thank goodness, you finally stopped screaming. You woke up the whole house." She releases me as I cover my face with my hands. I'm still here in Myzonia. It takes me a few seconds to shake off the disorientation.

"I'm sorry. I didn't even know." Tears stain my cheeks, and my skin is hot and damp with sweat. Looking up, I notice Adrian standing in the doorway being shoved aside as Gennet walks in. She moves with purpose to my bedside.

"Oh child, you are safe. Do not worry about waking us. It keeps us from getting lazy." Her eyes spark with both laughter and pity. I hate pity. I hate weakness. I'm tired of not sleeping well. I want to know where Meiora is, but I can't find the cryarsh within the shadows of the darkened room. My stomach clenches.

My thoughts drift to Aster's daughter, and I worry I have traumatized her with my screams.

Aster stands from my bed and walks out of the room without another word, nodding in acknowledgment of Adrian's presence as she passes by.

"Now, do you want to start telling me what wakes you in the dark of the night?" Gennet places a cool hand on my arm. "Would you also like to explain why you are still dressed so fancy?"

Her humor releases some of the tension in my chest, and I blush.

"I don't have any else. When I got back, my clothes were still missing, and I was too tired to look for anything else. Besides, Meiora was here with me to help me stay warm."

Adrian steps in carrying clothes that were handed to him by a servant a moment ago. They aren't my clothes, but they look more suited to sleeping than this dress. He sets a long-sleeved linen shirt and matching pants on the bed beside me.

"Here, these will probably be more comfortable." He steps away and walks back to the door. "Hopefully you can sleep better the rest of the night."

He lingers next to the bed, but his expression is strange. He looks at me with a question in his eyes. A question I don't think I can answer yet.

I turn my eyes back to Gennet. She waits expectantly for me to answer her first question. I sigh and smooth the blankets on my lap to give myself something to do. The fire crackles softly in the hearth. It's not as full as when I first came in here, but the coals are giving off enough heat.

"It's only a nightmare. One I've had for two years. Ever since my family died. I don't want to relive it, to be honest." I drop my eyes to my hands waiting for Gennet to prod more. But she stays quiet. The silence eats at me though, and I can't help but speak.

"I think it is a flashback to the day they invaded. I hear screaming. My children scream for me, and I run to them, chasing after my husband. But I fall and I'm too late." My throat is tight, and the last words are difficult to force out. "They are all dead before I can reach them."

My stomach aches at the memory, but the words leave a bitter taste in my mouth. It's not exactly a lie. It is what my dream has always been. Tonight, it was different. Everything about it was different and dark and more evil. I don't tell her that part. I don't tell her the dream has changed.

Adrian tenses and flexes his hands. It's not a happy story. Gennet reaches over and pats my knee through the covers. "Maybe you'll feel better since you shared this fear with someone. Keeping everything locked up inside of you is not good. It will only destroy you more."

I'm not entirely sure this is true. I don't know how I could be ruined any more than I already have been at the loss of my family. But I say nothing else.

Gennet smiles softly and then stands to leave.

"I'll let you get more comfortable and hopefully get back to sleep." She shuts the door gently behind her. Adrian lingers for a moment, and there is an awkwardness about the moment I don't know what to do with.

"I'm sorry I woke everyone up." I rub my forehead, wincing at the stickiness there.

"You don't have to be sorry. We can't control what haunts us at night." He looks at the fire before meeting my eyes again. "I'm sorry for your family. I can't imagine what it is like to lose everyone you love. Especially children."

"There are no words," I whisper.

"Goodnight, Darci." The words are a soft caress after the terror my mind put me through. My lips turn up slightly in response before he, too, steps out of the room. With the door shut, I inhale deeply, holding my breath for a couple of moments, before releasing it back out. The action releases some of the tension built up inside of me.

"Meiora," I whisper.

It appears at the window allowing me to see it against the light of the moon. I sigh in relief and then push the covers back and get up to change. The new clothes are light and loose on my body, but they fit well. I wonder who they belong to. As I step towards the window, I notice Meiora has vanished yet again. Frustration bubbles inside my chest.

My eyes sweep over the scenery outside following the tree line carefully. I freeze, and my heart beats harder. I can feel the room closing in around me as I stare at what stands against the tree line. A sparkling black mass, waxing and waning like waves on the shore, presses against the perimeter of the trees. A figure stands in the middle of the shadows. A being with eyes so white, I can see them from here. I think they might lack pupils altogether. I jerk backward, yanking the curtains closed before I hurry to the bed.

"Meiora, please!" I lose the struggle to keep my voice steady.

Meiora sweeps in around me in an instant. I don't know if hours pass, but it feels like the longest night of my life as I wait for dawn to cast the shadows away. At the first rays of light to peek through the crack of the curtain, I feel myself relax enough to slip into sleep.

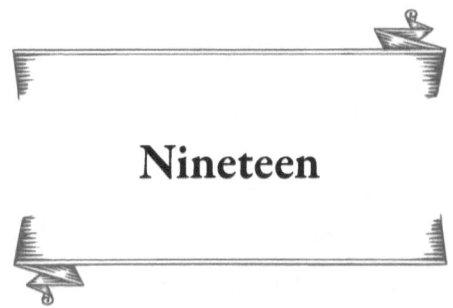

Nineteen

A gentle squeeze along my ankles wakes me up. I squint my eyes against a bright streak of light coming between the curtains. My body is stiff and achy like every muscle has been tensed all night, even into my sleeping hours. Meiora slides off my feet onto the floor and slips under the door leaving me to fend for myself this morning. I sit up slowly and rub my eyes as I get to my feet. There is a clock on the mantle above the fire which is nothing but ashes at this point. It's cold in the room, but I don't mind. The chill sharpens my senses and helps clear away the fog.

It's noon. I blink in surprise wondering why no one came to wake me up yet. Maybe Gennet kept everyone away. Or maybe everyone is afraid of me now. I walk to the window and pull the curtains open letting in warm sunlight. My muscles tense as I search the tree line for whoever, or whatever, was there last night. I need to tell Adrian. Or at least inform Marcus. Someone important should know.

I get the sinking feeling it's because of me. I don't want whatever it was to be after me, but it seems a little too much like a coincidence for my comfort. I use the washroom and wash my face with cold water before heading out the door with purpose. I doubt either man is in their rooms at this time of day, so I head straight for the stairs. As I trot down the steps, I halt in front of Aster at the foot of the staircase.

"It's about time you woke up. I thought we were going to have to summon a *marjol* to wake you." Her arms are crossed; everything about her stands in defiance against me.

"I'm sorry. I didn't sleep well. I didn't realize it was so late." I pause, but I can't resist. "What is a marjol?"

Her eyes narrow, but she still answers me. "A marjol is a death speaker. They communicate with the dead to give us answers or peace or relief. I thought maybe you had died of fright up there."

"Oh. Well, I didn't."

She smirks, but I continue.

"I need to speak with Adrian. Do you know where he is?"

A spark of anger flashes in her eyes again at my informal use of his name, but I can't change what I've grown used to.

"He's meeting with the commanders. I'm sure whatever it is you need from him, it can wait."

"Where are they meeting? I promise I won't interrupt. I'll wait outside the door." I lift my hands in a plea. I don't know how much I should tell her, and she dislikes me enough I'm not sure she'll take anything I have to say seriously.

She points down the hall towards the back of the house. "They're in his private study. I'm sure you are familiar with it?"

"Okay, thank you!" I don't linger and scurry to the back of the house where the study is that housed me on my first night in this world. When I reach the closed door, I hesitate, looking for somewhere to stand or sit as I wait for them to finish.

Multiple voices break out into arguments on the other side of the door. It's too difficult to understand exactly what is being said. Whatever is bothering them, it must be important. Maybe they already know about the creature. Could it be why they are meeting? To discuss plans for guarding the estate against the enemy?

Goosebumps appear on my arms when I picture the creature with solid white eyes staring at me amidst the writhing darkness.

It haunts me whether I'm awake or asleep. Another nightmare to follow me for the rest of my days.

Several minutes pass, and the sounds within the room become calmer and more focused. Next moment, I jump as the door opens, and men and women I've never seen before stream out. There are six of them; all dressed in warrior uniforms with swords strapped to their backs and ornate gold detailing in the form of what looks like a serpent on the upper right corner of the shirts. After what I learned last night, I realize the image must be that of a myrukim. Three men and three women walk out eyeing me suspiciously as I stand awkwardly to the side.

When the last one steps out, I move to enter the room and run into Marcus.

"Why must you always be in the way?" He grunts and moves me to the side with one shove of his hand. He doesn't give me the chance to apologize before he walks briskly down the hallway. Adrian smiles grimly at me from the chair by the fire.

"I hope you are feeling better this afternoon." I walk over to the bench under the window and sit down.

"Yes, I am. No, I don't know why I said that." I shake my head to clear my mind. "I didn't fall back asleep until dawn. It's why I slept so late, but it's not why I'm here. I need to talk to you about something I saw."

He raises an eyebrow but says nothing else, so I continue.

"I saw a creature of some sort and darkness that seemed very much alive along the edge of the woods last night. After everyone left. I don't know what it was. But I think it saw me in the window." I look down at my hands feeling oddly ashamed.

He rubs his brow, "I know what it was. It was not a creature. It was the Dark Lord of Daemons. He is the one we must be on guard against. Some patrols noticed the disturbance last night and it's what we were all discussing. How to prepare." He says nothing else, but my gut tells me this is not normal.

"Oh. I, uh, I wanted to make sure someone knew about it."

Adrian's eyes soften, "Are you okay? Were you able to get some restful sleep after your nightmare?"

"Yes. Eventually. I'm sorry for waking everyone up." My cheeks flush with embarrassment. The buzzing beneath my skin starts up again. My fingertips tingle, but I ignore the sensation for the moment.

Adrian studies my face. He wants to say something more, but he's keeping silent. Questions swirl to the front of my mind, and I break the stillness yet again.

"What is your magic?" He blinks in surprise at my question. "I mean, if you can tell me. If you want to. Tell me that is." I keep getting more awkward.

He clears his throat and holds his hands up for me to see. A green light glows across his fingers and expands up his arms. I hear a hum increase as the light strengthens. I'm awestruck as I watch the light form a shape and then soften as a flower appears in his hand.

"You...you just made a flower appear." I know my mouth hangs open, but I can't help it.

He laughs, "This is my favorite part of my magic. The part that allows me to create new things, new life." He flicks his wrist and flower petals cascade around me in the chair. A rainbow-colored bird bursts from the downpour of color and swoops around the room before landing near the window. With another twist of his wrist, the window opens and the bird escapes to freedom. Obviously, he can do more than just create.

"You can also heal things. The way you healed me." I gaze at his fingers before pulling my eyes up to his face.

"Yes. It sort of goes hand in hand with life, but magic can also be a weapon and used to manipulate peoples' minds and physical bodies. I can do great damage as well. But I prefer to heal."

"Is that all then? You create life. You heal things. You open windows." At this, he chuckles again, and I can't help but smile.

"Well, when you put it like that..." He stands and holds out his hand to pull me to my feet. "It sounds more impressive than it is. I guess I shouldn't tell you I can travel too." My face must convey my confusion. Instantly, he vanishes from my sight and appears beside the door leading outside.

"Oh, so that's what it means." I walk to his side as he opens the door and steps outside into the cool air.

"All people have magic here, but like I told you before, some are stronger than others. My strength is good for leading. Others contain raw energy in their hands so powerful they serve as excellent commanders of my army." Like Marcus, I wonder.

"Do you ever worry they will try to overthrow you?" It seems like a reasonable question.

"No. They are trustworthy, and they trust me. Plus, my best friend is more powerful than any of them."

"Marcus?"

"Yes. He is both strong and deadly."

We walk out into the yard and meander through what must be beautiful gardens in the spring and summer. The path we take has been cleared of snow. I remember the electric power that surged into me when Marcus knocked me out the first time I was here. I don't find it hard to believe he is as powerful and as deadly as Adrian suggests. He is also angry every time I see him.

"Tell me what you're thinking about." I jump and look over to Adrian on the stone path. "Your mind is always working, isn't it? Do you have other questions?"

I ponder this for a minute. "I'm sure I do have other questions. But I was mostly thinking about how scary Marcus is." Adrian laughs tilting his head back. It's a full body laugh, and I can't help but smile in response. "What? His magic hurts like death, and he is always angry."

He shakes his head. "He's not always angry."

"He is every time I see him." I point out.

"Well, okay. Maybe he is always angry when he's around you. But he has good reason to be guarded." I raise my eyebrows at this. "He does," Adrian reassures me.

"I didn't realize I was such a threat to him. Or maybe he just views me as a threat to you somehow."

"It's not that. I don't think you are dangerous. But this is all very strange. We have known about the other realms for as long as our history goes back, but as far as I know, they have always remained separate. My counselors have been searching the histories, but there is no record of anyone traveling unintentionally between realms. At least not consistently. We can use strong blood magic or a token to be used only twice, but it is dangerous and most of the time we avoid doing that. We've only ever known the gods to be able to manage the act at will. Your connection to me and your ability to bypass those laws is strange. He worries you are bringing something more dangerous with you. He lost his sisters in the war for the throne five years ago. He doesn't want to lose anyone else."

We stroll silently for a few minutes. I can understand his dislike of me. I can also understand why he wants to protect his friend and his people. It reminds me of his tenderness when I spoke of my family killed by war. We could be a little more alike than I thought. Though, instead of being angry and on guard, I feel numb and empty. There is no fire in me anymore.

I'm about to say something else because apparently, silence is hard to maintain when you've spent so much time forced into it by loneliness, but the buzzing I've felt under my skin since earlier suddenly increases in intensity.

I stop walking and rub my fingers together, closing my eyes as the tingling grows more insistent.

"What is it?" Adrian faces me; I feel his presence. I hear the hum of magic under his skin. Magic. That's what this is. It's buzzing and alive like a million tiny fires sparking across my body.

I swallow and grimace because it's getting painful. "I don't know." My head is pounding. I turn my body away from Adrian's and end up facing the woods. The fires in me die slightly. I take one step toward the tree line, and it softens even more.

It's not a conscious effort to go to the woods, but my body notices the reprieve the closer I get to them.

"Where are you going? Darci!" I feel his hand grasp my forearm. What feels like lightning flashes through my skin and burns as I scream and jerk away falling to the ground.

He stares at his hand, then at me. I know he felt it too. Two guards come running toward us, called to our location by my screaming. Black light pulses over my hands and my skin reddens with heat. Where his hand had touched my arm, blood seeps out from my pores. What is happening??

He's yelling something at the guards. Something about Gennet, but I can't hear the rest. I turn to my hands and knees and start crawling towards the trees. My ears pop, but the closer I get to the woods the more relief I feel. Adrian comes to my side and kneels beside me, afraid to touch me again but wanting to do something.

Suddenly, I feel velvet and coolness touch my back, and darkness envelops me. Meiora. It's instant relief at the same time I collapse to the cold, hard ground. My mind goes blank and dark, and the last thing I remember hearing is Adrian's panicked voice outside Meiora's shield.

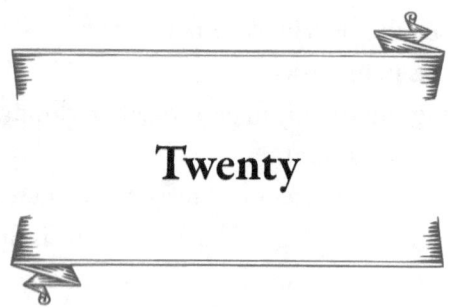

Twenty

I blink my eyes open to see nothing but shadows over my face, but I'm not afraid. This darkness is familiar and soft and tangible. Meiora saved me. It stopped whatever was happening to me, the horrendous pain I had been feeling. I let myself breathe deeply the scent of earth and spice. As my mind wakes up, my other senses follow suit. I'm lying on the ground curled in on myself. It is completely dark, but I know it is only the cryarsh. I hear voices speaking quickly and urgently around me.

Adrian and Gennet talk back and forth. I hear him telling Gennet what happened. Marcus' voice interjects with anger. There are two other voices murmuring softly to the side. Maybe the guards who came running to help. I slowly inhale and then look at my hands. There is something glowing around my fingers. It's barely discernible in the shadows of Meiora, but I think it's light. Black light. I clench my fists and the glow is snuffed out.

"Okay, Meiora. I think it's safe." I whisper. The velvet shadows caress my face and then begin to lighten and dissipate. I blink against the light of the sky and sit up slowly. Adrian drops to his knees next to me and slowly moves his fingers to my neck.

"Are you okay?" He stops before touching me. His eyes move down my body to the blood still oozing slowly from the handprint on my arm.

Gennet and Marcus step up beside him. Gennet looks concerned and *tsks* when she sees my arm. Marcus eyes me closely; all his walls up revealing nothing about what he truly feels.

"Umm..." I cough lightly. "Yes. I mean. I'm not dying anymore. Or at least that's what it felt like." I try to stand, but my legs feel useless and Gennet's hand rests on my shoulder to stop me.

"Give yourself a moment, child. Can you tell us what happened?"

My stomach churns. "It hurt. I heard or felt a buzzing. Then, pain like a fire. I couldn't get it to stop."

"There was light on your arms and hands. A black light I've never seen before." Adrian looks at my hands like he's expecting to still see it. I was hoping he hadn't. I keep the information to myself that I still saw it moments ago in the shelter of Meiora.

"I don't know what it was. It hurt, and it just kept growing."

"It's okay. You don't need to remember everything perfectly now. It was a buzzing you said?" Gennet pats my shoulder gently.

"Yes. I felt it earlier today, when I woke up. Actually, I've felt it a few times since being here, but it was so much worse this time. It was like I was burning from the inside out." I close my eyes and grimace.

"You burned me," Adrian says. Marcus jerks his gaze to Adrian and grabs his wrists forcing his palms up. The hand he touched my arm with looks like he held it to the fire for a second too long. Not too severe, but enough to make it angry and red. I look down at my arm again.

Gennet reaches towards me and places her cold hand along the bloody wound. I hiss in pain at the touch, but only for a moment. A cool sensation spreads out around the wound and the ache there slowly ebbs away. She's healing me. I glance up at Adrian and see his palm lighten again, the red giving way to healthy skin. Violet light dances there like it did on my wound the first time he healed me.

I stand slowly, accepting help from Adrian. I'm a little shaky but feeling better. The hum is still there under my skin, but nowhere near as amplified. It has to be magic. But why would I have any? Why now?

Gennet takes my arm and leads me back to the house.

I sneak a glance at Gennet's face. Marcus and Adrian stay behind talking heatedly. She looks pensive. Worried. I've never seen Gennet worried. Though I've only been around her for a short amount of time, she always seems so self-assured. Knowing all the little secrets of the realms and beyond. It's disquieting.

She hums in thought. "I don't know what exactly it was, but I think I can find out for you. Why don't I take you to your room to rest for a while, okay?"

"Oh, um, yes. That sounds good." Being locked away feels a bit ominous now.

"Actually, I think a trip into the village would be good," Adrian calls out. He watches for my response. He must notice the relief I feel at the suggestion.

"That sounds like a terrible idea." Marcus crosses his arms with all the fluidity of a mountain.

"I think Darci should have a chance to see our home. If you're feeling up to it, that is?"

I nod, "I'd like to."

He holds a hand out for me to take. "Come on, let me grab something inside first."

"Adrian, I don't think this is a good idea."

"Marcus, let him take her. It might do her some good. We'll talk later." Gennet moves ahead of us, disappearing to the side of the house instead of going up the back steps.

"Marcus, why don't you join us?" The smug look on Adrian's face is unexpected, and I have to cough to hide my laugh. Marcus smirks in return.

"Sure. Just what I want to do. Walk to the village today."

"I'll buy dinner." With that settled, Marcus falls into step behind us.

As we walk into the house, I notice the servants avert their eyes from me. There is a tension that wasn't there the day before when I made bread alongside Aster with Risa bouncing between us joyfully. Now, I feel like a prisoner who has committed some terrible crime. I sense their unease at my presence. The appearance of my cryarsh may be the cause of a lot of this discomfort, too.

Adrian grabs a cloak off the hook by the front door, and I'm surprised to find my cloak hanging next to where his had been. It's cold here, but not bitter. The stroll through the garden was brief, but the walk into the village must take longer.

At my confusion, Adrian hands me my cloak. "The house probably put it here after it was washed. Come on. It doesn't take too long to walk into Zaiven."

Marcus steps through the front door ahead of us and sets a brisk pace down the path toward a slightly wider dirt road. Only a single wagon could come through at a time on this path. We walk in silence for a few minutes. I use the time to absorb the surroundings. Open fields border each side of the road with a scattering of trees here and there. Everything is coated in a thin blanket of white snow. A few birds caw from the treetops, and the sun creates diamonds as we walk. Thankfully, the air is cold enough the road is solid, and not the muddy mess I imagine it to be in the spring when everything thaws.

"How big is the village? Zai...?"

"Zaiven. It is the home of a few hundred people. Large enough to warrant a market and a pub. But small enough no secrets are safe." Marcus snorts ahead of us.

"It sounds nice. To be known and to know others. My town is too far away to justify going there often. And there isn't much left of it. One store to buy things, but not many people still live there. Everyone went to Novundo. The capital."

"Is your capital nice? Is it ruled well?" He looks at me expectantly.

"No. Well, I don't know since I have never been there. But the new sovereign is one of the results of the war and keeps any wealth of Oria to himself and those he favors. I don't imagine he cares much about the poor or forgotten."

He nods and turns back to the road. We walk in companionable silence then. Marcus doesn't slow down for us, but Adrian doesn't seem bothered by the privacy his distance gives us. It isn't much longer until the road widens and small huts with smoking chimneys come into view. Cozy homes line the streets. They're not extravagant, but neither do they appear destitute. The road widens until we come into a large circular section and the houses are traded for wooden stalls in a charming market. It bustles with activity—-people, children, and animals. A few dogs bound around legs while chickens peck at the ground behind makeshift pens of glowing strings. Magic permeates the air. The hum reaching out to me and awakening the strange light under my skin. This place is wonderful.

I stare wide eyed as children dart back and forth chasing each other and a few stray goats. Lights pulsing with power illuminate each stall where all sorts of wares are being sold. Sweet smelling breads and cakes at one. Baskets and colorful woven blankets at another. Beautiful hand carved bowls and spoons adorn the counter of one stand; trinkets and salves another. People haggle good naturedly with each other, passing coins and other items back and forth.

A sign reading G&G's hangs outside a stone building on the far side of the circle that must be the pub Adrian and Marcus spoke of. Laughter and chatter spill out of the door every time it opens. I finally turn my gaze to Adrian who stands there beaming at me.

"This place is amazing. Can I live here?"

He laughs. "We could arrange for you to stay, I'm sure."

"No, we can't," Marcus grumbles before striding towards a booth selling what looks like arrows and daggers.

"Well, not all of your natives are friendly." At this point, I'm beginning to find Marcus' behavior endearing. He is definitely growing on me, though I can't say the same for him.

"You can't expect perfection everywhere, I guess." Adrian's eyes twinkle as he gestures around the market. "Where would you like to look first?"

I spot a stand selling beaded necklaces and bracelets alongside one selling wood carvings of myrukim. "Can we start over there?" I point to the dragon stand.

"Lead the way."

The carvings are beautiful and painted an array of colors. The serpent bodies of the dragons display clawed feet and large, wise eyes gazing outward. Some are made curled into themselves like a cat. Others show the creatures raised up on their back feet, powerful jaws open wide to destroy. These are the images I've seen carved into the mantles around Adrian's house.

An old woman with olive skin and gray streaked hair hobbles over to me. "What can I help you with, dear?" Her voice carries a unique accent I've yet to hear from the others.

"Oh, I don't have any money." Adrian steps up beside me, and the woman gasps.

"Your Highness, what brings you to my stall today?" She clasps a cane made of a black wood with a myrukim carved into the top.

"Meesha, this is Darci. She is a friend of mine. I'll cover anything she wants."

"Oh, you don't have to." I try to stop him, but Adrian gently takes my hand and squeezes. Butterflies come to life inside of me.

Meesha smiles. "Well, it is a pleasure to meet you, Darci." Her eyes are a cobalt blue. "You are such a beautiful creature to grace us with your presence here. I've no doubt His Highness has noticed." She winks.

I blush and shift on my feet. "Oh, uh, thank you." My eye catches on a smaller myrukim curled into a restful pose. The wood is polished and painted blue and violet. It reminds me of peace. No war. No fighting. No death.

I glance at Adrian before pointing to the piece. "What about this one?"

Meesha picks up the small figurine and hands it to me. The wood is surprisingly warm and the hum of magic swells in my chest again. "This one is a favorite of mine."

Adrian hands her a silver coin which she stashes quickly into a pouch. "Always a pleasure, your Highness."

I clutch the myrukim to me as we walk through the rest of the market. Adrian purchases a couple of pastries that smell of cloves and cinnamon and melt the moment they hit your tongue. They are divine. I laugh and marvel at the magic on blatant display around me, and I'm more than ready for food by the time we sit at a worn table in the corner of the pub with Marcus.

"What do the Gs stand for in the name?" I ask, taking in all the noise and laughter around us. A few people nodded in greeting to Adrian and a couple of men even clapped Marcus on the back as we passed.

"Ginger and Gwenyth. They're twins who inherited the business from their father." Adrian explains. Before I can inquire further, Marcus directs a question to Adrian.

"Did you find anything useful to waste your money on today?" He chooses to act like I don't exist. It's fine.

"We bought only what was absolutely necessary." Marcus doesn't miss the bite of sarcasm in Adrian's voice.

Adrian shifts his body towards me. "Gwenyth and Ginger make the best cider in the kingdom. It's spiced perfectly, and you can't visit Zaiven without trying some."

"I guess I'm trying some then." I chuckle. Marcus rolls his eyes.

A beautiful blonde woman with fair skin saunters over and rests her hands on the back of Marcus' chair. "Well, well, well, look who the myrukim brought in." Adrian smiles at her while Marcus remains resolute. Not stiff but not relaxed. I wonder if he would be different without me here. Her purple eyes move around the table, falling on me last.

She is riveting. I know I'm staring.

"And who might you be?" The question breaks the trance. A pulse of magic stretches from her before washing over me. Do they ever get tired of being bombarded by magic all the time? I imagine it would get annoying after a while.

"I'm Darci."

"Gwenyth, she is a guest of ours. She's new to the area." Adrian gives her a knowing look she obviously understands.

"Well, your first cider is on the house then, and I recommend the chicken pie tonight. Ginger has been getting a little creative with the stew recipe. She hasn't touched the chicken pie, though." Gwenyth tilts her head towards me like she's sharing a secret between friends. "I don't recommend being an experiment for her. Her food is divine, once she's figured it out. Until then, you can never be sure what you will get."

Adrian and Marcus both chuckle at this which surprises me.

"I trust your judgment then."

She smiles at me and then boldly reaches forward and massages Marcus' shoulders.

"And what about you, gentlemen? The same? Goodness, Marcus, you're as stiff as a stone statue sitting here." She leans forward to whisper something in his ear I don't catch, but the warmth rising into his cheeks says all I need to know.

"We'll take the same," Adrian says through a laugh. She slips away through the tables back into the kitchen with the same grace she descended upon us.

"She seems nice. And her eyes are mesmerizing." Marcus ignores me and instead searches the room for...well, I'm not sure what he's searching for.

"They're both kind and generous. Many of the people here are like family to one another. The war a few years ago stole a lot of loved ones from us all. We make it work now with those left behind." I understand. War and death break and destroy all in the name of power or greed. A somber mood settles on us all, and we remain silent until our food arrives.

The rest of the evening passes with laughter and stories from Gwenyth and an appearance by Ginger. The only physical difference between the two women is Ginger wears her hair short. Ginger also seems a bit bubblier and full of manic energy. I can easily picture her experimenting with seasonings in her kitchen, attempting to create a new bestselling dish for their clientele. I'm lost in thought, mesmerized by the community here when she directs a question toward me.

"So, Darci, how are you liking your visit to our little town? I know we can be a bit much. But it's really a lovely place to live. It's wonderful to have so many good friends to surround oneself with." Ginger stops only to look expectantly at me. I'm not entirely certain how to respond.

"I..." I'm not quick enough for her though.

"I know, it is hard to be in new places. But you should really stick around. We can always use more ladies to add to our group. Do you like the cider?"

"It is really good." Ginger's enthusiasm doesn't require much from me in the form of communication apparently.

"Oh, wonderful! Glad you like it! Would you like more cider?" Her wide eyes glow with exuberance.

"Ginger, love, please shut up. You aren't even letting her get a word in." Saved by Gwenyth. The others stifle their laughter, but she is unbothered by their reactions.

"Oh yes! Sorry, I talk too much. I need to go check on the stew. Nice to meet you! We'll chat soon!" And just like that Ginger disappears. Not sure I would actually be able to chat with her. I stare dumbfounded for a moment, then turn back to Gwenyth.

"Does she actually expect me to carry a conversation or is it okay if I just sit here?"

Marcus chokes on his cider while Adrian laughs hard.

Gwenyth chuckles. "That's Ginger for you. Best part is you don't have to do much to keep her carrying on."

"I can tell!" I smile and feel the knot in my chest unravel more. Community, friendship, belonging. Maybe there is hope for me here in Myzonia. Maybe I could make a life among these people.

Marcus loosens up as the cider flows, and I feel a little woozy myself from the one cider I drank. I drink water the rest of the time since I don't want to embarrass myself on the walk back to the house. By the time we stand to leave, Ginger and Gwenyth have invited me to visit with them at the end of the week, stating no woman should be left to the companionship of His Highness and the High Commander alone.

I wrap my cloak tighter around me as we step into the cold of the night. Torches adorn the road out, and the warm glow of firelight escaping the windows of the homes we pass has me feeling nostalgic. It's a relief to be out of the pub with everyone's magic bombarding me. Perhaps, I'm more sensitive to it now that I have been here longer. Adrian notices my reticence the farther we get from the village.

"Hey, are you okay?" His fingers brush my arm. Marcus sets a fast pace ahead of us and is far enough away, I don't think he'll hear us.

"Just thinking about how beautiful it is here." I pause for a few more steps. "I like it. I've missed being a part of something more. For some reason, I feel like I've been on the outside looking in for all of my life. Always wanting more. Always longing to be the person people like and want to be around. Instead, I think I'm the villain of my own story." The feeling is painful to articulate, but it's true. I rub the small myrukim carving with my thumb as we walk—-a new nervous habit. I've felt like the villain of my life for as long as I can remember, and all I've ever wanted was to be a needed member of the community.

"You're not the villain. I don't believe that. You are kind and gracious. I've watched your interactions with everyone today and yesterday. There is a gentleness to you." He glances at his feet before stopping me with a hand on my shoulder. His deep brown eyes search mine. "Besides, we're connected, you and I. If you're a villain, so am I."

I smile softly but don't have any words to say. We walk in silence the rest of the way.

Back at the house, Adrian walks me to my room and leaves me at the door whispering goodnight as he walks to the end of the hall. I step inside and lean against the closed door.

"Meiora? Meiora, are you here?"

The shadow appears instantly in the corner of the room and holds the shape of a man. I breathe a sigh of relief at its presence.

"I don't think I belong here, Meiora. I think it's time for me to go. There is something wrong with me." I stare down at my hands, palms out. I don't see anything on my pale skin.

Meiora moves towards me hovering across the ground. It stops in front of me; wispy shadows fanning out around the shape it holds.

"Is there magic in me?" I whisper, afraid to know what might be living beneath the surface of my skin.

Then, Meiora does something I've never seen it do before. It forms a hand out of the shadows extending on a wispy arm. The shape looks more solid and begins to sparkle. Its hand turns over palm up, and a light glows and forms, sparkling like frost in sunshine. The fingers flex and curl, and the light grows in intensity. I gasp as Meiora closes its fist and then points a finger toward me.

I look down at my hands. Spreading my fingers wide, I focus on the buzzing beneath the surface. The ever-present hum is so much more noticeable now. I imagine the black light I saw before. I imagine seeing it glowing across my knuckles and fingertips.

But nothing happens. I exhale and close my eyes. When I open them, Meiora still hovers in front of me. It points again at me, but this time emphasizes the area over my chest. Directly above my heart.

"You know, that's not incredibly helpful, right?"

If a shadow can be sassy, Meiora pulls it off. Its presence sags and shifts in a way that makes me giggle, which feels absolutely absurd right now.

"Okay, okay. I'll try again."

I close my eyes and take another deep breath. I focus on the hum beneath my skin. How it tingles and pulses with energy. It's electric and fiery at the same time. The sensation intensifies almost to the point of getting a little painful. I feel my breathing quicken and my heartbeat race.

Suddenly, something warms my hands burning through my fingertips. I open my eyes and see black light dancing across my hands. It swells and grows, becoming hotter. It is pure power and strength. It is magic. Meiora moves and sways in excitement, but I begin to sweat because whatever it is doing to me, it hurts.

My skin prickles, and the light scatters up my arms and around my body. It reminds me of Meiora's shadows, but this black light is more aggressive. This magic wants to get out of me, but I'm afraid it will consume me in the process.

Fear pulses in my chest now. As my fear grows so does the reckless nature of this power.

"Meiora, help me!" I hear the panic in my voice. It swells in size and then drapes across me. Instantly, the cryarsh smothers the light, and the magic blinks out. The pain is gone, and Meiora releases me from its embrace.

I pull in a breath and stumble towards the bed. Collapsing there, I close my eyes and feel myself sink into oblivion. My mind lingers on one thing. I have magic, and it might be deadly.

Twenty-One

The silent darkness around me is not empty. Something watches me from the shadows. I feel the weight of their presence. I can't see anything. Not even my own hands as I reach out around me searching for some tangible object. My heart pounds, but I hear nothing else.

Hello?

I take a step forward and what feels like a stick cracks under my feet. I look down, though I don't know why I think I will see anything there. Squatting, I use my fingers to explore the ground. There is something sharp here. The sting of a cut makes me pull my hand back, hissing through my teeth. I feel the warmth of blood trickle into my palm from my fingertips. I'm more cautious this time, seeking the object on the ground. I feel a broken edge of a long, smooth object.

I explore a moment longer only to realize with dread I'm holding the long bone of a leg. I drop it and bolt upright. The movement knocks me off balance, causing me to stumble back a couple of steps hearing the crunch of what is undoubtedly more bones.

My skin crawls. There is a slight intake of air behind me, coming out of the shadows. I whip my head around. Still nothing. I feel panicky and might be on the verge of hyperventilating. This is nothing like I remembered. There is a stillness here that makes no sense. The line between dream and reality is blurred.

I clench my fists and squeeze my eyes shut. A tingling sensation crawls along the surface of my skin. It burns and warms me. I know this feeling. I felt it not long ago.

I look down at my hands to see a glow of dark light flickering there. The flames dance across my knuckles and wrists and begin to climb up my arms. Every inch gained causes more pain, more burning. I try to resist. I try to make the light go away, to force it down into my tight fists to be snuffed out.

But the more I fight it, the more it grows and overwhelms my senses.

A hiss slithers out of the darkness around me. Words whispered that I don't understand. I blink and look up to see solid white eyes staring back at me.

I want to scream, but the sound dies in my throat. I step backward and look down at my hands again. Only magic can help me in this situation; I have nothing else to defend myself with. But I also have no control over this power coursing through my veins.

This isn't real. This isn't real. It's just a dream.

I relax my hold on the magic. I smash down all my walls and feel power sweep my senses and my body. Light explodes from my skin. Black shadows are at the core of it, and white flames lick along the edges of the shadows.

It stands before me—white eyes watching and its solemn mouth in a straight line. I don't see the mouth move, but I hear whispers.

Words fill my mind. Words I don't want to hear. A sudden clarity about what they all mean. I scream and fall backwards to my back feeling a stabbing pain through my spine. Light glows around the stark point of deadly bone jutting out through my core. I fell on a bone.

I'm going numb.

I'm dying.

I'm dead.

I JOLT AWAKE, MY MOUTH open in a silent scream. I'm clutching my stomach, but there is no bone. Magic dances across my skin. It stings a little, but it is nowhere near as painful as before. I shut my mind down on the memories of the words it spoke to me in the nightmare. Instantly the magic vanishes like blowing out a candle.

Sticky with sweat, the fog around my mind clears, and I start to hear other sounds outside my door in the hallway. Voices talking urgently back and forth, and footsteps moving quickly toward the stairs. Something is wrong.

I throw the covers off me and rush to the door. Opening it carefully, I peek out hoping I don't run into anyone less than thrilled with my presence here. The hall is empty, but I hear an anguished scream downstairs. A knot forms in my throat as a weight settles in my stomach.

I whisper, "Meiora, come with me." Instantly my shadow is there by my side, hugging the wall to look less conspicuous. I hurry out of my room and down the stairs. People are running back and forth. I follow the cries to the study in the back of the house. A servant brushes past me quickly carrying blankets and linens. I step into the room; my mind whirring as it takes in the focused chaos of the scene.

Adrian kneels next to a man sprawled out on the sofa near the fireplace, but I can't see his face. Gennet rests a hand on Adrian's shoulder. Marcus holds someone back from the man. A child cries in the corner. *Risa.*

My stomach churns. It's Aster fighting Marcus. Aster trying to get to the man lying on the sofa. Her husband. She has a husband. Instantly it's like my brain clicks on all the way. Marcus yells for someone to take her away. To get her and Risa out of the room. Another woman I recognize from the kitchen grabs Aster and pulls her, but Aster is strong with grief. She finds me and the hatred in her eyes forces me back a step.

"It's your fault! You did this!" She screams. A guard joins to help contain the fury and pain giving her so much strength to fight. Someone scoops up Risa and soon the screams and cries are contained to outside of the closed door. My hands shake at her words. Did my presence lure danger here?

Marcus steps up to put more linens on the man's bleeding abdomen. Adrian holds his hands over the wounds and light pulses out of him. But there's so much blood. It's pooling on the floor. Gashes split his tunic in several places. I'm sure each gash penetrates deep into the soft tissues of his body. Places that don't heal easily. The magic under my skin rumbles to life when I hear the man struggle to say words.

I don't realize I have walked over to him until Gennet places a gentle hand on my lower back. Adrian glances up briefly. The man is still speaking. *Hoku.*

His name is Hoku.

I feel the burning under my skin; the power is so close to the surface. But I am not afraid. I don't resist it. I let it swell inside of me. I let my breathing calm and slow. This is familiar. My instincts lead the way, and I know what to do for some reason.

Hoku mumbles, "I just... just want to... see..." His words slur and his brow is damp with sweat.

Adrian shakes his head towards Marcus. The blood-soaked linens pile up on the floor next to us. Marcus removes the pressure from the wounds. The blood slows but doesn't stop.

I kneel next to Hoku's head. His eyes lock onto mine, and he gasps. Adrian stares at my hands. Black light dances across my skin. I know it does because I feel it, though I can't unlock my eyes from Hoku's. Meiora slithers over his body, and I know it offers only comfort and warmth and velvety shadows like it has done for me so many times.

He whispers as his eyes search mine. "You." His voice is weak but unafraid, speaking like old friends reunited again.

I don't know what I'm doing, but I feel it. The magic controlling my movements. I place my hands on his chest. The shadows within me seep into him into all the places hidden by Meiora and the ones that are not. He stills and his labored breathing eases.

He smiles for a moment. His eyes look strangely at peace. My skin warms and then cools, like fire and ice. Something slips into me. There is more to me now than there was before.

A moment passes, and the light in his eyes slips away into shadows. He sees nothing now. No pain in this world anymore. The magic in my blood shuts down as quickly as it came.

"To Arawnia now," Gennet whispers.

The word is foreign to me, but the magic in my blood sparks in recognition. This is right. This is the way it was supposed to be. I want to ask what Arawnia is, but the reverence of the moment demands silence.

The nightmare. Whatever it was I went through in my mind. I did what I was supposed to do because of it. At least in this, there is peace.

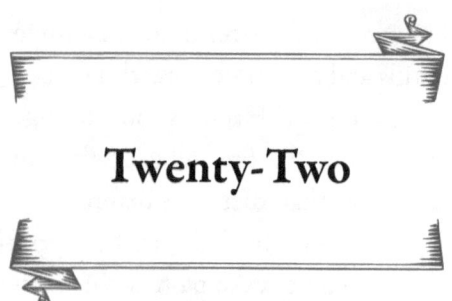

Twenty-Two

Gennet whispers what sounds like more prayers as she turns her eyes toward me. I see the questions and wonder in her gaze. Adrian's stare feels heavy at my back, but I don't turn around. Marcus curses and then throws another sodden rag on the ground. Pain is palpable in his voice.

I can't take my eyes off Hoku. The pain and sorrow that Aster and Risa will soon feel overwhelm me. It is a pain I am deeply aware of. I have tasted death and have known it intimately. I don't wish this on them, but I can rest knowing that for a brief moment, he was peaceful. He did not struggle as his soul slipped away.

"What did you do?" Marcus snarls. His voice breaks the spell I'm under, and I rise to face him. Adrian moves quickly to stand between us.

"I... I don't know." It's only a partial lie.

"What did you do? Where did you get that magic?" His voice gets louder with every word.

"Marcus, stop. Hoku was beyond even the help of our magic. There wasn't anything else we could have done for him." Adrian tries to reason. But his friend's rage grows, and dangerous light crackles across his knuckles and forearms.

"I wasn't trying to hurt him. I only..."

"You did something to him!" he interrupts.

I step back bumping into Gennet who has finished her prayers. Marcus lunges towards me; and though he is only slightly taller than Adrian, he is fueled by grief and rage. He pushes past Adrian and clasps my wrist, burning with icy-cold wrath. I gasp, but before anyone else can react, Meiora appears and shrouds us in black.

My arm is released as Marcus lets out a pained cry.

"No! Meiora!" I cry out and the strange black light sparks from my fingers and reveals the room to me. Marcus stumbles backward gripping his arm; Adrian reaches to steady him as Meiora swells up in size and freezes at the sound of my voice.

I take a shaky breath. "No, Meiora. No more. Please." Meiora shrinks back down and slides around my legs reminding me of a cat once again. It doesn't leave my side, acting as a guard and protector. The room lights up again as Meiora reels the shadows back in.

Adrian looks at the dark mark staining Marcus' arm. I step over quickly not caring that he had tried to harm me. Marcus seethes, but I grab his other hand pulling it free from his injured arm. Blue light sparkles along our joined palms, but it doesn't burn. I release his hand to place both of mine on the dark mark as he winces. Adrian steadies him before looking at me.

"What are you doing?"

"I'm not entirely sure yet."

Marcus scoffs, "Well, that's a relief."

I narrow my eyes at him while Gennet tells him to hold still. She still watches me like she's seeing me for the first time. Curious and intrigued. It unsettles me.

I concentrate and feel the shadows change under my hands. The black mark on his light, brown skin begins to seep into my hands, leaving behind no mark or blemish. The shadows simply came back to me. I feel the muscles of his forearm tense and then ease, and his breathing slows.

Lifting my hands away, I turn my eyes to his. He still looks at me with suspicion, but it feels less hostile, if only a little bit less. I'll take what I can get. I'm going to need to talk to Meiora about attacking people, though I know it was only protecting me.

"Very interesting." Gennet mutters. It's enough to make me shift my eyes away from Marcus'. "Adrian, why don't you and Marcus find Aster."

My stomach feels tight again, remembering that cries of the grieving will consume the rest of the night no matter what.

Both men stiffen at the reminder. Marcus pivots and walks quickly to the door. Adrian lingers only a moment, trying to figure me out before he follows his friend. They shut the door behind them.

"I don't know what happened. I wasn't trying to hurt him, I promise." I ramble my defense before this woman; my voice coming out in choked gasps. I think she truly sees me, and I am terrified by this.

"Child, peace. I think it is time for us to talk." She gestures to the door and guides me from the room, leaving Hoku's body behind. We step down a narrow hall off to the side of the main one and end up in a tiny study I haven't been in before. Everything about the room reminds me of Gennet. This must be her private space.

I sit in a small armchair across from a larger one. A crate contains red hot coals to keep the room warm though an active fire isn't burning in it. I consider speaking again but decide it would be better to wait and let her do the talking first. On the back wall is a portrait of what must be Araina—I see the resemblance between the dress I wore at dinner and the one on this beautiful goddess before me. The pulse in my throat skips a beat.

She tilts her head as she watches me. The undivided attention makes me squirm. I clear my throat a couple of times but remain silent.

"I have not seen magic like yours before. I have heard of it. But I have not seen it."

"I don't know what it is." My hands are moving of their own accord at this point. "This is insane. I have lived in a world without magic all my life. Why would I have magic now?" I press my palm to my forehead, forcing myself to still the jittery movements.

"You didn't seem completely lost when using your magic now." She's right, and she's wrong. The magic seemed to control me more than anything, but it also feels like an old friend. Or like pulling on a favorite sweater on a cold day. Comforting. Familiar. Warm.

"It seemed to know what to do more than me."

One side of her mouth curves in question.

"A long time ago, when the realms were created, there were only the gods and goddesses. They created the realms out of a desire for goodness and beauty. Each one brought something to the creation it deemed necessary. Many of the deities controlled opposite strengths.

"Luna is the Goddess of Wind and Space. Movement and stillness. Khitaen is the God of War and Peace. Markyr is the God of Fire and Ice.

"But not all of them contained opposites of their powers. Araina is the Goddess of Light but not of darkness. Cryirz contains the power of darkness but not light as the God of Night. And finally, the one who brings death and destruction. The one we do not name as the God of Death, but not of life. All the gods and goddesses worked together until something caused a break in their work. War broke out among the gods because the God of Death thought he should have more power than he should. Instead of working for the good of his realm, he slaughtered his subjects. I'm not as well-versed in his history. Not like the priestesses in the temple would be, but I know the other deities fought to restrain his power and subject him to an obscure existence. I believe you should do some learning of your own at the nearest temple. I think you are connected to this place in a way we haven't yet seen."

My heart pounds. These words are so familiar. These gods and goddesses remind me of a place I have been, but it's not Oria. It's not what I've known as home. A part of me suspects this isn't entirely true either. There's more to the story even Gennet doesn't understand.

Gennet continues, "We do not know the names of all the realms. Only that they exist. For one to continue without magic does not feel right to me. I think there is more to your world than you know, Darci. I think there is more to you than we have discovered. For some reason, you have been brought to this world. You did something to Hoku that released him from this realm. I don't think it was evil. But you did it. And you did it well. Not as someone who has never tasted magic before or felt its power surging through your veins."

"But I don't know anything about it. That's what I'm trying to say. The magic controlled me. It moved on its own."

"It wants out. That's why it hurts when you suppress it. When we deny who we are, pain is the only natural response."

We stare at each other for a moment. Finally, she speaks again, but her words are anything but comforting.

"You need to use this magic. Learn what it can do. You need to go to the temple closest to us."

"I don't know where that is." I'm being sent away. Banished. Always on the outside, never accepted within.

"Marcus will take you." She doesn't even hesitate.

"What?! He...he hates me." She looks deeply into my eyes, and I see a spark of concern there.

"He will not be swayed by you should you prove to be...unable to contain the power within you." I nod slowly as I realize what she's saying. She doesn't trust me alone with Adrian. Not away from this house at least. I am a mystery to her now, and I know the way he looks at me. Like he's intrigued but also drawn to me. Drawn dangerously, and he is their sovereign.

"Okay. I will go to this temple. When do I have to leave?"

"Tomorrow morning. I will speak with Marcus tonight."

I stand to leave but stop at Gennet's calm voice. "Oh, and Darci, try to get some good sleep. It is a bit of a journey to get there." Annoyance flares in my chest. I suppress it, but it is there nonetheless. Before I pass the threshold, I remember the question I wanted to ask.

"Oh, Gennet?" Her eyes capture mine, waiting. "What is Arawnia?"

Her smile is sad. "It is the afterlife. Paradise."

I nod but say nothing else. Passing the threshold, the magic moving through me drains away until I feel no buzz or hum.

Dread weighs my feet down every step I take up the stairs. Soft crying and moaning come from the back of the house. I hate this. I hate the pain and suffering death has brought. I didn't ask for what happened to him. I didn't ask for him to be injured. But I have a good idea who it might have been. Tension sits heavy in my body. A pulling apart of what I did and the pain death brought too.

I reach my room and gently close the door behind me. The fire crackles softly; the darkness outside is still heavy. I won't need to get up for a few more hours at least.

Meiora curls around my feet as I crawl back into bed after cleaning my hands of Hoku's blood. Staring at the ceiling, everything feels different and dangerous. Being alone with Marcus tomorrow weighs heavily on my mind. I hope we can make it to this temple without anything else going wrong. I fall asleep clutching the myrukim figurine.

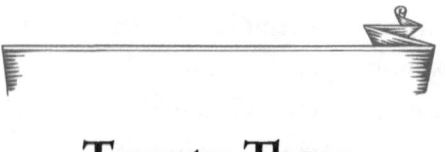

Twenty-Three

Adrian

"This is madness." Marcus exudes frustration as Gennet attempts to reason with him about taking Darci to the temple. It's at least a three-day journey there, and neither of them will let me consider taking her. It makes sense, but I don't have to like it. I have too many things to address back in the capital. A messenger arrived bringing news about a rebel group faithful to my father's legacy attacking random markets throughout the city. I am not the sovereign my father would have left behind. I know they need me to be there for leadership and to condemn the violence.

But I would rather go with Darci to find answers to our questions–especially the one I want to ask about our connection. I could easily shift us to the temple to save time, but Gennet is insistent I cannot go with Darci. She looks worried which is out of character for her. Her concern is the only reason I defer to her wisdom in this. However, it doesn't stop me from suggesting it once again.

"I could take her myself."

"No!" They both shout. I'm dumbfounded by Gennet actually raising her voice. I don't remember her ever shouting at me before. I shake my head to clear my thoughts and try again to change their minds.

"Marcus doesn't want to take her. I can take her a lot quicker than he can. I'll be back with answers before you even miss me."

"If you think I'm letting you wander off with that witch, you are insane. Yes, you are powerful; your magic stands alone as far as we know. But we don't *know* anything about her power. *She* doesn't seem to know anything about it. I'm not letting our Sovereign walk alone with her and risk her harming you." Marcus huffs in exasperation.

Gennet bites her lip, turning towards the window. She watches the woods, and I wonder what she is looking for.

"Why do you assume there is something wrong about her? Maybe she's supposed to be in this world. I can't explain it, but I feel like I'm supposed to know her." I feel uneasy because I understand why Marcus is against her. When she dreamt the other night and screamed loud enough to wake the dead, I heard her whispering words in a language I did not recognize. Her voice carried through the walls to me.

The memory of them leaves me unsettled. A part of my mind screams that I know the language, but I can't place it. I also know there is goodness in her. I've seen it in her interactions with others. She wants to belong somewhere. She doesn't want to be alone. I don't think she would intentionally harm any of us.

She did do something to Hoku, though. I tried desperately to heal him, but Marcus and I both knew he wouldn't survive. She came and seemed to call him into her. She gave him peace in those final moments. I shudder slightly at the memory. If Gennet thinks we can all get answers from the temple, then we will go to temple.

"Adrian, you can't expect her to be good. You can't expect kindness and good intentions from everyone you meet. Sometimes, people are bad no matter how much you wish they weren't." His eyes betray the hurt buried deep. He is a tortured soul.

"Marcus, I am not a fool. But I would rather hope for goodness and be prepared for evil. Besides, we need answers. Right, Gennet?"

She finally turns toward us, her face haggard and full of something I'm not used to seeing there. Fear. The realization startles me.

"Adrian, we do need answers. You will not get them with her. Marcus will go." He starts to protest, but her hand silences him. "There is nothing else to discuss. She needs to go to one of the temples; and if something is to be done with her, Marcus is the one strong enough to do it."

A knot forms in my stomach. "What do you mean? Gennet, we are a peaceful people. I'm trying to make a better world for us here! I don't want to resort to violence when we don't have to."

"Sometimes, a better world requires great sacrifice. Whatever draws you two together will dampen your senses and alter your focus. Marcus will not hesitate."

That's why she wants to send him. She knows Marcus would already have killed Darci if given permission. He doesn't trust or like her.

"For Araina's sake, Gennet!" I turn toward Marcus and point. "You better not do anything without absolute just cause."

Marcus holds his hands up. "I will only do what is necessary to ensure our survival."

"It's all I ask." I turn my attention back to Gennet. She knows more than she's telling us. Or she is at least suspicious. It worries me, but if she thinks this is the best course of action, I trust her judgment even if I hate the potential outcomes.

Marcus sighs, "Well, I guess I should try to get some sleep if I'm doing this." He leaves the room without another word. I'm exhausted, but I don't want to sleep. Gennet watches me closely, but she leaves keeping her thoughts to herself. I'm left alone with the fire in the hearth and shadows on the wall.

Twenty-Four

Darci

My eyes snap open. The room is mostly dark, but the gray light of morning seeps through the curtains. It must be before dawn when the sun hasn't quite crossed the horizon. Meiora slips from the foot of the bed onto the floor and slinks to a dark corner. Waiting for my command. What woke me up?

Insistent knocking resumes on the door. I jump up, grabbing pants and a tunic before running to the washroom to dress. Pulling my top over my head, I hear the door to my room open. I yank it down over my head, shoving my arms into the sleeves when I hear cursing and angry footsteps coming to the washroom. Quickly, I step into my pants and get them buttoned when the door swings open. I shriek at the sight of Marcus standing there in black pants, a navy tunic, and a scowl on his face.

"What are you doing!?"

"Why aren't you ready?"

"No one told me when we were leaving. And I am ready." I gesture to my hastily covered body. His eyes scan me before snagging on my bare feet. I roll my eyes. "Well, I'm almost ready. Don't you have any manners?"

"We need to leave now, and preferably without waking up the entire house with your squeals."

My mouth drops open. I must look ridiculous, but is he blaming me for my squeals when he barged into my room first? And I don't

squeal. He hasn't moved from his place in the doorway. I cross my
arms and raise my eyebrows.

"Well, are you going to move?"

His jaw tenses, and he steps back. There's another knock at my
door before it creaks open a crack. I see Adrian poke his head in and
look around. I squeeze past Marcus and go to grab my boots next to
the bed.

"Is everything okay in here?" Adrian steps the rest of the way in,
glancing toward Marcus.

Marcus is about to blame me, I'm sure. So, I interrupt before he
has a chance. "Yes, everything is fine. I was just startled for a moment.
There. I'm ready." Meiora moves from the corner and drapes itself
over my shoulders like a cloak. I slip the myrukim into my pocket.

"Are you sure you want to do this?" Adrian's voice betrays his
concern. Marcus' jaw tightens, but he doesn't say a word.

"Yes, I'm sure. I want answers. You need answers. If this is the
best way to get them, then I'm willing to go." I lower my voice
slightly, "But if it were up to me, I'd rather go with you." Marcus
crosses his arms and grunts in annoyance. Adrian smiles down at me.
It makes my heart flutter.

I turn to my guide and point to the door. "Shall we?" He stomps
from the room, and I follow. I don't know if I need supplies, but I
notice he carries two pouches for water and his weapons. I guess we
aren't expected to bring anything else.

I hesitate for only a moment as I think about the possibility that
he will kill me the moment we get far enough away from here. I don't
have much choice in the matter at the moment. Meiora offers me the
only comfort as we move down the stairs and into the foyer. Adrian
grabs my hand before I go out the door.

"He only wants to protect Myzonia, and he is loyal to me and
like a brother. He won't hurt you. I don't think you're a danger to us."
I swallow back the knot in my throat. I understand Marcus. More

than he realizes. I nod at Adrian and follow his friend toward the woods. I wish I felt the same way, but this magic inside me doesn't feel innocent.

MARCUS IS TALL. I'M more aware of this than ever considering how hard it is for me to keep up as we take a narrow trail through the trees. For every stride he takes, I need to take three, and at this rate, I'm going to be exhausted before we even get through the first day. Surely, we'll rest at some point. Meiora follows the path, moving quietly around trees and branches. It doesn't cling to me, but it is there, watching and following as we move through the shadows of the trees.

Despite the cool air, sweat trickles down my back and my lungs ache. We haven't spoken a word to each other in the past few hours. We march onward into the depths of the forest around us. Life bustles about with birds singing and critters chattering. The occasional deer is spooked by our approach and dashes into the shadows. My stomach growls reminding me of the haste in which we left, but he shows no sign of stopping.

More time passes and at this point, I might need to intervene. Even if it's just to rest for a few minutes. The trail we walk is narrow and full of rocks and roots. A thin layer of snow cushions are steps, and the soft crunch of our boots fills the air. Branches reach inward towards us clawing and grabbing at our cloaks. I hear a screech behind me and make the mistake of turning my head towards the sound only to trip on a root jutting up in the path.

I stumble and fall barely managing to catch myself with my hands before my face does. The snow stings my hands. A moan escapes my lips as I push up to my knees. Boots step into my line of sight, but he doesn't offer me a hand up. He simply stands there. I decide to take advantage of this moment and remain kneeling on the forest floor to catch my breath. I inhale slowly before letting it out, feeling my heart rate slow down.

"Are you done?" He sounds more annoyed than ever.

I glare up at him. "I need a minute to catch my breath." I debate saying nothing else, but my mouth gets the best of me. "Do you have any water?"

He snatches one of the pouches from his belt and hands it to me. I gulp down cool water like a fish stranded on shore for too long. I expect him to snatch it from me. But he doesn't, and I'm smart enough to know I shouldn't drink all of it. I leave it half full, secure the lid, and hand it back to him. I move to stand feeling the aches in my knees and hands.

He watches me closely for a minute. Then holds his hand in front of him, and a spark of magic flashes in his palm. When it's gone some type of pink fruit rests in its place. He offers it to me.

"Wha...how did you do that?" He tilts his head; his expression saying I shouldn't have to ask. "I mean, I didn't know that was possible. Especially from you." I grumble the last part, but I see his eyes spark with annoyance.

"If you don't want it, you don't have to eat it."

Suspicious, I reach out and take it from his hand, careful not to let any part of my fingers touch his skin. "Is it safe to eat?" I sniff the strange fruit. It smells sweet and warm like a summer peach but mingled with the tartness of an apple.

He laughs, and I jump at the sound. It is such an uncharacteristic sound coming out of him—it makes me smile.

"If I wanted to kill you, I would do it. I don't think poisoning you would be my first choice. Why waste the time it would take to wait?"

"I wouldn't put anything past you at this point. But what is this?" I take a small bite out of the pink fruit. Sweet juices flood my mouth.

It tastes like a cross between an apple and a strawberry. Or maybe a blueberry. It's nothing like I remember tasting back in Oria.

"It's a *stygo*. They keep you feeling full longer, so you don't need to stop as frequently for food." He turns back to the path and walks away.

I hurry to take a few more bites and then jog to catch up. Between stealing bites of stygo and avoiding falling on my face again, I don't know how I managed to finish the rest of the fruit without choking.

"How long will it take to get there?" I breathe out as the trail winds around a cluster of giant trees.

"Three days."

"Three days? At this pace? With rests, right?" He doesn't answer. Three days at this blistering pace? I might be dead by the time we reach the temple. I wonder if the priestesses there can bring me back to life.

I try three more times to start up a conversation, but Marcus refuses to engage. I give up and focus on breathing and keeping up with him instead. After another couple of hours, we step into a small clearing full of leaves and logs from fallen trees. He slows to a stop and sits on a log pulling out the pouch of water and drinking.

I glance around and sit down away from him. I don't ask for my water. I need to conserve it. I haven't seen any place for us to refill them along our path so far. It makes me wonder if we will find any as we walk.

"You're tougher than I thought you would be." He steals a glance at me but does not explain.

"What? You thought I couldn't handle running after you through the forest for the past several hours?" My feet ache, and I'm starting to feel chilled from the dampness of my shirt against my skin. But I don't shiver. I hide any weakness from him as much as possible.

He smirks, "I didn't expect you to complain so little. You haven't even asked for more water yet."

"I haven't seen us pass any water on this journey yet. I know how to conserve resources. You're not the only one who has learned how to survive."

He is thoughtful as he watches me. Then, he unclips my water pouch and hands it to me. "Here. We're about two hours away from a stream where we can drink our fill and refill these. Drink what you want."

I don't take my eyes off him as I drink the rest of mine. I hand the empty pouch back to him as my stomach rumbles again. He pulls something wrapped in cloth out of his pocket. Unrolling it, I see two pieces of flatbread. He takes one and gives me the other.

"No magic this time?"

"I can only summon small items of food. Besides, I wanted to get as far into our journey as possible before eating. We'll have to hunt along the way some. But this should keep you going until nightfall."

We eat in silence and then continue our journey.

"Why do you hate me so much?" His shoulders stiffen at my question.

"I don't hate you. I just don't trust you. There's a difference."

"Could have fooled me," I mutter.

He stops abruptly forcing me to do the same to avoid colliding with him. "Listen, I don't know who you are or why you have magic no one knows much about. There is something about you we don't understand. Adrian is my sovereign and my friend. I see how he looks at you, and he trusts this situation too easily. Maybe the gods are testing us—testing him. I will do whatever I have to in order to protect him even if it means protecting him from himself."

"I don't want to hurt anyone." My mind sticks to the one sentence he spoke I shouldn't focus on. *I see how he looks at you.* I shouldn't say anything else. "What do you mean how he looks at me?" Obviously, I can't take my own advice.

"Like he is intrigued enough to jeopardize his safety. You don't belong here, and the sooner we find out why you are here. The sooner you can leave. I don't care whether you two are connected or not."

I cringe at the words. I finally thought I had found a place where I wouldn't be so alone. A place where I could belong after everything I have lost, but I seem to be an outsider no matter where I go. Aster doesn't like me, and I'm sure she will hate me even more when she finds out what I did with Hoku. Maybe this is for the best. Maybe I'm meant to be all alone.

I don't know if he sees how his words have wounded me. I avert my eyes from his and nod toward the trail behind him.

"I guess we better get going then." He watches me. I feel him wait for me to look at his face. I don't. I steel myself against the emotions tightening my chest. I lock down my feelings and let the numbness I am so used to wash over me again.

Marcus covers his pain with anger. I cover mine with apathy. It hurts too much to feel. Being here has opened all my scars again letting them bleed. Being here gave me a small taste of community. It also reminded me why I have sequestered myself in my house on the hill, tucked near the woods. Where death and shadows are the only friends I have. I feel the sting of tears behind my eyes for only a moment before I harden myself against them. Show no weakness. Admit no defeat. Not yet.

Maybe he sees this on my face—sees the iron locking into place around my body like a shield. Meiora lingers in the shadows but keeps its distance. In my peripheral vision, I see his shoulders soften. I see him slightly lift a hand to do what, I don't know. Then, he turns and continues down the path, slower this time. I shouldn't have to rush to keep up, but the weight of my existence makes every step feel labored. Everything is hard, and I'm tired of it.

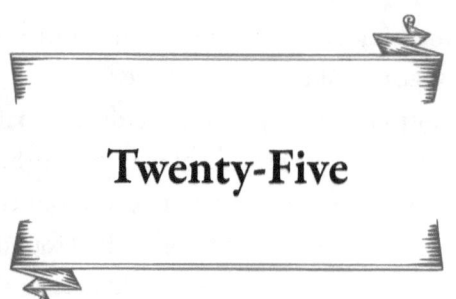

Twenty-Five

Believe it or not, the path narrows further. Old growth takes over a lot of where our feet are stepping. I shiver constantly at this point. My clothes are not warm enough; and in my haste to leave this morning, I didn't think to put on extra layers. Combined with my sweat, it feels even more frigid. I notice Meiora out of the corner of my eye, and I finally decide I can't wait for us to stop and start a fire.

"Meiora, please," I whisper, but I see Marcus hesitate briefly ahead of me. He slows down and looks over his shoulder watching as Meiora sweeps in quickly to wrap itself around me. I instantly feel a bit warmer, though it's not as much as I was hoping it would be.

He stops and takes in our surroundings. "If we walk about ten more minutes, we can stop to camp for the night."

Clenching my teeth to control their chattering, I nod and follow him again. True to his word, there is a small cove on our right with what looks like a cave tucked in among the trees and dry grass. He gathers up fallen twigs and branches and walks to the cave opening. I reach to grab some sticks myself, but his warm hand grabs my arm when I reach out of Meiora's covering.

"Go sit down. We can't make a big fire anyway. This will be enough." I say nothing as I walk toward one of the larger rocks by the cave and plop down. I'm so tired, physically and mentally. My body hurts all over. My feet and fingers are numb, and my jaw hurts from biting down every time my teeth start to chatter.

Marcus sets up the sticks and branches near me, pulls some grass away from the cave, and holds up a glowing ember of fire in the palm of his hand. In mere minutes a crackling fire spreads its warmth toward me, and I feel tension slowly release from my body.

He disappears into the woods, and I'm beginning to wonder where he has gone. "Maybe, he decided to leave me here to be eaten by...well, I don't know what I would be eaten by here, Meiora." The cryarsh moves off my shoulders and curls around my lower legs.

"What am I even doing? I'm not wanted here. I'm wasting everyone's time." I take a deep breath, letting the pain buried so deeply bubble to the surface. Tears slip unbidden down my cheeks. Shadows stretch across the ground as the sun sinks lower.

"I think it's time to go home, Meiora. I don't need to disrupt everyone's lives here." I picture my sad house. The emptiness of the rooms. The shadows haunting my dreams and the terrors watching my steps. I wish I'd never found this place. I wish this magic inside me had stayed dormant never to wake up. If I leave now, I might find a way to slip back into my world. I have no idea how that would work, but it might. I need to leave before Marcus gets back.

And if I don't survive, well, I don't care at this point. I push myself to my feet, swaying from the fatigue coursing through my veins. Every muscle protests as I walk. I look around for anything to take with me, but everything was with Marcus. I'll have to trust I can find what I need on the way.

"Come on, Meiora. Let's go home."

I watch the path we came on. No sign of Marcus yet. I can't follow it or he'll find me too easily. Instead, I turn toward the tangle of branches and trees extending behind the cave entrance. With no idea where I'll go, I push past them slowly and quietly. I have enough experience hunting to know how to disappear.

I slip along silently for ten minutes before I hear a loud crack of a branch snapping. I whip my head around to look behind me, but I don't see anything. I turn to go forward and run straight into a hard tree trunk. I grab my head and feel the warm trickle of blood oozing out of scratches across my forehead.

"Just great," I murmur.

I move a few more steps only to be stopped by strong hands grabbing my arms and hauling me backwards against a strong body. I scream but stop when I'm forced around to face my captor, only to see Marcus' deep blue eyes and permanent scowl glaring back at me.

I sag in relief. Then, remember I don't want to be caught.

"Where do you think you're going?"

I yank myself free. "Let me go."

"Why would I do that? How would I explain to them my inability to keep track of you?"

"You can tell them I disappeared again. I vanished while we slept."

"And how exactly were you going to vanish?" His tone drips with disdain. "You have no idea how to travel between realms. You don't know anything about the dangers you could unlock by doing so."

I throw my arms up in exasperation. "I don't know what you want from me! You want me gone. You don't want me to ruin your world by leaving and letting something else in. I can't do this anymore! Please, let me go. You...you can..." I stammer, not quite having the fortitude to declare what I think he should do.

"I can do what?" He demands.

My throat constricts, and the ache in my chest deepens. Tired. I remind myself. I'm so tired.

"If you won't let me leave, kill me now instead." His eyes widen briefly and something like shock crosses his face.

"I won't harm you. I promised Adrian that I would get you to the temple and back and that's what I'm going to do. Do you think I'm dishonorable?"

"Then let me go. Please." I hate how weak I sound. I hate how tight my voice is.

"Where would you go? You'll die out here from exposure or an animal attack."

I capture his eyes with mine and will him to see this is okay. I don't need to keep going. I can be done with all of this. I can be done being the monster—the villain of the story here. He softens briefly.

"You're not dying. Not today at least. I don't know who you are. But you don't get to ruin my friendship to make yourself feel better." He grabs my upper arm and burns my skin.

I scream and go to tug away from him. He releases me quickly looking at his hand in surprise at the magic glowing there. Between lack of food and half running all day through the woods, my body has finally had enough. The pain of the icy burn pushes me over the edge and my vision goes dark as I lock eyes with Marcus. The last thing I remember is him reaching for me quickly as my knees buckle. Then, there are only shadows.

MY SKIN IS TINGLING. I blink my eyes open and squint against the orange, flickering light of a fire. The smell of roasting meat makes my stomachache. I sit up slowly and notice a cloak draped across my body.

"Take it easy. Don't move too quickly." Marcus kneels next to me holding up roasted meat of some sort. "Here, eat this."

"What is it?" I gingerly take it from him feeling a stinging sensation across my upper arm.

"I know what you're thinking, and it's not poisoned." Is he making a joke? I catch his eye and see mischief hidden under the mask of annoyance. It's a side of himself he rarely shows me, but I like it. I smile back.

"I meant what *kind* of meat is it?" I take a bite. "Rabbit." I close my eyes and let the warmth spread across my tongue. Hot food never tasted so good.

"Impressive. You didn't even need to ask." I open my eyes to find him holding up more meat for me to take. He notices the question in my eyes. "I've already eaten one. You can have all this one."

As I reach to take the rest of the meat, I wince at the pain in my arm. "May I?" He asks.

I shrug and continue eating. He gently rolls up my sleeve exposing the raw skin to the crisp air. Right where his hand had grasped me, I have a burn mark in the shape of his fingers. Just like our first encounter.

"I'm beginning to think this is the norm with you." I joke. He jerks his head toward me. "I only mean, you left your mark on me the first time we met too."

"Unfortunately, I can't heal you. I'm sorry. His fingertips brush across the angry mark, and I suppress a shiver. He holds my arm in his hands softly. "I can wrap it."

He goes to tear the hem of his tunic.

"No." He stops and looks at me. This is the closest he's ever been to me. His blue eyes hold mine unwaveringly. "No. It's cold enough; we don't need to lose fabric that keeps us warm. It will be fine for now."

He lingers and then stands and sits across from me.

"Why would you want to die?"

I'm startled by his question. I didn't expect to speak with him at all tonight.

"I... I'm tired of having to try so hard to make it another day. It's too much, and since I seem to be condemned to a life alone, what is there to live for anyway?"

"And who condemned you to such a life?" I ponder the question for a moment.

"I think I did. It doesn't matter." A sad smile ghosts my lips. "I'm not wanted anywhere. Everyone who ever cared about me is dead. No one would miss me."

He waits, watching me closely to see what I'll say next. I swallow and stare at the fire. "I've lived by myself for two years. Too many friends or neighbors I knew either died or moved as far away from the woods as they could get. There's not much point in me being home. But it's better than being a burden on everyone here."

I laugh but it holds no joy. "I thought I might find a place at your house. With Adrian. I might find friendship with Aster or maybe Gwenyth and Ginger." My words die out. Marcus looks down at the fire. "I was wrong though. It's time we stop believing it could be otherwise."

Neither of us speaks for a while. He opens his mouth to say something, but I hold my hand up. "I don't need your sympathy."

I stand and walk over to him, handing him his cloak back.

"You keep it." His eyes never leave mine.

"No," I say letting it drop into his lap. "I will get you back to your people safe and well. You won't end up sick or dead from the cold because of me."

I lay down on the ground with my back toward the fire, toward Marcus. Meiora lays across me as a cloak in place of his. I feel him watching me. I know he wants to say something, but thankfully he doesn't. It doesn't take long for me to fall asleep.

Twenty-Six

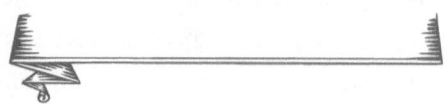

I stand alone in nothing but darkness. Shadows and white eyes watch me. Someone screams behind me. It sounds like a child–maybe more than one. My heart races as the pitch changes. I recognize those screams. Explosions of black fire rip through the air behind me. I want to turn. I want to run after them. I want to stop this madness, but I can't take my eyes off this thing in front of me.

Whispers seep into my ears, my skin, my soul. The words shake me to the core. Lies! They're nothing but lies. This isn't happening.

I step back feeling the crunch of bones under my feet. He steps forward. Eyes wide seeing all of me. His hand reaches out and shadows erupt out of his fingers, twining around me like ropes and making me stumble to the ground. They burn. I'm dragged backward feeling the crunch of my knees on jagged bones and blood seeping from wounds. I try to scream, but no sound comes out of my mouth.

My throat constricts. This is it. This is what was supposed to happen. Their screams fade away to silence. Everything is ending, including me. I hate this. I hate who I am and who I will never be.

I let myself go limp, surrendering to the sweet embrace of nothingness. The sound of great wings beating through the air somewhere reaches me. As I give in, I hear the creature or man or whatever it is speak.

"Your time has finally run out, Ancient One." Nothing but pain burns through my skin, and all I hear are those wingbeats.

"DARCI!" SOMEONE IS smothering me. I can't breathe! He's not in the dream anymore, and I'm being taken. Where is Marcus? Did he escape?

"Shhh! Shhhh! It's okay. Everything is okay." There is something familiar about his voice. I let my breathing slow. I stop resisting as warm magic slips into my skin from the hand over my mouth. I must have been screaming. As my senses become more focused, I take in the smell of smoke from the fire. The scent of mint and earth and smoke is all around me. A warm, strong chest is pressed to my back. One arm is wrapped around my waist, the other is slowly loosening from my mouth.

Marcus.

He sits behind me, holding me tight. The more I relax and calm down, the more I feel the tension release from his body. He slowly pulls his hand away from my mouth. I can't move. I stay leaning back, ensnared by his other arm.

"Was I screaming?" I whisper.

"Yes." He pauses. "I'm sorry for silencing you. But I couldn't risk you drawing more attention to us."

I nod, understanding there are shadows in the darkness we don't want to encounter. I become painfully aware of his presence around me. The beating of his heart. The rise and fall of his chest. I sit up and hug my knees into my chest, resting my chin on the tops of them. He moves out from behind me and returns to his position on the other side of the now-smoldering fire.

"What do you see?" I blink up at him but say nothing. "I've known you for only a short time, but I've seen you have multiple nightmares. So, what do you see when you dream?"

I chew on my bottom lip, then take a deep breath before responding. "It's changed. It's not the same anymore. Not what it used to be." I search his face to find questions there unasked. He waits for me to continue. "I have relived my family dying over and over again for more than two years. Their screams. Trying to save them and being too late." He doesn't look away. He holds my eyes with his, unwaveringly. It's a little mesmerizing.

"You said they've changed? How so?"

"There's always been darkness mixed with their deaths. Always sorrow and pain. But lately, I've noticed a change. Something seems to be reaching out to me in my dreams. It–it wants me. I either wake up because I'm stabbed or dying or falling. But darkness always consumes me in the midst of it, and it hurts when I resist." I stop myself before I say too much. I don't know whether to share about the creature or man in my dream. I don't know if I should tell him what it called me. *Ancient one.* What does it even mean?

We sit in silence for a few minutes.

"My family all died too. During the war that allowed us to place Adrian on the throne. They were killed then. I couldn't do anything to stop it. I know what your nightmares are because I have the same ones."

I don't turn away from his pain or the grief I see deep in his eyes. He offered me the respect of looking at the sorrow inside of me; I do the same for him.

"I'm sorry. For your family. I would wish this pain on no one. Even someone who wants me gone."

He smiles softly and looks down at the fire. "I may not want you here, but I don't think you're bad. Maybe Adrian is right in thinking there is goodness in you."

I think he's wrong. The more I remember about the war in my world, the more I think nothing I have been through makes sense. Everything feels broken and displaced inside of me, like a puzzle with the wrong pieces forced together. I want to be someone other than me.

"Well, you could help me figure out how to get back, and I would be off your hands." He purses his lips but remains thoughtful. "Anyway, I'll try not to wake the forest this time." I shift around to face away from the fire again. Keeping my back turned to the one person most interested in getting me out of his world.

I hear him shift on the dirt and sigh. We both lay there pretending to sleep for the longest time. As the fire dims, I hear the soft rhythmic breathing of sleep coming from him. I shift my body to sit up again. I won't sleep the rest of the night. It isn't safe.

Instead, I keep watch over the fire and listen to the night noises coming from the darkness around us. In the distance, I hear the occasional beat of something familiar, but it doesn't draw closer.

The night drags on until a soft glow finally breaks through the trees. The sun is rising, and the world will soon be awake. Meiora slips away after spending the darkest hours with me. Marcus slept deeply all night. I wonder what it would be like to sleep so soundly even in strange surroundings. I creep away from the cave to relieve myself and return to find a shadow creature hovering only a few feet away from a wide-awake Marcus. He sees me shaking his head to get me to stop.

At first, I think it's Meiora, but there is an ominous presence about this one. This shadow doesn't like us. This shadow intends to harm. My heart thuds as the tendrils of darkness spread out from the creature toward Marcus who cautiously rises to his feet allowing magic to stir at his fingertips. I've never had to consider how to kill a cryarsh. Meiora has never posed a threat to me before. Will magic do the trick? Or does it have to be a certain type of magic?

It moves like a snake seeking prey. Only this snake is far more frightening than any others I would encounter here. My mind races through ways I can help. As Marcus slowly lifts his hands toward the creature, it senses the movement and expands so quickly I don't notice it move.

In the next instant, Marcus is shrouded by darkness and screams of pain pierce my ears. "No!" I run forward without hesitation, feeling the burn of my magic swell inside my veins. Strange black light erupts from my hands towards the cryarsh. The creature pulls back as quickly as it has attacked. It cowers on the ground near a tree as I rush to Marcus' side.

His skin is sliced and bleeding. It looks like someone tried to carve him with a knife across his arms and sides. My hands rush to expose his wounds; his face contorts in pain as I pull the sleeves up. I'm not thinking anymore. The magic is controlling it all. I sense the power searching his body. It takes an inventory of the wounds and their severity. None are fatal. I reacted quickly enough to prevent the cryarsh from doing more damage.

In the corner of my eye, I see Meiora move and form a man's silhouette between us and the other creature, standing guard. Marcus has an especially nasty cut on his right side, but there's nothing I can do other than apply pressure. I don't know how, but I know my magic doesn't heal.

He blinks his eyes open, and I see the moment he notices the cowering cryarsh.

"How did you do that?" I look into his face and see nothing but wonder there.

"I don't know. I told it to stop."

"I knew you were friends with one cryarsh, but I didn't know all would bow before you."

I roll my eyes, "It's not bowing before me. And neither does Meiora for that matter." He lifts an eyebrow in question. "I call my cryarsh Meiora. It needed a name, and we agreed on one."

"You—agreed?"

I laugh. "Yes. I made some suggestions, and it made it quite clear to me those were not worthy of it."

He winces as I lift his shirt to check the wound. It isn't bleeding any more. Of course, I also used his shirt to stop the bleeding; so, he might not be as grateful as I would hope.

"Thank you. For helping me."

"You would have done the same for me." The expression on his face says this is debatable, but it makes me laugh all the same. "I'm sorry I can't heal you. I wish I could. I can at least tell you won't die."

This makes him laugh. "How would you know? Although, I do agree. The wounds ache, but they aren't deep."

"I don't know. It's like my magic evaluated you. I knew you were safe from death like I knew Hoku could not escape it." His eyes lose some of their light, but he doesn't seem angry at my words. Only sad at the memory of his friend.

I stand and move to Meiora, stepping around my shadow creature to face the one on the ground.

"What are you doing, little one?" The creature responds to my voice and question by rising slightly. I watch it, but I know it won't hurt me. My magic sparkles along my arms. "You cannot harm him. None of your kind will harm him."

I can almost imagine it nodding its agreement. The shadows swirl and move in such subtle and beautiful ways. They are amazing creatures.

"Go." Why I feel so in control around these monsters, I don't know. Maybe I'm a monster too.

I turn back to Marcus and help him gather up our meager camp. The fire is out, and the adrenaline is wearing off. I catch him watching me with curiosity now. I don't have any answers about the cryarsh submitting to me. I wish I did. I hope we can find some answers at the temple. My body feels heavy again, but I know we still have a long way to go. As we step back onto the path, a roar shakes the trees behind us. Cold dread rushes to the surface of my skin.

Marcus freezes and looks behind us. He grabs my hand and drags me into the cave before pressing me into the back wall of it with his back to my front. The stone is cold and slightly damp and his entire body is taut with energy—ready to fight at a moment's notice.

"What was that?" I whisper.

He shakes his head. I can barely see the opening of the cave and the early morning light peeking through. We stand there pressed together--my body shielded by his. That's when I hear it. Beating wings—like my dream. The same sound I heard last night while sitting awake. These wings are close though.

A shadow passes over the opening of the cave. Whatever it was, it flew over us. The wingbeats fade before building in intensity again. It is circling back around. I breathe Meiora's name, and the cryarsh spreads in front of our cave entrance blocking out the rest of the light.

I feel the beat of Marcus' heart in my chest. He breathes steady and controlled, but I know whatever it is that is out there, he is afraid of it. My fingers twitch and brush the palm of his hand in front of me. He grabs a hold of my hand and intertwines our fingers. The wingbeats fade into the distance, and the tension seeps out of my body.

He lets go of my fingers after a few more minutes. Meiora melts away from the entrance, and Marcus steps towards the opening. When I go to follow, he holds a hand back to stop me. I wait as he steps out into the daylight. After a few more agonizing minutes, he appears again and holds his hand out to take mine.

"Ready?" He asks.

"Are you sure?" He nods. He helps me out of the cave, and I squint at the brightness of the sky. "What was it, Marcus?"

"Dragon." His reaction strikes me as odd.

"I thought the myrukim were highly revered?"

He shakes his head before tightening his cloak around him more. "That was not a myrukim. The myrukim are revered serpent dragons. They do not have wings. What flew over us was an abomination. A dragon created in a similar image to the myrukim by the God of Death thousands of years ago. I haven't heard of one in this area in my lifetime, maybe not even for hundreds of years."

The God of Death. Dragons. Wingbeats. My throat tightens as I begin to wonder who the figure haunting my dreams might be. I can't think of anything else to say, but Marcus doesn't expect a reaction. He steps back onto the trail, and we walk in silence at a brisk pace. This time fear drives me forward. I hope the next place we stop for camp also has a place to hide.

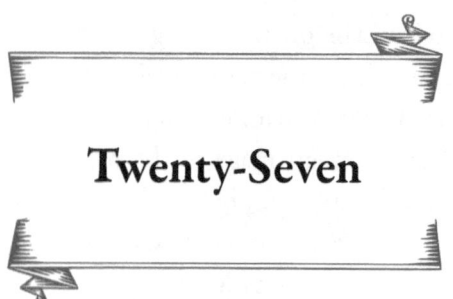

Twenty-Seven

Three days. It did, in fact, take us three days to get to this point. Yesterday was uneventful, and no more dragons were spotted during the rest of our journey. We walked for hours and only rested to eat and drink twice. Every bone and muscle ache in my body. I did sleep more last night than the previous one, and I think it was mostly because I was completely exhausted. Even my dreams couldn't wake me.

Marcus pointed out creatures along the way and spoke some about his childhood and how he met Adrian. How they grew up together in Rizyrk, the capital of Myzonia. How Adrian's father ruled with hate in his heart and oppression as his tool. Marcus' father served alongside the sovereign as general but never felt quite as strongly as his leader did about the supposed enemy among them. Adrian's father wanted blind followers and hated anyone who wouldn't fall in line. When a new dam was to be built through a heavily populated area, Adrian's father didn't hesitate to remove any people longing to stay in their ancestral homes. Those who resisted were enslaved to help build the dam that redirected water toward the palace, essentially destroying the land when the water was diverted.

Adrian hated the man, and the man hated him. He thought of Adrian as weak, but his heart was too kind and generous to be anything like the man who fathered him. It sounds to me like Adrian's father would do anything to ensure absolute power. That kind of person is dangerous.

Marcus and Adrian grew up in the shadows of this great evil, but also under the influence of a great good found in Gennet–the high mother and grandmother to Adrian.

To create an heir as mighty as himself, the Sovereign trained Adrian to use his magic to destroy, but the magic itself was good and would not bend to his will. Gennet taught Adrian how to heal and create instead of harm and destroy. Ultimately, Adrian and Marcus both saw the disastrous effects of war and massacre. A resistance formed against the armies of Myzonia, and somehow good triumphed. Marcus wouldn't talk much about the details of the war. Or how Adrian ended up being successful in overthrowing his father. But it fascinated me nonetheless.

Adrian had been working for the past five years to restore peace and order to his realm. It was not easy. Many of his father's supporters resented the changes. Many still oppressed those in their midst and sought to destroy any good that stirred among them. That's where people like Hoku and Aster came in. They fled their home to escape the madness of those seeking any with special seer magic who might thwart their plans to eliminate Adrian.

Adrian's power scared them though. He could heal but also defend. His power cast out shadows and darkness. His power saved thousands from certain death when he took out the remaining members of the army still in allegiance with the nobles who followed his father. His magic burned them with the power of the sun.

The thought scares me. The idea of any one man possessing enough power to wipe out hundreds at one time with light alone made my skin crawl. My magic pulsed at the idea—it felt—hungry. Marcus said he had been gifted the power of Araina–their Goddess of light. But did Araina's power destroy so soundly?

Her name scares me. What does it say about me when the magic in my veins is black, and the shadows respond to my call willingly and without hesitation? The work Adrian's father put into molding his son into a weapon hadn't been entirely fruitless, had it? I wonder what exactly his father did to make his son so powerful.

Marcus asked me some things about my world, but by the time we set up camp for the night, I had been too tired to share anything more than the bare minimum.

That was yesterday. Today, we stand drinking water before a long stone staircase stretched up the side of a mountain. I can't see the end of the steps, but the mountain is covered in trees and mist and snow. It feels sacred here. Holy.

"We have to get up the stairs, and we'll be at the entrance to the temple." Marcus takes another sip of water and then pulls his cloak tighter around his body. The air has grown cold, and tiny snowflakes fall on our hoods.

"Just climb those stairs?" I eye the frosty steps. "Yeah, sure. It shouldn't be a problem." He smiles at me, and it feels like a prize at this point. His jaw is covered in scruff from our days on the road. I smile in return.

"Come on." He nudges my shoulder. "You've made it this far. What's a few hundred more steps?"

"You forgot to say those steps were straight up the side of a mountain." I hand him my water pouch and tap my shoulder. Meiora gathers around me like a cloak once again.

We climb the stairs, slowly and carefully. The snow is gathering in places on the steps, adding a slippery coating to the already smooth stone. I keep my eyes fixed on Marcus' back refusing to look behind me and see how far I might fall.

The higher we get the colder the air and deeper the snow. I try to step into his footprints to make it easier.

"You doing okay back there?"

"I'm doing fi–" The word dies in my throat as my foot slips and my shin collides with the stone instead. I gasp as I manage to avoid slipping farther by dropping my other knee to the ground too.

He spins effortlessly without so much as a wobble to keep his balance. "Darci, are you okay?" He reaches down to offer me a hand up. The ice between us has been thawing over the past few days.

"Well, I've been better." I pause, "But I've also been worse." I take his hand and let him guide me to my feet.

"Maybe you should walk in front of me."

I give him my most appalled look. "Are you suggesting I am clumsy and can't be trusted not to plummet to my death?"

His face shows no emotion, but there's mischief in his eyes, "That's exactly what I'm saying. Only, I wouldn't put it so bluntly."

"Well, fine. But only because I don't want you to knock me down when you slip and fall first." A slight curve of his lips is the only evidence he wants to smile. I like this, whatever it is, that is budding between us. He might end up calling me a friend by the end of our journey.

I step in the lead, and we manage to make it to the top after thirty minutes of steady climbing. The sight takes my breath away. Up here, the world is blanketed in a deep layer of undisturbed snow. The temple is carved directly into the mountainside. Black stone columns frame a tall ornately carved door. Images of myrukim and serpents and fairies adorn the entrance. The pine trees tower majestically on either side of the temple, and the narrow path between the last step and the doorway is bordered by lanterns, glowing warm and welcoming. Our steps through the snow reveal a ruby-red stone beneath our feet as we step up to the door.

Marcus knocks on the door, but it opens quickly enough someone had to know we arrived. A young woman with light brown skin and sparkling blue eyes stands before us in purple robes.

"Welcome to the Temple of Markyr." Her voice is soft and lilting. We're at the temple of the God of Fire and Ice. She steps back giving us room to enter.

"We're here to see the high priestess. There are questions we think she might be able to answer." Marcus holds both hands open to appear less intimidating. Not sure it works for him when he towers over the young priestess, but she is unbothered by his or my presence. She nods in understanding and turns to lead us through the labyrinth of hallways to the right of the entrance.

Everything about this temple is stunning. The carved images from the front door are echoed throughout the space. More ruby red stones glisten, standing in stark contrast to the black rock forming the foundation this mountain is made of.

"Are there six temples?" The question surprises me because I didn't plan on asking anything yet.

Marcus gives me a questioning look, but the priestess doesn't hesitate to answer. "There are five temples. One for each of the gods and goddesses. They are spread throughout the kingdom so everyone can access one of them at any given time."

"I thought there were six gods and goddesses though." Marcus shakes his head, but I'm not sure why he is being resistant.

"Death needs no temple. He isn't recognized as one of the revered. The other gods and goddesses sought to banish the one who held death after the Thousand Years War. I don't know if they were successful, but there is nothing Death can offer we would want."

Chills crawl up my arms. Marcus' expression looks annoyed more than anything. I'm not sure why this revelation bothers me so much. Death needs no place to rest so why would it need a temple to be adored at? And who would adore death?

My mind drifts to the strange man I've encountered in my dreams and this realm. If anyone is the God of Death, it is him. Adrian called him the Dark Lord of Daemons, but what if he isn't who they think he is? I shake the thoughts from my mind and follow the young woman farther in.

We round a final corner and stand before a plain wooden door. It seems out of place compared to the lavish surroundings. I attempt to catch Marcus' eye, but he stands resolute behind our hostess and waits for her to let us in.

She holds her hands out in front of the door and whispers words in a language I don't recognize. The door glows a bright red before it eases open on its own. She steps in and waits for us to join her before announcing us to the elderly woman who sits before a table full of books. It's a simple library bursting with books and scrolls of varying degrees of age. A roaring fire warms the space, and I am dumbstruck at the vastness of so much knowledge in one place.

"Mother Jaden, may I introduce Marcus Kaniko and Darci." The room no longer holds my attention. We never said our names, but she knows them. The magic tickles the back of my neck; I notice it if I focus on it. She didn't say my surname. Why?

"Thank you, Sister Cleo. Welcome. I'm sure you are weary and ready to rest. We can offer you warm food and drink?" The mother priestess rises to her feet and moves slowly toward the fireplace where a sofa and two armchairs sit unoccupied. A small square table is at the center of them and with a wave of her wrist, steaming mugs and warm plates full of meats and cheeses appear.

"Why couldn't you have this form of magic, *Mr. Kaniko*? You could have summoned a whole meal instead of a small stygo." I whisper to Marcus. The glare he sends my way delights me more than it should. I suppress a smile and lower myself to the sofa. Marcus sits to my right on one of the armchairs, while the priestess sits in the armchair to the left.

"Go ahead; warm yourselves. We have plenty of time to discuss all you wish to know."

I reach forward to take one of the mugs, careful not to spill it as I bring it towards my nose to smell. It smells like hot cocoa, rich and creamy. Marcus picks up pieces of food first. Our priorities do not align apparently. Taking a tentative sip, the sweetness hits my tongue, and instantly my whole-body warms. Of course, it would be magical hot cocoa. I close my eyes and sip again feeling every muscle in my body instantly eased of every ache and pain. Even the bruise on my shin feels less tender.

When I open my eyes, I find myself staring at Mother Jaden. Her skin is a creamy olive color and her hair is white and wavy. Wrinkles adorn her face, but her hazel eyes spark with fire. She is not to be underestimated.

Marcus waits for Mother Jaden to open the discussion. He contents himself with eating and drinking, so I follow his lead. By the time we finish, I feel warm and drowsy and strangely at peace.

"Now, what brings you two to our doorstep this time of year? Surely, you have hot cocoa and seasoned foods back in Zaiven."

Before Marcus can speak, my mouth gets away from me. "I need to know why I'm here." She stares at me, so I clarify. "In Myzonia. Here in Myzonia. Instead of in Oria. That's my home. Oria." Marcus stares at me like my brain is malfunctioning before his very eyes. I'm not sure he's wrong.

I take a deep breath and try again. "I'm from a different realm. A world called Oria with no magic. For some reason, I keep getting drawn back to this world–back to Adrian. And..." I hesitate but continue regardless, "And I have magic. I have no idea how or what it does or means. But it's inside of me."

Mother Jaden tilts her head and looks to Marcus who sits stiff as a board with wide eyes. He clears his throat to speak but doesn't say anything. "What an interesting mystery you bring to us. I think you are here for something other than world walking, though." My mind races back through my conversation with Gennet. Does this woman communicate with Gennet in some way? Gennet was more concerned about the type of magic I wielded. She had never shown concern when it came to my presence around Adrian or in this world. Not until she saw me use magic on Hoku.

"Her magic." Marcus finally speaks. "We've come to ask about the magic she possesses. Gennet seems to think there was something unusual about it."

"Interesting. What kind of magic do you have, Darci?"

I look at my hands unsure of what to say. I don't know anything about magic or about what it does. Even as these thoughts flicker to the front of my mind, I can feel the warm build-up of magic beneath my skin. Like a monster waking up from a deep sleep.

"I don't know. I don't know exactly what it can do either. It sort of does what it wants to."

"Come with me. I'll take you into the Chamber of Silence. It will be safer there than here with so many...books." She stands slowly, and we follow her out of the room. She takes us into a room a few doors down from the library. It is empty inside. The walls glow with red stone and the floor shimmers with black onyx. But there are no pieces of furniture.

"This is a place of thought and solitude. Any priestess may come in here to dwell on the work she does for the temple. Or simply to find rest and peace from the noise within."

Peace is not the first thing I think of when I see this room. I see a prison. My heart beats faster and a cool sweat forms on my back. The space feels too small though it's cavernous.

Mother Jaden opens her hands towards me. "Okay, show me your magic."

"Right here? Right now?" My voice sounds shrill even to me. Marcus tenses beside me. I know he has seen my magic already, and I'm sure he is wondering why I'm protesting so much when this was the whole reason we came here. Blue magic sparks across his hands.

"Yes, Darci. Right here." She watches me closely. My skin burns as I resist the call of my power.

"Okay, I can do that." I shake my hands out at my sides and take a deep breath. I allow the magic to surface, opening the door for it to come out. Closing my eyes, I feel the burning warmth of the black flames and light on my arms. I open my eyes feeling the power swell and build. It feels like an ocean being held back by a beaver's dam. Sweat trickles down the back of my neck. It hurts.

I watch Mother Jaden's eyes widen. I see the flash of terror in them before she masks the emotion. Marcus' magic is building next to me ready to subdue me if I don't bring mine under control.

"Darci." He warns. My breathing grows ragged.

"Help me." When I think Marcus is about to burn me with his magic to stop me, Meiora appears out of thin air and engulfs me in shadows. The pain subsides, and I regulate my breathing.

The high priestess gasps at the sight before her. I merely think the thought to Meiora that I'm okay now, and the cryarsh vanishes as quickly as it came.

"How did you do that?"

I look up at her eyes with tears of pain in my own. "I don't know. It feels like more than I can subdue now."

"No, not your magic. The cryarsh. How did you summon it?"

"It's been with me for months now. Even in my world. It follows me."

"No cryarsh can be summoned. They are freer and wilder than any creature in any known world." She covers her mouth with her hand as she turns away from me to pace.

"What does it mean?" Marcus questions. She stops and turns back to face us.

"I don't know. But I need some time to research the ancient scrolls." Her eyes drift to mine, inquiring and concerned. She reminds me of Gennet. "Your magic is an ancient one. I have never heard of anyone possessing it who was mortal. You said your world has no magic?" I nod. "This is impossible though. All worlds have some magic. Some magic is buried deeper in the earth than others, but it is there all the same. I need to think about this. You will be shown to rooms for the time being. I do not know how long this will last."

She exits the room and is greeted by Sister Cleo instantly. It's as if they all communicate telepathically in this place.

Before any more can be said, Mother Jaden is gone and we are left alone with the young priestess again.

"Come this way. I'll show you to your rooms."

We exchange a look, but there isn't anywhere else for us to go while we wait. We follow her back through the labyrinth until she stops next to two black doors, one on either side of the hall. She points to one and Marcus steps through without a backward glance.

I hesitate only a moment before doing the same with the other door. "We will have dinner ready in a few hours. You'll know when it's time. Enjoy your rest." She smiles and leaves the way we came.

I have no idea how I'll find my way back through the maze of this place. I focus on the room in front of me. Closing the door, I notice the room is full of icy blue and white stones. A simple bed with wool blankets and a small fireplace, across from the bed, are the only adornments in the space.

The same sensation of entrapment overwhelms my senses again. I close my eyes against the panic and force myself to slow my heartbeat and breathing. I can't afford to lose control of my magic again. It ebbs and flows under the surface still. Like it is knocking against my skin, trying to find a way out.

I open my eyes and sit down on the bed. A prison. This feels like a prison, and I have no idea why.

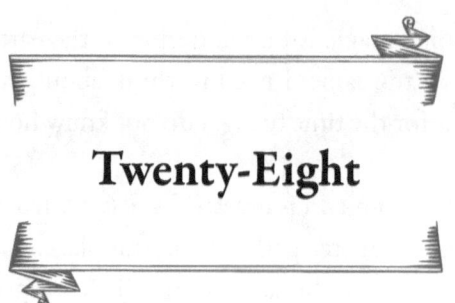

Twenty-Eight

We spend the next seven days stuck here. Mother Jaden studies volume after volume of books and scrolls in the ancient library. She breaks periodically to discuss what she is searching for and what she is finding with other priestesses and occasionally with Marcus. She doesn't speak with me, though. She watches me closely when I enter the library but never invites me to join her. Something about my magic frightened her. I know it did, and I know she's not ready to confront me about it.

I honestly thought my life in Oria was boring, but now I have nothing to keep my mind and hands occupied. No food to hunt for and cook. No bread to bake or firewood to gather. I've lost all sense of purpose in favor of walking these strange halls and daydreaming about snowy woods and good conversation. The one positive is I haven't had any nightmares in this place. I don't know if it is something about the room I sleep in or merely being in the temple that does it, but I feel relief regardless.

Some of the priestesses speak with me, but they do so reluctantly. The same can't be said of Marcus. I've caught several young ladies watching him closely or stealing glances at him when he has his back turned. He's handsome and rugged and a warrior, and this place is void of all other men as far as I can tell.

He spends his time reading scrolls with Mother Jaden and studying maps on the walls of the library. I have caught him going to the Chamber of Silence on occasion, but I haven't been brave enough to follow him in or ask what he does there. The beginnings of our newfound tolerance of each other continue to grow. If anything, he doesn't seem to despise me as much as before, but I don't know if I would call us friends.

I kind of wish we were.

I slip into the library to find the priestess and Marcus whispering about some passage they recently found. Two young priestesses wipe the shelves nearby and keep eyeing Marcus, exchanging giggles and knowing glances with one another. I roll my eyes and plop down into one of the chairs by the fire, staring at the angry flames as they lick across the wood within the hearth.

The whispering stops, and I hear footsteps softly padding across the room towards me. My magic sparks and writhes as he gets closer. I sense his presence behind me when the footsteps stop, but he remains quiet.

"As fascinating as I might be, the front of my head is more interesting than the back." I can't hide the smile in my voice. I've grown used to pestering him. I find it to be the one joyful thing I can do in this place—see how much I can get away with before Marcus' aggravation with me snaps.

"You're not as funny as you think you are." He sighs, annoyed.

"Well, that's debatable." I look over my shoulder at him and point to the chair across from mine.

He reluctantly moves to sit, and I feel it again—the spark of magic building under my skin. The tingling heightens when he is around me. I think it knows I'm afraid of what he could do to me if he wanted. At least that's what I tell myself. He doesn't say anything at first, only stares into the fire alongside me. I never remove my gaze from him, though. I study his features, his eyes. The softness starting to grace his jaw instead of the tension he always holds there is new. This place has proved to be more of a sanctuary for him than for me.

"Your admirers grow by the day." When he jerks his head toward me, I shift my eyes in the direction of the young women who busily finish their work before briskly walking out the door.

He rolls his eyes, "I don't have admirers." The look I give tells him I'm not that stupid. "Well, they're not used to men being in the temple for extended stays. I'm an anomaly to them."

"Mmmhmm. It doesn't hurt you are the epitome of a strong, handsome warrior."

His cheeks warm to a deeper color, and he squirms in his seat slightly. I wouldn't normally notice the movement, but I'm bored and have only my senses to entertain myself. Is he embarrassed I called him a warrior or handsome? Or that I pointed out his deflection in the first place. I spare him any more needling and change the conversation.

"What did you come over here to discuss?" I ease my eyes back to the fire, giving him space in other ways.

He clears his throat a couple of times. "I–we found some interesting things in today's scrolls."

I wait for him to continue, still not looking in his direction. My arms start to feel like they are burning. I'll need to leave the room soon. I can't risk catching the library on fire with uncontrolled magic.

"We think your magic comes from Death himself. The flames of black light you generate were used only by the God of Death in the Thousand Years War. He decimated armies with a simple wave of his hand. I think–I think it's why they seem to hurt you when you resist. Mother Jaden believes the magic is too strong for you, and you might be used as a weapon to wipe out an entire world should the magic swell beyond your control."

My mouth is dry, and my chest grows tight. I suck in a deep breath feeling the tension in my chest release only slightly. "What do you mean an entire world?" I rasp.

"The magic may grow to the point where you would burn with a fire so potent, it would be catastrophic. It would destroy you and anything in its path. The God of Death is notoriously powerful." I face him now, and I hate what I see in his eyes. Fear. Deep, uncontrolled, soul-crushing fear.

"Can I destroy it? I never asked for this. How did I get cursed with it?" Panic laces my words. I stop myself from asking more.

"I've never heard of someone destroying magic within themselves. We don't know how you got it. It's almost as if you have been infected." He looks away.

"If I can learn to control it, will it stay locked away?" I'm desperate for something. An answer to this terror now coursing through my veins. I stand abruptly and launch myself toward the door stumbling over my own feet. I have to get out of here. My distress is causing the magic to swell more.

"Darci, wait. Where are you going?" He jumps to his feet to follow me. I make it into the hallway, and the pain grows more debilitating.

My words are almost swallowed up in my cries of pain. I feel him grab my waist as I double over. I try to voice them again, but only one word comes out. "Silence."

He scrunches his brow in confusion at first, then clarity passes over his face. "Hold on. I'll get you there."

He scoops me up into his arms, and I think I hear him hiss in pain before he starts running down the hallway toward the room I hate. Priestesses squeal as we rush past them; I hear Mother Jaden call out behind us. But he never stops.

Skidding to a stop next to the door, we are both panting as he grabs the handle and shoves the door open. He drops to his knees in the middle of the room and sets me on the ground. Shadows swirl around me and flames of black and white spread across my skin.

I need him to leave. I need Meiora. I need to not die right now which surprises me because it has been a long time since I have wanted to live.

"Get. Out." I grind through my clenched teeth.

"Darci. Just wait. I'll figure something out." I shake my head and hold a hand up—-magic stretching off my fingertips. I point to the door. Mother Jaden appears at the door.

"What is..." Her words die in her throat at the sight of the monster I have become. "Marcus, get out of the room now!"

"We have to help her!" He's on his feet now but hasn't moved to leave yet.

"There is no time. Get out now!" She looks at me. "Control your emotions! You can still control it if you focus on its source."

My flesh is hot. I'm on fire, but I nod and keep my hand pointed at the door. "Go!" I manage to yell.

Mother Jaden summons her magic and a tendril of pink light wraps around Marcus' arm, tugging him towards the open door. When the door shuts, I force myself to breathe through the pain. My thoughts drift to Meiora, and it isn't long before my shadow appears at my side swirling over top of me. In Meiora, I feel safe and sheltered. Instantly, my emotions regulate and calm down. The intensity of this power is familiar. I sense its source deep in my soul, and I'm not afraid for a moment.

My heartbeats slow, and the pain ebbs away. I release my hold on some of the magic. It bursts from my hands into the walls around me heating the ruby rock to a white glow. The release eases the pressure inside of me. As the magic subsides, I feel Meiora wrap around my body, cooling me and bringing my mind back to the room I am in.

I feel spent. My head aches, and one look at my arms shows angry red burns along my skin. I try to sit up, but the sudden movement makes my vision go black and my stomach roll. I curl up on my side trying to hide inside of myself. I think about Marcus carrying me.

I had to have burned him. There is no way he touched me without feeling the heat of my magic. Or whoever's magic this is.

The door eases open, and I hear him suck in a breath before approaching me carefully. "Darci?" I lay still with my eyes closed. I don't want to vomit on his boots.

"Darci, are you okay now?" Mother Jaden's voice is calm and soothing. I whimper as I nod. The pain lessens more each minute, and Meiora releases me from its wrap.

"Marcus, you should get your burns assessed by one of the healing priestesses. I'll send one to your room."

"I'd rather stay with Darci right now." I feel him kneel next to me brushing my hair back from my face.

"Very well. Darci, you can open your eyes. I'm impressed you managed to suppress it. You are stronger than I thought you would be." My eyes open a sliver. Mother Jaden stands nearby looking around at the now cooling stones of the walls. Marcus lifts my chin so I look at him and nod. Fear still dances behind his eyes, but there is also pity. Sorrow at the news he has given me.

"I want to train you. We must soon teach you how to control and use your magic without letting it control you." I slowly look at the old woman marveling at how calm she appears in the face of potential destruction.

"Can it be stopped?" I swallow, my throat feeling parched and ragged. "Can I control it forever?" She knows what I am asking. She smiles sadly at me.

"We have to try, my dear."

I don't want to ask the next question, but I force myself anyway. "And if it doesn't work?"

"Then, you will have to choose, won't you? We'll begin your training here tomorrow." She says nothing else. But I understand her. If I cannot control this magic. If it grows beyond what I can manage, I will destroy the entire world we live in, myself included.

I wonder. If I die, does it go with me? And if it does, then maybe that's what I'll be choosing. To die before I can accidentally destroy everyone else.

Death has come for me after all.

After making it back to our rooms later, I lie in my bed listening to the quiet of the temple around me. The healer soothed our burns, but the ache in my chest remains. Marcus nodded goodnight when he left the room to go to his, and I ended up alone. Nothing but Meiora and my thoughts to keep me company. I don't think about my magic. I don't think about what is to come or the possible choices I might have to make.

In the stillness, I feel a buzz in my skull build slightly. A presence telling me I'm not entirely alone right now. I focus on the hum and the soft breathing of another being in the room. Goosebumps rise on my arms, and I shiver from the sensation. I close my eyes, and I feel more than hear him. Adrian. It's like his mind is reaching toward me. Murmuring comes to my ears, but it feels muffled and distant. I know it's him though. It's the same feeling I would get when he was in my house and the words began to appear on the door.

Something inside of me calls out to something inside of him. We are connected for some reason, and I still don't know why.

I drift asleep to the sound of voices, shuffling feet, and the crackling fire.

Twenty-Nine

"What's your favorite color?"

"Gray."

I can't help the snort laugh escaping my lips. "Of course it's gray."

"What's that supposed to mean?" Marcus' face betrays the mischief he hides in his eyes at times. "Why can't I like gray?"

"Of all the colors, you pick gray? It's so bland. What about blue?" I tap my chin, dragging my eyes up and down his clothes.

"I like gray. It's like snow clouds on a winter's day."

"But you would look good in blue."

"I'm allowed to like gray, okay?" He takes another sip of his hot tea as we sit in his room. Unlike me, he has two armchairs and a table next to his fireplace. I knew they liked him more than me.

"I still think you should pick blue." We've taken to eating breakfast together in his room ever since I almost incinerated him with my magic a week ago in the Chamber of Silence.

"You think I should pick blue as my favorite color? What shade of blue? Light blue, dark blue?" He smiles. It's soft, and I return the gesture.

"I think any shade of blue would do. It's a lot better than gray though, right?" I bite into a piece of buttered bread.

"Gray. It's still gray." He sighs in feigned annoyance. "What about you? What's your favorite color?"

I avert my eyes as I grab my teacup.

"It's blue, isn't it?"

I fight the smile on my lips, but there's no deceiving him. "What if it is?"

"You expect me to say blue is mine because you like blue the best. That doesn't seem fair to me."

"Who said anything about fair?" I mock. "Besides, blue is the superior color," I mumble.

He smirks. "Okay. My turn. What's your favorite—fruit?"

We have been playing this game lately where we share random facts about ourselves. Nothing too serious. Nothing too exciting. Sometimes it's about our childhoods or growing up. The more I talk with Marcus, the more I realize I don't remember a lot about growing up. A whole segment of my life lies dormant in my mind. But today, we discuss the shallow facts about ourselves. Favorite colors, favorite foods. I enjoy this more than I should.

I tilt my head. "My favorite fruit in Oria or Myzonia?"

"Oria."

I pretend to marinate on the question. Humming slightly as I take another sip of tea. "I would have to say melonberries."

"I've never heard of them before. Must be native to your home. Personally, I prefer stygo."

I can give him that. Stygo is delicious. "Melonberries are the perfect blend of tangy and sweet. They only grow for a month at home. So, we don't get to enjoy them for very long." I sit back and sigh.

Neither of us speaks for a while. But this has been nice. This almost feels comfortable. I wonder if we might be able to be friends after all. He still doesn't talk about who he lost, but I don't talk about my family either. Dwelling on the past won't help me here. I need to focus on controlling my magic and hopefully not killing an entire world in the process.

Mother Jaden trains me every day for multiple hours. I'm getting better at accessing my magic, and the regular expenditure of magic eases the pressure from the power growing inside of me. It still grows though. I know it can't be good; I'm beginning to fear it is only a matter of time before it consumes me entirely. I can't let that happen. I've already decided I won't let it happen. I'll die before then.

The buzz of Adrian's presence stirs around the room and my eyes follow shadows moving on their own across the wall.

"Is he there again?" Marcus' voice is tight. Uneasy. I see the tension build up in his tight shoulders and stiffened back. His eyes lose some of their mirth as well.

"Yes. He's there." If Adrian can sense me as much as I do him, I don't know. It's hard to tell when all I get are glimpses of shadows and whispers. I can never hear his words clearly. But as my magic grows in strength, I see him or feel him more. There is a tether anchoring me to his soul. It's still a mystery to all of us.

Marcus scans the room willing his eyes and ears to see and hear the things I do. He won't of course, but it doesn't stop him from trying. Our easiness from before dissipates. I'm not sure why, but I think it's because Adrian reminds Marcus of what is at stake–of what we all stand to lose should my magic overpower me.

"Okay, show me what you can do." He stands and steps behind his chair waiting.

"What? Right here? In here?" We always train and practice in the Chamber of Silence.

He smirks, "Unless you're too afraid to try." How does he do that? How does he shift the mood around us so quickly?

"I'm not afraid." I'm terrified I'll burn his bed down. Maybe even destroy the rest of the furniture, but feigning bravado seems to be my default mode most days.

I take my position on the other side of the room. Focusing on my breathing, I close my eyes for a few breaths to focus on the well of power stirring beneath my skin. When I open them, my skin burns with black flames up and down my arms. I focus my attention on separating a flame from my body to create a floating ball of magic in the center of the room. A trickle of sweat slides down my temple.

"Good. Now hold it there next to the fireplace. Good. You're doing great." Blue magic dances across Marcus' knuckles. Adrenaline forces his body to prepare for a fight that shouldn't happen. Hopefully.

I snatch my fingers into a fist, instantly extinguishing the ball. I blow out a breath causing the loose strands of hair to lift around my cheeks. I forget to completely shut my magic down, though; and when my hands relax, a burst of power launches my chair across the room towards my face. I scream and drop to a crouch before it bangs against the door.

I cringe and reach for the chair. It isn't smashed so I guess that's a positive. Marcus chuckles as he crosses the room to take the chair back to its rightful place.

"You're getting better." His eyes spark with amusement.

"Are you referring to the part where I controlled the magic in ball form? Or where I tried to smash myself into the wall with your furniture?" I pause when I see him try to hide a smile. "Wait, was that part of the plan? Eliminate Darci with her magic by making her train in a non-empty room?" I put my hands on my hips.

"Now where would be the fun in that?"

"Oh, right. The magic will take care of me anyway." I say it jokingly, but the room fills with heaviness at the truth I've spoken. I'm living on borrowed time.

"You know, I actually don't want to see you self-combust and destroy the world."

I force a smile, "I know. Then you and all you care about would be gone too." He opens his mouth to say something but closes it again. "I won't let it get to that point."

He startles at the words. "Darci, I—I think it's safe to say I've grown to—" his eyes dart around the room.

"Tolerate my company?" I offer.

He sighs, exasperated. "No, it's—it's more than that. I know you wouldn't want to hurt any of us. I'll figure out how to help you control it, okay?"

"And if I can't? What then?"

"We'll find another way." His voice tightens and seeing the sadness in his eyes makes a lump form in my throat.

"Marcus, I will do all I can to learn how to control this. But you and I both know this is more of a curse than a blessing. I... if it is too much...if I fail...I'll need you to help me get back to Oria. I'd rather die there where my family is. Okay?"

He looks down fighting emotions I don't fully understand.

"Please, Marcus. Please promise me you'll help me leave. It'll be okay. I..." I swallow and clear my throat, forcing the sorrows of my life down. "I'm the only one left anyway. No one will miss me when I'm gone." The last part comes out as a whisper. One last hope that the words aren't a lie. I force a sad smile and meet his eyes.

We stand there for a moment, a million unspoken words passing between us. But he doesn't disagree with me, and I know ultimately this all ends with me leaving every world behind.

A knock on the door breaks the connection between us. Marcus walks over and opens the door to find Mother Jaden standing there. "Is everything all right in here?" Her eyes scan the room past his shoulder, landing on me for a moment. "A priestess said she heard a loud bang and a scream."

Marcus rubs the back of his neck awkwardly, looking very much like a young boy caught stealing treats from the kitchen. "Yeah, everything is fine. Darci was just practicing."

Mother Jaden squints her eyes, but she doesn't chastise us. "Very well. Darci, you've been working hard lately. Why don't we take a break from the training for the day?"

"Whatever you think is best." I shrug.

"I'll be working in the library if you need me."

She continues down the hallway without another word. Marcus stands frozen in the doorway for a minute before he spins back to face me. But he doesn't look at me. His eyes look everywhere but at me.

"I—uh—I need to go see if there's any word from Adrian." He points over his shoulder. I can take a hint.

"Of course, I'll leave you to it." I squeeze past him to get out; my shoulder gently brushing against his.

He follows, closing the door behind him. "I'll see you at dinner."

Dinner? I wonder what he plans to do all day to stay away from me until then. I watch as he strides away without looking back at me. My heart hurts, maybe even my soul. I want to belong–to have someone miss me when I'm gone. But everyone who cared has long since left this life. Sighing, I move down the hallway to the Chamber of Silence. Perhaps time spent alone will help me make the decision I know will need to be made.

Hours pass, and I completely skip lunch. I don't feel hungry though. The pit in my stomach makes the thought of eating sound terrible. It must be getting late though, and I am completely burnt out from trying to manipulate and master my magic throughout the day. Meiora keeps me company but also serves as a flame retardant for when my control slips.

I'm lying on the floor spread eagle, bone tired and sticky with sweat when the door flies open.

"Darci!" Marcus skids to a stop. "What are you doing?"

I push myself to my feet. "Waiting to explode. What's going on?"

He shakes his head having grown used to my humor at this point. "I received news from Adrian."

One look at his face and I know something has happened. It doesn't look like good news. "What? What's wrong?"

"Unrest is building in the capital. People have been getting attacked by Lord Daemon's night creatures, and there's talk of an uprising. They don't feel safe. Adrian had to go to Rizyrk to try to get control of the situation. I think some of his father's supporters are trying to cause an insurrection. I wouldn't put it past them."

I notice a slight change in what he calls the Dark Lord. It must be an actual name and not only a title. Attacks? Unrest? "What else has happened?"

"While Adrian was gone, the house was attacked."

I suck in a breath. The house. Adrian's house. The place where Gennet, Aster, and Risa all live. My heart pounds in my ears. "Risa?"

"Aster and Risa are okay. But not everyone was as fortunate." He pauses. "We have to go back."

"Of course." I nod and stride to the door. He stops me with a hand on my shoulder.

"If you need to stay here—"

"No. I'm coming. Let me help."

He nods and together we move to the library to let Mother Jaden know our plans. I have the sinking feeling it won't be an easy trip back and I'll be missing something by leaving this place. I'm not letting Marcus travel alone; I want to help. But I'm afraid of what we'll find when we get there.

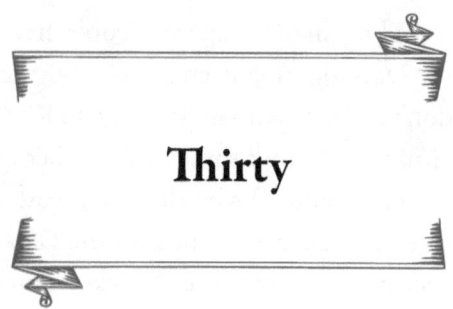

Thirty

The journey back to Zaiven and the house is tedious. I know it will take us three days, but with a blanket of urgency weighing heavily on us, each day lasts an eternity. Meiora follows close by, and occasionally, I catch sight of another cryarsh moving in the treetops. Nothing threatens us, and nothing attacks us. The presence of cryarsh among us might be enough of a deterrent to keep other enemies away. At least temporarily. I never hear the wingbeats in the distance.

I sleep as little as possible at night. My deepest fear is my nightmares will return since I've left the protection of the temple. We can't afford for my screams to draw attention to our location. My magic writhes under my skin. Adrenaline coursing through my veins agitates it even more.

I know I must look awful. My body and mind are growing weary, but we are finally less than a day away from the house. Marcus watches me closely from time to time. He sees me wearing down, but he hasn't slowed down yet. He hasn't said anything more. Conflicting emotions battle across his face.

Suddenly, he halts in front of me, causing me to stumble into his back before catching myself. He pivots towards me and grabs my shoulders forcing my gaze to meet his.

"What's wrong?" I search his eyes.

"Are you feeling overwhelmed?" The concern lacing his voice makes my heartbeat faster.

"I...uh... yeah, I'm nervous. But I want to get there. We don't have time to stand here."

He holds me firmly, ducking his head to bring our eyes level. "You haven't slept well in two days. Your skin looks sickly. The dark circles under your eyes are more prevalent than before. And every other hour I hear you grimace in pain. The magic is building, isn't it?"

I drop his gaze looking off to the side. "I'm tired, and I haven't slept because I didn't want nightmares making our journey harder. But I'm okay. I can do this."

"We're resting. We're resting and you are going to use some of the magic right now." He drops his hands from my arms, and my skin feels cold without his touch. He searches the canopy of branches above for something. Finally, he takes my hand in his and pulls me toward a log a few steps off the trail.

"This can't be a good idea. What if it summons something?" I bite my lip thinking about my tendency to lose control of my magic. There's an awful lot of flammable things in our vicinity.

"Meiora!" He steps back and whips his head around. "Meiora, we need you."

No one has ever called for the cryarsh other than me. I don't even know if it will respond to him. But sure enough, the shadow slips across the log I'm sitting on and pools on the ground between us.

"Meiora, can you subdue her magic if she loses control?"

The cryarsh rises taking on its wispy human form. *Yes.*

He turns his attention back to me. "Okay, it's the same thing we've always practiced. Your nerves are causing it to grow, and if you don't make a conscious effort to use it, it will use you instead." He takes a deep breath. "Form the ball like you normally do."

I nod and then tap into the monster beneath my skin. The magic moves like it is sentient, responding to the door I'm cracking open within me. Instead of a trickle, a burning fire erupts across my arms and hands, and my concentration wavers only a moment from the sudden rush of power.

"Breathe. Feel it within you. But don't resist it."

"I'm trying." I squeeze my eyes shut, but it's like a tidal wave washing over me. My eyes water, and my heart pounds so hard, I might pass out. *You can do this. Hold it steady.* "I'm losing it, Marcus. I can't hold it." I pant, and I hear Marcus move to get closer to me. He says something to Meiora, but I can't hear anything else. One moment I hear the movements of him around me, and the next moment everything grows eerily still.

Wingbeats and whispers touch my ears and my skin. The breath of some creature or force syncs up with my own. I can't understand the words, but I know these sounds. I hear them in my nightmares. Did I pass out from lack of sleep and the strain of my power? I don't think I did. I open my eyes, and I see Marcus and Meiora, but they are secondary to the white eyes staring straight into my own.

A name brushes across my mind. A name I know well and recognize. The heat in my blood turns to ice. I can hear myself screaming, but mostly my mind zeros in on the voices rushing into me until one voice, gravelly and low, silences them all.

"Hello, Ancient One. I've been looking for you."

I know I don't speak the words, but I think them and somehow, I know the Dark Lord hears them. *"What do you want?"*

"Your time is up. The payment is due. I'm here to collect your debt. No more hiding."

"I don't know what you're talking about. I'm not the Ancient One. I don't even know who that is."

"You do even if you have made yourself forget."

He whispers a name–*that* name—again. A name that is both familiar and terrifying. My mind races with all the implications of it. Memories flash into my mind. Pictures of *the* room in my house, my family, darkness, death, and nothingness.

My mind locks onto it, and all I hear is my voice screaming and the powerful rhythm of wings beating before shadows swallow me up.

Thirty-One

A velvety black blanket shrouds my vision. The soft and tangible warmth of Meiora slides across my skin, my face. The burning of magic has dulled to a low hum, and I feel cold streaks of tears cutting paths down my cheeks. As I blink my eyes open, Meiora senses my consciousness and begins to unwind from around me.

Warm hands shakily push my hair back from my face, but they aren't mine. I squint against the gray light of the sky and let my eyes focus on Marcus' eyes. His eyes are so blue like the sky on an early summer day. His fear is painted on his face. We both know this magic is too much. I won't be able to control it, and eventually, I'll have to end this. It makes me sad. Not because of me, but because of the loss of this friendship blossoming between us. Because that's what this is. A friendship.

"Hey." He breathes the word out searching me for answers, for injuries.

"Hi." I push off the ground, feeling a little dizzy and even more exhausted than before.

"Are you okay?" He reaches under my arms and pulls me to standing, holding on until he feels my balance even out.

My mouth goes dry as I remember the encounter, and I feel panic build in my chest. "Did you see him? Did you hear him?" I grab his arms and search the woods around us.

"What are you talking about?"

"The Dark Lord. He was here. He was talking to me!" My voice rises and I wish I didn't sound so hysterical. "I heard dragon wings!"

"Darci, it was you and me and Meiora. There is no one else here."

My wild eyes snap back to his. "That's impossible. He was right here standing in front of me. White eyes." My voice shakes. I think I might be sick.

His eyes widen in fear as he grabs my face with both hands to steady me. "He wasn't here. At least, he wasn't here in the flesh."

He releases me for a moment and turns away from me thinking. "Have you seen him before? In your mind I mean?"

"Yes." The word comes out as barely a whisper. I'm not sure how he even heard it.

"Where? When?" The questions pierce me, and I feel like I may have made a grave mistake.

"I have seen him in my dreams. He speaks to me, but I usually don't understand. It's in a different language. But he–" I stop myself. Can I tell him the name he calls me? I doubt I should. Instinct tells me to keep this a secret.

"What does he say? Does he say anything you can understand?" Those piercing blue eyes pierce my soul. I give him a partial truth.

"He calls me the Ancient One." I watch his reaction carefully. He furrows his brow in confusion though which isn't exactly what I was expecting.

"The Ancient One." He murmurs and paces on the narrow path. "We have to get back to the house. We have to see if Gennet still lives. She will know."

"Well, let's go. What are we waiting for?"

"Okay." He says more to himself than to me. "Okay, let's go. Are you sure you're okay?"

"I'm fine."

But I'm not really. Everything I believe about myself breaks down like a snake shedding its old skin. But instead of something new, I'm reverting to something I tried to escape a long time ago. A destiny I never wanted to fulfill in its entirety. I'll get back to Zaiven and the house, but I know time is running out.

We move quickly now, setting a blistering pace in an effort to get to the house before dark. Every little noise in the forest around me has me jumping and checking over my shoulder. The idea the Dark Lord knows how to access me through my mind, through my magic, urges me on faster. The sooner we leave the trees, the better.

As the sun begins to dip towards the horizon, a familiar hill appears up ahead and the trees thin. The path before us shifts to stone. In moments, we step out of the shadows of the trees. When Marcus reaches back to take my hand as we step over the log in the middle of the path, I hear Adrian yell our names.

I turn my eyes toward the house and see charred wood and broken windows. Guards bustle about, and other council members give orders to what look like warriors arriving to set up a perimeter.

Marcus releases my hand, and pain explodes across my body. I'm being torn apart. Is the magic consuming me now of all times? But no, this is familiar. This is pain I know. I cry out as Marcus whips back toward me to reach for me. Adrian is running down the hill. But the next instant everything goes black.

I GASP CLUTCHING AT my head with both hands kneeling in a foot of fresh fallen snow. A lot of snow that wasn't present in Myzonia. Opening my eyes, I realize I'm kneeling in the snow at the bottom of my hill facing my old, worn-out house. Meiora flies across the trees and moves ahead of me. There is a presence here. Something watching me from the trees at my back.

I stumble to my feet and make my way up the hill. I'm back in Oria. I don't know why I was ripped from one world into another, but I am here. I'm too tired, and I've expended too much strength to think clearly.

The cold bites at my skin. It is so much colder here. So much more dead and empty. I start to shiver as I reach the front door. When I touch the handle, the door creaks open of its own accord. Someone is here. I have no idea how long I have been gone—-how much time has passed while I lived amongst the others. I don't know if time works the same in both worlds. But I don't think my house would be open. The sensation I'm not alone—someone is watching—floods my system with adrenaline, though I'm not sure how I'm not completely spent by now. The hum of my magic beneath my skin surprises me. I've never fully felt it here. But it's there, waiting for me to act. For me to summon it and release it from its cage.

My heart pounds so hard, and I do my best to step quietly into the house. I was right.

Meiora stands in the corner of my vision like it did so many months ago. But it makes no move to help or comfort. It simply waits.

A fire crackles in the other room. The warm glow of light dances on the walls bathing the room in an orange glow.

"Hello?" My voice sounds weak. I hate it.

As I step into the living room where the fire warms the air, I find myself face to face with someone I never expected to see.

"I've been waiting for you."

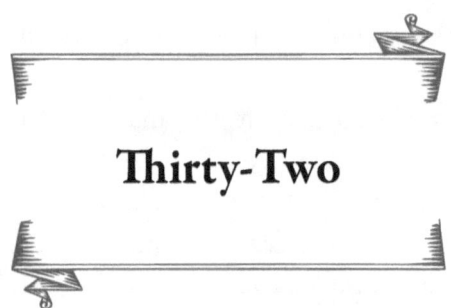

Thirty-Two

Adrian

Chaos. Everything burst into chaos. One moment, she was here. The next, she vanished from this realm. I didn't stop until I was standing next to Marcus who was frantically calling for her and searching the trees for any sign of her. But I know she's not there. She's back in Oria. At least, I hope it's where she ended up.

I grab Marcus firmly by the shoulder and force him to face me. "Marcus, she's gone. She's traveled back into the other realm."

He looks panicked. Where did the man who hated this woman go during their time away? It's been a few weeks, but he seems to be more bothered by her disappearance than even me.

He shrugs my hand off and takes one more look at the woods and the shadows lying beyond. I think I spot more than one cryarsh hovering amongst the barren branches. But they, too, vanish, as if called away.

"Marcus, what did you find out?"

"I have to go find her. How did you get to her world the last time?" He pivots and marches up the hill toward the house.

"Marcus, what did you find out?" My voice is stern, commanding. He knows something, and he is afraid. I can't remember the last time my friend was this afraid.

He presses on up the hill. "I don't have time to explain this to you. But I need to find her. I need to bring her back. She can't be there by herself. She isn't safe."

"*You* need to bring her back? Since when do you care about her safety?" I grab his arm and force him to stop moving, to look at me and explain what happened with them.

He opens and closes his mouth a couple of times before finally wrestling the words out. "I—she—I don't know." He focuses on the house, avoiding eye contact. "I think we're friends now. I care enough to not want her to get hurt."

"Friends? Is that all?"

He swallows. "Yes. Why? Does that bother you? I thought you of all people would be worried about her safety."

"I don't even know what is going on. You haven't told me anything."

Glancing around to be sure we are still isolated enough, he faces me. "The high priestess seems to believe Darci has somehow been infected by a certain form of magic." I wait for him to continue. "It's magic belonging to Death. Magic only used by Death." I feel the blood drain from my face.

"How is this possible?"

He shakes his head. "We don't know. We couldn't figure it out or figure out why you and she are connected. But we do know this magic is more than she can control. We were trying to train her to use it and let some of it out." He won't look at me now.

"But?"

"I don't think it's working. It's getting stronger, and Mother Jaden believes it will eventually overpower her."

I might be sick at this point. That much power contained in a mortal is unheard of. It's not possible for it to be fully controlled. There's a reason it belongs to a god.

"If it overpowers her—" I don't want to finish the statement.

"She and any world she is in will be completely destroyed."

We stare at one another for a minute. The implications of this are more far reaching than I could have imagined.

"There's another thing."

Of course, there is. "Say it, Marcus."

"Well, there's two things. The Dark Lord has been making contact with her. He's been in her nightmares and right before we got here, she encountered him when she used her magic. I don't know what he wants with her. But if he gets a hold of the magic—"

I finish for him. "We will have war on our hands and possible extinction." I rub my hand along my jaw. "What's the other thing? You said there were two."

I see his mask slip–the one he wears to protect himself from the pain the outside world causes. His jaw quivers slightly before he hardens himself again.

"If Darci can't control the magic, she was going to go back to her world." He stops and swallows.

"What? To destroy her world? That doesn't sound like her."

"No, she was going to die. Mother Jaden seems to think if Darci cuts off the life source, the magic will die with her. I don't think she was going to be able to stop the magic, Adrian. She'll choose to die instead of destroying everyone. I–we can't let her die. There has to be a way."

I close my eyes, feeling both dread and shock at the revelation. The part of my soul tied to hers screams at the thought. When I open them again, I find Marcus staring at the forest.

"Okay, this is important. But right now, she's not in our world. We have to address the issues here before we can think about doing anything else. Our people need us; your people need you, Marcus."

He turns away from the woods and follows me up the hill. "What have you done to secure the area since the latest attacks?" There's the commander I know.

"The armies have been deployed around the village and the capital, but we are spread thin. We don't know when he will attack or where. I'm having the servants move into the town. The soldiers are here to assist with transporting them all safely. I couldn't spread our forces thin to protect the house. We have to leave here."

His steps falter but only for a moment before walking on. "If we leave and she comes back, how will she find us? She'll be our world's problem then."

"We can only do what is best for the moment. I'm not risking anymore lives." He nods.

"Gennet?"

"She made it. But too many others didn't. It's time to prepare for a war we can win before we wait and are doomed to fail."

Neither of us speaks the rest of the way to the house. I stop at the back entrance and look one more time at the woods. There is no sign of Darci. No evidence she was there, but a slight movement out of the corner of my eye draws my attention. A shadow.

When I look, it's gone.

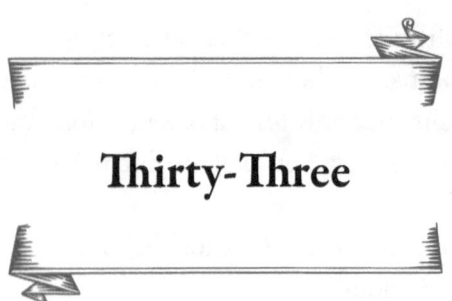

Thirty-Three

Darci

"Mr. McClane? What are you doing in my house?" My magic responds to my obvious distress at finding my home invaded. I feel it burning under my skin.

He assesses me with a cold look; one filled with disdain. His eyes seem vacant of life, of humanity. I clench my fists tight to force the flames sparking on my fingertips back to where they belong, locking down on the power within me even if it's temporary.

"We've been keeping an eye on you for a while now. But you have been up to something." He stands next to the fire, poking it with a charred stick.

"I don't know what you're talking about. I told you and Mrs. McClane I'm okay by myself. I don't need any looking after." I try to keep my voice calm, to play dumb—to act like I don't suspect his ill intentions.

He *tsks* at me before setting the stick amongst the flames. "You don't have to pretend anymore. He has been wanting to see if you would remember. If you would wake up so to speak. We do our part to ensure this world remains safe and void of energy it shouldn't possess. Isn't that what you wanted since the beginning?"

I scrunch my brow in confusion. "Wanted? I don't know what you're talking about."

"A magic-less world, Darci. A place where no powers could find you and destroy you and your family. It's a bit ironic."

My mind drifts back to what Mother Jaden said. Magic is always there in every realm and every world. No world is without it. Some are more obvious than others. Oria has always been a world where the magic lies buried deep within suppressed and contained.

"I have no desire to know anything about magic. I just want to keep living." Mr. McClane mentioned a *him*. Who is he talking about?

"I'm not here to hurt you. But I am here to tell you he knows where you have been and where you have gone. He knows what you can do now. Unfortunately, I don't think it will end well for you." He walks towards me, and I stumble back. "Be ready. Darci." He says my name like it's a shared secret between us. A private joke. Like one of us is lying, and I don't want to say who.

His eyes are dead with flecks of white along the brown irises. The pupil in the middle is a little foggy. Goosebumps form on my arms. He appears possessed by some force.

I offer a weak smile. "I, uh, I don't know what you want or what you're even talking about."

He chuckles and steps past me to the front door. "You make very good bread, Darci. I think the missus would enjoy one more loaf, don't you?"

He steps onto the porch, pulling the door shut behind him. I sink to the floor and hug my knees to my chest. My hands are shaking, and my heart pounds in its cage. I knew my instincts were telling me something wasn't right about Mr. McClane. Could it be the Dark Lord of Daemons is here? Is he in this world and has been using the McClanes to spy on me.

If so, why? How could he have possibly known I would get magic? Questions swarm my mind and my head aches. I try to remember everything that happened after the invasion. The nightmares have disturbed my sleep for months now playing on repeat in my memories.

I know the truth lies somewhere close. My heart tells me the Dark Lord is the God of Death. It makes sense. Everything about him is dark, violent, and terrifying. Could he have imbued his powers within me? Am I a walking firebomb waiting to destroy this world? But maybe it's not this world he is after. Maybe he wants to destroy Myzonia. I imagine he doesn't want me holding onto his powers for much longer.

Meiora slides around my knees, and I relax my posture to allow it to comfort me more easily. In the forest, when I used my magic, I saw him. He talked to me and called me the Ancient One. Perhaps this magic is why he calls me by that name. I also saw flashes of memories and thoughts and names. A name I never wanted to hear again. It is burned into my mind. I'm not sure why, but I know the truth of that name is something I don't want to discover.

But I have to know. I need to face this truth screaming at me from so close. The monster writhing beneath my skin wants out.

I push myself to my feet and walk to the door–to the room where all the treasures of my sons are held. I haven't walked into this room since they died. I have been too afraid to face the darkness inside there. The shadows and death of my past torture me if I dwell on them too long.

But I can't hide anymore. I must go in.

My hand trembles as I reach for the knob. Part of me screams to stop. To shut out the past and the truths there and simply continue to exist. But this magic inside of me calls out to whatever I will face in there. I hear it humming in my ears. I feel the tingle of it along my skin like pins and needles.

Shadows creep out of my fingers, reaching for the door. I can feel it–the dread and terror of what is underneath pushing out of me into the room around me. I don't see Meiora. I see only the darkness inside of me enveloping the room.

Taking one more deep breath, I turn the handle and crack the door. It's like all sound has been sucked from the house. The magic quiets within me. The buzz and hum of it is gone. Even the crackle of the fire is strangely still. All I hear is silence.

The door creaks open the rest of the way. Black flames tinged in white sparkle across the floor and walls. A floodgate is opened. Memory after memory pours into me—a vast wave of all I have suppressed for too long. Each terrible moment grows worse and more wicked than the one before. The laughter of children dying out, replaced by horror.

I remember all of it.

I remember. Death was my friend once.

I cover my mouth with my hands as a surge of magic explodes from my soul. The agony of being ripped apart more than I can bear. My sobs reach my ears. Gut-wrenching sobs tear my throat as tears stream down my cheeks. Shadows and fire burn through me, and my skin feels hot and prickly. The door deep within my soul is open, and a darkness, more evil than my worst nightmares, awakens.

Even Meiora doesn't come. It is me left alone with the monster.

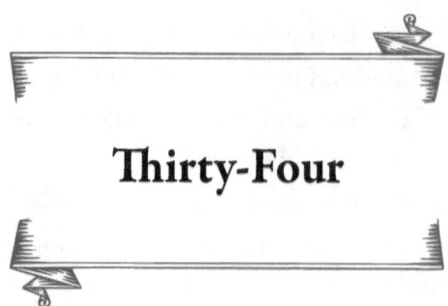

Thirty-Four

Hours pass. Maybe days. The pain throbbing in my chest ebbs away and the numbness I'm so used to takes its place again. I refuse to let it consume me. Not now that I remember everything. I know how this has to end. The world is in danger, and I might be the only one able to stop the coming catastrophe. Only one being can help me during this. Part of me doesn't want to believe this is the path laid out before me, but fate has other plans.

I tried this already. I ran away from my responsibilities–from the call placed on me. The gift that is my life. I created a new one hoping this somehow redeemed me from all my sins. I'm not blind anymore. There is no redemption story for me.

The war, all of it, meant something and nothing.

I crawl out of the room and into the light of the fire. The furniture is aged and broken. Slashes cut through the walls. A film of dust and death lingers on every surface. I have been gone for too long.

I can't go back.

"Meiora." I rasp. My voice, hoarse with sobs, barely makes a noise. But the cryarsh, my shadow, appears at my side. I rock back on my heels and let my fingers brush against the shadows dancing before me. Warm and velvet and home.

I am home in the darkness. Unafraid of what waits for me through the shadows. They belong to me and I to them.

He expects me to come–to face retribution. I need to save this land. If my death will protect the worlds around me, then I need to face it. I have to do it. Once time is up, only I'll be able to end it.

But who am I to stand against this madness?

Together, Meiora and I move through the house passing through rooms. I wave my hand in front of the fire, closing my fingers. The flames die instantly. Smothered by shadows.

Standing in the middle of my bedroom, I peel the snow-damp clothes off my body leaving them in a pile on the floor. I walk to the wardrobe and pull out a pair of insulated leather pants and a black tunic. Clothes I have kept tucked away in here for years. They fit like a familiar friend.

I slide a dagger out from under the mattress and secure it to my thigh under the hem of the tunic. I don't think I'll need it though. Wrapping my cloak around me, I slip my boots back on and walk to the front door. I take one more look behind me at the house I have called home. Saying goodbye and knowing it's the best decision I could have made. For Adrian. And Marcus. For Oria and Myzonia.

The door clicks shut behind me as the cruel winter wind bites my skin. Time is running out.

THIS MAY NOT HAVE BEEN my best idea. My self-preservation instincts scream I should turn around. The snow isn't as deep once I cross into the woods, but drifts caused by the uneven ground cause me to lose my footing or sink to my hips in the cold, wet piles. My ankles and calves are burning from walking, but I press on keeping my eyes out for Meiora and also making sure I don't veer too far off course. I'm not completely sure this will help me get to him, but it's the only idea I have right now. Nothing will ever be the same again. It shouldn't be.

Something has shifted in the air around me ever since I encountered Meiora a few months ago. It's inevitable that war would unleash monsters upon us. Meiora is a safe friend; though I can't deny I noticed how Adrian and Marcus looked at it at first. A mixture of awe and fear especially at the fact Meiora is territorial of me as well. The monster favors me a little too much. For good reason.

I pause to catch my breath and look around. I take note of the trees and branches. I turn around to look at the trail I'm leaving behind. It looks to be a straight line. When I fled from the darkness the last time, I moved straight through the trees and straight up the hill to my home. Now a hum vibrates along the ground drawing me back towards its source.

Meiora passes from tree to tree. Hovering in wispy clouds of black made more beautiful by the cold white of the snow around us. The trees with their skeletal branches cast dark gray shadows crisscrossing on the forest floor beneath my feet.

"Meiora, I wish I knew what you thought. I wish you could tell me what to do." It doesn't move to reassure me. It doesn't approve of my plan. I sense the frustration from the creature.

"I don't know how else to find him." I give the cryarsh a look that says I know it doesn't approve of this. It has somehow grown even more attached to me. This cryarsh reflects the speck of goodness in my soul.

"I know. I could have waited to see if he came, but it's time to finish this. I won't sit still and wait for whatever bad thing is coming. It's time to face my demons."

They do feel like demons. The darkness that pulled me to the avgrunn felt like an evil looking for me in this world. Seeking me out—to destroy me or to capture me or to crown me. I can feel it. A part of me reaches out to the shadows as if I belong to it. I smirk in disdain. I do belong to it, and it belongs to me. Knowing this scares me, but not enough.

I resume walking, getting farther and farther from my home. The land has leveled out, and I know the hill continues to fade away from me. There's a beat starting at the base of my neck. A call growing louder the closer I get to it. My magic hums to life and swells within me. A tide being pulled by something greater than the moon. I know I'm going the right way.

After several minutes of walking, I turn to find Meiora gone. A quickening of panic surges into my blood. I didn't want it to leave without saying goodbye. I've grown fond of my friend, but it can't get close to the avgrunn. Even my monster avoids it.

A pulse drums against me like a heartbeat. The first time around I didn't notice it. With my magic awake inside of me now, I sense other forms of magic more easily. The power inside of me beats in time with the monster inside the hole. The darkest part of me grows in anticipation. I'm connected to this, and the dark inside of me calls to the shadows inside of it.

Wings moving through the air draw closer. A large shadow flies over my head. I look up to marvel at the black, scaled dragon flying past me towards the shadows. There are more wings; more dragons coming. An army of monsters ready to destroy.

My heart beats faster as I notice the strange clearing coming into view up ahead. The black bottomless hole right in the middle of the clearing comes into view. I wonder if there's any life at all underneath the snow in the clearing; or if all the life there died in the presence of such evil.

I slow my steps as I get closer. I remind myself to breathe. The sounds of the forest have died out around me. The untainted snow on the outside edges of the trees in the circle reminds me no creature crosses into the clearing. I stop walking about five feet away from the edge. I hope this is close enough to trigger something from the other realm. I pray Adrian and Marcus will not be out looking for me. I don't want them anywhere near this place.

The darkness from the hole might come to swallow me up, or the Dark Lord will appear like I anticipate him to do. Despite how ominous the avgrunn appears, it's not as dangerous as I am.

I open my hands and let my magic come to the surface. It writhes and burns its way through me, but I have control. It isn't overwhelming. My mind clears all other thoughts as I center myself and let the power push out toward the abyss. The pit in my stomach feels heavier, and dread grows inside of me. I turn slowly, searching for any sign of the white-eyed man. Nothing. The woods sit silent–the trees watchmen in this strange place. No one else will hear me if I scream.

Then, as if a door opens, I sense someone behind me in the direction of the clearing. A presence fills the air and makes my heart race, and I haven't even turned around yet. I take a deep breath and face the clearing once again. Only there isn't only a clearing there. The black hole moves and twists with a distorted form of life. Before, a darkness seemed to seep outward from it, not too unlike Meiora moving across my house to envelop me. Now, someone is coming out of the shadows. A figure forms and grows in height and detail. A man's face takes shape, but it's not like any human I've ever been in the presence of. No, this man emanates power, darkness, and evil.

He came.

I'm riveted watching as his form becomes more tangible. Something beneath my skin hums in response to the power growing around me. The tips of my fingers tingle, and I hold my breath for a long moment. I start to step backward, but the snow makes it awkward. I want to be brave, but consequences for evil are rarely ever pleasant. My body reacts appropriately to what is coming. He faces me. The cruel jaw and hard eyes of my nightmares stand before me. What I used to think were completely white eyes, I realize are even more bizarre. They take in every muscle twitching on my body. A black pupil is surrounded by a white iris, and it conjures up images of pain and darkness and death. My stomach roils. It takes all my willpower to face him. To not run away and flee the unholy creature standing here.

A strong force seizes both of my arms and my body lurches from the pull. Shadows wrap around my wrists and upper arms shackling me with such power my skin burns beneath it. The magic buzzing under my skin amplifies in response. I struggle, kicking and tossing my weight forward; but it's not enough. My body resists, but my mind accepts and so the magic within me dulls instead of sharpening.

The Dark Lord of Daemons moves steadily through the branches and snow stepping out of the clearing and into the woods. It's his power holding me here. The abyss behind him pulses and ripples outward like a pond disturbed by a stone. He is dressed in black pants and a black cloak with his hood pulled up. He is dressed, strangely, like me. He doesn't rush. He doesn't need to. I'm not going anywhere.

I stiffen my spine as he approaches. The shadows won't even let me turn around. I don't know how he plans to destroy me–perhaps he'll use the magic in these shadows. The only question is whether I will die looking terrified or defiant. My mind flashes back to the day death attached itself once again to my life. No, I will defy death this time. It doesn't come to steal what I freely give. I welcome it and the payment due.

I school my features trying to appear calm and turn my gaze away from the clearing and away from him. I stare straight ahead and still my body. Empty, silent trees stare back. Meiora hovers in its humanoid shape deep in the trees away from me. Watching, but not interfering.

I blink back the sorrow threatening to reveal itself. Instead, I focus on his presence as he comes right up to my back and then slowly steps around to my front. He towers over me, and I am not afraid when I stare right back at him.

My heart pounds; he must hear it. A cold sweat breaks out on my forehead and down my back. Every part of me tenses—a snake coiled to strike. The shadows holding tight to my arms expand to encompass my legs too. No part of me can move on its own now except for my head.

Fog and mist seep out of the surrounding trees. Pale, cold fingers grab my chin and force my face upward, inspecting me. I recoil, inwardly, because my body remains frozen by the shadows on the outside.

The burning under my skin amplifies to a roaring blaze. It calls out to whatever this is standing before me. Everything human about him seems to be a facade quickly replaced by the evil lying beneath the surface. Those pale white eyes latch onto mine, and I shake involuntarily. Before I would have thought he was death personified, and that might be true for me. Because he will be my death and destruction. He will end my existence once and for all.

He examines me carefully, reading all the tells my body gives away. I don't remember ever feeling fear quite like this. Even when my family was ripped away from me. My effort to be strong in the face of this creature strengthens as I remember he is not the only monster here.

His low voice echoes in my ears.

"I knew you would come back." I stand taller though my heart is in my throat now. Of course, he knew. He knew I couldn't stay away once I remembered the truth.

I try to speak, but no sound leaves me. He releases my chin and quickly looks over his shoulder in the direction I know Meiora stands when I hear another voice. Someone calls my name like a question. I know them, and I feel defeat burrow deep in my soul. He can't be here. The strange connection to Adrian crosses worlds and draws our souls together. He sees me as a shadow now like I have seen him over the months. His tone tells me he is as surprised to be encountering me at this moment as I am to be hearing him. I cast my eyes toward him. He's covered in shadows and fog; relief floods my veins. He's not in my world. I think he is safe for now.

The Dark Lord looks back at me. A wicked smirk plays on his lips. His pupils have dilated, reminding me of a predator on the hunt.

I whisper the only word I can think to say. "Please."

The magic inside me is burning through my skin now and fully alive.

"You don't want him. You are here for me." I steady my voice with resolve. I cannot live with myself if I don't at least try. Whispers fill the air all around me. Like thousands of ghosts speaking all at once, and he is the only one who understands them. Or he was. He acknowledges them. Then, he reaches out and places a hand on my chest.

Just like that, everything goes black.

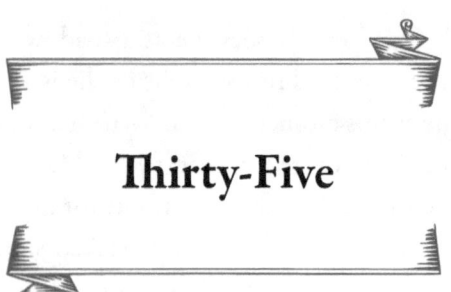

Thirty-Five

I'm drowning. There is no air to breathe, and no light to see. I can't feel any part of my body other than my lungs, which protest my lack of oxygen. This isn't like when I've been ripped from Oria into Myzonia. That always hurts, but it doesn't feel deadly. We might be moving, but I feel frozen in place. Other than my lungs burning, there is no other pain. No tearing apart of my soul and body as we move.

It doesn't matter if I open or close my eyes; it looks the same. I wish I were unconscious. It would be better than this unbearable weight on my chest and the taste of death on my lips. If the Dark Lord still holds me, I don't feel him.

A few more minutes pass, and the pressure builds in my lungs. I open my mouth to gulp air but find no relief. My body concedes as my mind slips into oblivion.

Adrian

"ADRIAN. ADRIAN!" THE fog clears from my mind, and I feel Marcus shaking my shoulders jolting me back to the present. I saw her. Marcus and I were discussing the next steps to prepare for a potential invasion from the Dark Lord when I blacked out. It reminded me of the times in this very room when I noticed a shadow moving around the space or would hear footsteps passing by. The moments when I was seeing Darci before I even knew who she was.

But this time was more intense. I saw her instantly, standing in the very place I met her. In the woods, near the avgrunn.

She wasn't alone.

"Adrian, what happened?" Marcus' bright blue eyes come into view.

"I saw Darci."

"You saw her? Like a shadow? Or a vision?" His face betrays the hope buried within.

"It was like before I met her. These encounters were mere shadows or sounds. I knew she was there before I even laid eyes on her. I felt her presence."

He nods. "She said it was similar with you. When we were at the temple, I knew there were moments when she heard you or sensed your presence. In whatever way you two are connected."

"This time, it was more like a vision. I saw her clearly. She was at the avgrunn, Marcus. The Dark Lord–he has her."

Terror paints Marcus' face. I'm sure I don't look much better. All our worst fears are coming true. If the Dark Lord somehow takes her magic, he'll be more powerful than any of us. This world will fall to him, and possibly countless others.

We shouldn't have wasted time keeping things from her. I should have told her more clearly the dangers the Dark Lord posed, but my advisors had been afraid she was in league with the Dark Lord himself. I didn't know how to explain our connection. I couldn't exactly put it into words. Something must have happened when she was taken back to Oria. Did *he* summon her there? To be isolated?

She had been trapped in the shadows he controlled, and I couldn't do anything to help her. They were gone before I even had a chance—the avgrunn sitting silent and ominous in their wake.

Marcus swears, digging his fingers into his scalp. Pressure builds in my head while he paces the room.

"Marcus, I couldn't help her! She saw me, and she didn't want me to come for her. I think she offered herself to him." The implications taint the air between us.

"No. She wouldn't do that. She knows he would gain too much power. She knows it would destroy worlds." Marcus breathes heavily and terror haunts his eyes. I don't know how to understand his denial.

"She wasn't fighting, Marcus. She accepted it like it was fate." I force myself to take a deep breath. "You said she was learning how to use her magic. But I didn't see any sign of it."

"She was going to sacrifice herself before the magic controlled her! She was going to give up her life to save us. You can't honestly believe she would allow this magic to fall into *his* hands?!" Marcus' voice grows louder.

"Stop. You're going to draw unnecessary attention." I hold my breath listening for any indication someone is going to walk through the door to us. Where had Meiora been? Why did the shadow creature not stop her?

"There is a reason you and her are connected. I don't know why, but I know there is goodness in her. The Dark Lord must have overpowered her senses. Or seduced her into the forest." Anger replaces the fear in Marcus' eyes now.

"Marcus, I don't know what happened between you two, but we have to think about the worlds most in danger. We need to get her back from him, but if there is any indication she is working with him, we need to be ready to end it." The words taste bitter in my mouth. My soul is tied to hers, but I also have to be the ruler my people need me to be.

I watch my friend steady himself. We both understand what needs to be done as much as we both hate the idea.

"We might be too late. He might have already destroyed her by the time we find a way to get there." Grief-soaked words escape

Marcus' lips. I might not be the only one now connected to Darci. It might make it that much harder to kill her when the time comes.

Darci

BLOOD. I SMELL BLOOD. Keeping my eyes closed, I let my other senses reach out. Behind my eyelids, I see light. I can breathe. The air smells strange and metallic. It's cold, and the ground I lay on is hard like stone. I force myself to stay still and silent, taking slow deep breaths. My ears become acutely aware of some sort of movement in the space with me. Footsteps. Someone is here with me.

No time like the present to face your end, I suppose. I let one eyelid crack open and then the other. I'm relieved to find the room I'm in is not dark, but I soon find this presents a problem of its own. It's solid white. Blindingly so. My eyes burn from it, and it takes me a minute to get them adjusted. As if by command, pain floods my body, spreading outward from my chest to my fingertips and toes.

A small moan leaves me before I can suppress it. The footsteps halt. I take this moment to turn my head towards the ceiling and try to force myself into a seated position. It is too bright here. My head pounds and stars spark in the corners of my vision. A voice so slithery, I imagine it's what snakes sound like if they could talk, responds to my movement.

"I wouldn't do that if I were you." Its accent is strange and wispy, stirring deep-rooted fears in my soul. I blink my eyes and wrap my forearms around my knees, trying to calm my churning stomach. Deep breaths in through my nose and out through my mouth.

"You'll be purging your stomach soon enough if you keep moving." It hisses at me. I can't tell if it's female or male. Footsteps head in my direction. I keep my body still when two bare feet, callused with toes bent in strange directions, step into my line of sight. I slowly look up to see who they belong to. It takes all my willpower not to move suddenly and scurry away from this creature. I think it is female. Its hair is thin and scraggly and white as snow to the point it almost disappears in the background of white in this room. It has cat eyes and jagged teeth. Wrinkles adorn its skin, and it stands slightly hunched but does not give the impression of weakness. I don't doubt this creature could kill me effortlessly if it wanted to. Well, at least it could have before.

It tilts its head and speaks in its strange voice again, "What does *he* want with you? What did you do to end up here with me?"

My blood chills, but I answer anyway. "I'm only here because I allowed it to be so."

At the sound of my voice, the creature's eyes widen, and it hisses at me showing me all its jagged teeth. It laughs in disbelief before schooling its features.

"Of course you did." It taps a clawed finger to its chin. "He doesn't put just anyone in here with me. Only those he deems most dangerous."

Magic burns under my skin in response to the threat. "Who are you? Or what are you?" I can feel sweat building up on my skin again. This creature reminds me of something I've seen or known before. The part of me buried deep inside—the part slowly waking up—remembers this monster. Cracks form in my deeply scarred heart.

"My name is Nidra. I don't think I am that different from you, woman. If that is what you are called."

"I don't think I've ever seen anything like you before." I swallow back the bile rising in my throat. I lie. I have seen her before. Puzzle pieces click into place.

"Males of my kind are quicker to kill. I prefer to decide for myself how quickly or slowly one should go. And whether they are worthy of—" She pauses and a gleam of excitement shines in her eyes. "Death." I ignore her explanation.

"Where am I?" I take this moment to look around the room. It is entirely white like freshly fallen snow. White and made of stone as pure as pearls. No shadows come from our bodies. There is no darkness in this cell.

She chuckles and follows my gaze around the room. "The white room is meant for those who summon darkness. No darkness or shadows, no power." She singsongs. She's wrong.

"I don't have any powers. I don't use darkness." I'm curious to discover what she knows. I avoid letting my eyes linger on hers, though her gaze never wavers from me.

"I feast on darkness. But I am here for fun today." She blinks her eyes slowly, observing. "You are right when you say you don't use darkness." She murmurs under her breath. Confusion masks her eyes momentarily.

"Why do I need to be observed?" What is he waiting for? What does he want?

"I'm here for him. He does what he wants. Who are we to question?" The Dark Lord who haunts me now. I look to see if there is a door in this space. I stand shakily to my feet and search every inch of the white stone. Nothing stands out offering a means of escape. But I'm not here to escape. Nidra sneers at me with a hunger in her eyes I know is being held back by only a thin thread.

I ask the only question I can think of right now. "And what do you think gave you your power, death eater?"

Terror replaces the hunger in her eyes. Maybe even realization. "He is the giver of power. He is the angel of death!" She stumbles away from me looking enraged now. "He is the most feared in this land."

I know she speaks a partial truth. I saw only death in his eyes. Yet he knows me. Every passing minute, a hardness settles deeper into my marrow and my heart. A crystallization of the person I wanted to be. I cling to the kernel of light in my soul. But death is here for me. I will not allow myself to persist past this. The magic flowing through my veins settles coming to rest inside of me. I no longer fight it or resist it. She claims he is the most fearful ruler of all. Yet, the horror building in her eyes betrays her.

"Is there some way out of here?" I feel no more fear. She nervously chuckles, and I tilt my head as I soak up the sight of her. This creature of jagged teeth and ragged bones. I'm dizzy from the traveling I did with the Dark Lord. I briefly close my eyes to calm my stomach again, letting another sliver of steel harden my resolve. When I open my eyes again, she is gone; and I smile.

Thirty-Six

I grow weary waiting here. When Nidra vanished, I assumed *he* would arrive shortly after. But he didn't. Instead, I sit in this blindingly white room longer than I should have to. I have no idea what day it is or what time it is. The room is disorienting, and I'm feeling bored and hungry. My heart beats slowly.

There is nothing else in the room. No bed or chairs. Not even another giant rock to use as a seat. I have walked the entire room countless times, running my fingers over the walls attempting to feel some crack in the rock to suggest a door. I do this mostly to keep myself entertained. Nidra didn't use a door to leave. She simply disappeared. Every pass around the room grants me more knowledge about the magic containing me here, and knowledge is power.

I push on the floors and the corners of the room. No give in the ground anywhere. I could see how someone might go mad in a place like this. The well of power inside of me continues to grow and the tiny light I cling to is fading. I give up my attempts and sit crisscrossed on the floor in the center of the room.

No sound penetrates the walls. The longer I sit, the more I notice my magic responding to the magic in the stones. I close my eyes and allow myself to focus on it. It's an undercurrent of something alive calling out to me. The room has a source of magic all its own. The more I still my body, the easier it is to hear and feel the electric nature of it.

The room is alive, and the magic remembers me. Swells of power grow under my skin until I open my eyes to see tiny sparks of black flames on my fingertips. They are small, but I keep them suppressed. I wonder. There might be no shadows in this room, but I don't need them to access my power. They have always underestimated me.

I concentrate on my fingers, holding my hands palms up on my knees. I keep my eyes closed and imagine grabbing the current by a thread under my skin. Behind my eyelids, in the darkness of my mind, I see a little blue light, faintly there. It's the magic of this room. I imagine holding my hand out and balancing this ball of blue gently in my palms. Without noticing, I move my hand away from my knee as if I'm going to touch it.

In my mind, I see the light in my hand, and a fire swells up inside of me. The power pushing at the limits I set around it. My hand grows hot and soon the ball of blue light mingles with the black flames. A smirk reaches my lips.

I know exactly who I am, and now the room does too.

A crack like thunder rumbles in the room and the air changes. He is finally here. I stand up casually. I am not afraid. I remember exactly who he is and why he wants me. I hope he is smart enough to finish what was started.

His entire essence emanates power. Those white eyes drink me in and survey every inch of my body. He lingers on my right hand sensing the magic dancing on my skin moments ago. He frowns.

"What are you waiting for?"

He stares intently for a minute, studying me. I do not look away.

"You remember everything, don't you?" His frown deepens.

"Yes," I say matter of fact. "I remember all of it, and I remember you."

He smirks. "You may think you can trick me, but I'm not easily thwarted." He steps closer to me, and I let him. I remember the pain of his touch. Those eyes whisper death to me. Death only I can allow.

"Let's not pretend you think I am contained fully here. I'm only here because I allow it."

He narrows his eyes and steps forward again towering over me. I have nowhere to run in a room with no doors, and I plan on facing this unashamed. He stands mere inches from me now. I feel the power slipping from him and around me. It occurs to me the shadows he weaponized against me before aren't available this time. Yet the magic inside of him obviously longs for access to them. He has other magic, though, since he managed to get into this room without using normal means.

"If you are so willing now, why did you resist for so long?" I don't respond. He's suspicious.

"It's gone on long enough." The goodness in me melts a little more. Time is running out, and I can sense the shadows of my soul crawling to the surface. He needs to hurry.

He chuckles. "You thought you could do it, didn't you? You thought you could exist in peace and happiness without hurting everyone around you."

I ignore this and ask the one question I have for him. One mystery I haven't quite figured out. "How did you remember? And why you and not the others?"

"You made a mistake the day you befriended the cryarsh. It cracked the foundation of everything you created. I can't quite figure out what you did to the Sovereign of Myzonia, though. How you connected yourself to him?"

My lips are sealed.

He steps back and before I have a chance to ask any other questions, the crack of thunder follows his quick departure. I'm alone in the room again. I let out a breath and rub my hands along my arms. Chilled and empty, my cloak is a poor excuse for protection against the cold emanating from the stones. The others had still forgotten who I was. Even the histories were changed. I learned this much in Myzonia. Yet he managed to squeeze through the fault line caused by friendship.

Moving to the center of the room, I sit back down and close my eyes. I focus on the good I have known. My husband, my sons. Marcus. Adrian. Risa. Hoku's death. Meiora. There is never enough time. I wish I had been able to do more–live better. But these are moments in the tapestry I created, and now it is torn in two.

Khitaen, the God of War and Peace, will be back for me soon.

SILENCE MEETS ME. THE dark woods all around me carry no sounds at all. It's like every creature left in the presence of the figure who stands in front of me shrouded in black. My heart pounds. I've been here before. I've been in the darkness. It is absolute, and my head throbs.

My ears pop and I open my jaw trying to relieve the pressure. I look down at my bare feet. Blood is everywhere, pooling out from under my soles. I know what comes next. Intense pain slices up my spine, and I fall to my knees, leaves and twigs snapping under my body. Where are they? I scream it, but I know where they are. No sound carries through this vacuum. The figure is walking toward me, tall and graceful, moving like a wraith through the night. The trees stand as sentinels around me, and I know death is coming. I have called it here.

Death came for them. It came for the people and world I called my own. Nothing I attempted could change what is true. The monster still arrived, and it showed no mercy. My body is being ripped apart.

I plead, but there is no sound. The figure stands over me and all I see is darkness pouring into all of who I am wiping out the essence of my soul.

MY SCREAM WAKES ME. I didn't realize I had fallen asleep. I'm fighting with my cloak, trying to rip it off my body only to get myself more tangled up in it. My eyes burn against the white of the stones. I force myself to still. The emptiness in my stomach along with the adrenaline now racing through my veins makes my stomach lurch. I turn over quickly before I vomit up what little remained in my belly. When I finish gagging, I crawl towards a corner of the room and prop myself up. My physical body has grown weak, trying to survive the internal war I'm waging. I close my eyes, breathing, forcing myself to calm. It is almost finished.

"Are you sure I should stay here?" Nidra's voice echoes in my mind. I open my eyes to find her standing in the middle of the room wringing her hands in his presence. She is scared.

"Yes. You must stay here. I want to see what she does." Khitaen looks briefly toward me. I offer a wicked smile in return.

"But–" Nidra protests.

Khitaen holds up a hand to silence her. He won't tolerate any arguments about the matter. I know why he plans to leave her with me. As my body weakens, my magic strengthens. It's getting harder to keep it subdued. Nidra isn't safe with me. I am his weapon. At least, he thinks I am.

He vanishes from sight, and the death eater faces me. I tilt my head, feeling every bit the predator I am. She cowers into the corner farthest from me. She knows what I am now. She wasn't sure before, but now there is no question.

2.5 Years Earlier

"NO! NO! DON'T!" I SCREAM as I barrel down the hillside, bare feet sliced open by broken nuts and sticks. Kiran, my husband follows close behind. I see the shadows. The creatures grabbing my boys and running into the woods with them. Hordes of jagged teeth and

monstrous claws smashing through branches and entire trees like blades of grass. Death eaters. My death eaters. Dragons soar overhead, and Kiran gasps.

"What is going on?! Darci! Wait!"

I don't wait. I keep going. Not this time. I will get to them! I trip and stumble into a ravine, feeling my ankle sprain and my head crack against a branch on the way down.

Kiran hesitates only a moment before I see him jump over me and run after the boys. Black dots cover my vision, but I fight the urge to black out. I see them. I just have to get up.

A tsunami of fiery power flows through my veins. I scream, but I can't stop what I was made to be. Black fire explodes out of me incinerating everything—-everyone—-in my path. Until there is nothing but ash and bones. Darkness sweeps over me.

I am the darkness.

Thirty-Seven

Adrian

I pace back and forth in Gennet's small study. She is taking too long, but I can't rush her. She has to be able to help. She opened the door for me the last time. Marcus comes into the room, closing the door roughly and turning to face me. He crosses his arms and frowns at me.

"You're going to wear a trench into the floor if you keep that up."

I scowl, "We have to get to Oria."

"I know." He drops his arms and blocks my path. "I spoke with Gennet. I'm coming with you this time."

I shake my head. "I need you here. I need you to help move everyone to the village and secure the people while I'm gone."

"And I'm coming with you to make sure you don't kill her before she has a chance to explain."

"Marcus, I won't make any rash decisions. But I think you are too biased to make a good decision."

"There is good in her. We can't just let her die."

Neither of us wants her death. My connection to Darci grows taut inside me. For some reason, I feel like I belong to her, and she belongs to me. Marcus' attachment to her seems as profound as mine. I can't keep the question to myself any longer.

"Do you love her?" He startles at my direct tone.

"What—why would you ask that?" My friend looks flustered, and he won't meet my eyes. I can't help the smile playing on my lips.

I don't get a chance to say more though because Gennet bustles into the room.

"I assume you are both going this time? The portal will not take you farther than her house. I don't know if you can leave the house and get into her world entirely." She pauses and the look she gives me is full of sympathy. "I'm not sure she is actually in Oria any longer."

Marcus looks away, his jaw tightening. I sense defeat from him.

"We have to at least try to find some answers." I watch Marcus, but address Gennet. "And we need to protect the world from whatever is coming."

Darci may have gotten under my skin, but I think she got into his heart.

I've never regretted any of the choices I've had to make since becoming the sovereign of my people. They were necessary choices even if they were painful. If I need to, I'll make another painful choice when we find Darci.

Gennet smiles sadly and nods her head. "Okay, give me a moment."

She walks to the threshold and shuts the door. Pulling out a dagger, Marcus cringes as she swipes the blade quickly across her palm. None of this surprises me. I've seen her do this before. Dipping two fingers into her own blood, she marks three points on the door frame. One on the top and two marks of blood on each side. Stepping back, she summons her magic to her fingertips. The bright orange light spreads out to meet the marks of blood. With eyes closed, she mouths phrases in an ancient language and the doorframe glows.

Soon the solid wood of the door fades and shadows and mist swirl in its absence. I look at Marcus and check to make sure my dagger is secured along my side.

"Ready?" I ask him.

"Let's go find her."

Darci

THERE IS A WAR OF TWO natures waging within me. I've done what I can to keep one side contained, but I feel myself losing ground slowly. Goodness in me is dying. I hope Marcus and Adrian stay far away. I can't continue like this much longer. If I don't end this soon, I won't be able to do what needs to be done.

"Please." Nidra hisses. Her voice sounds more and more animalistic as she gives in to her fear. I grimace at the sound.

"I thought you expected me to fear you." The words scratch my throat. I feel my pupils dilate as I watch the creature still cowering in the corner.

"I didn't know. I didn't realize." She's begging now. It's pitiful.

"I'm thirsty." I scratch out quietly. Power pulls at my mind. Darkness pollutes my once clear mission. I think I have passed the moment when I would willingly succumb to death. There won't be anything to stop me if Khitaen doesn't quit playing these games.

"If you spare me, perhaps I can help you." Her eyes brighten slightly at the idea.

"There is nothing you can do to help me. This would be over if I let it be."

Any hope she had vanishes. I know why he left her here. He doesn't intend for her to leave.

"What you need is not very far away. Confirm what he knows to be true about you." Her eyes dart around the room before settling on me again. She averts them as soon as she sees the gleam in mine. "If you will only submit to his demands, then you will be saved."

I close my eyes and laugh bitterly. "You're a fool." Confusion emanates from her demeanor. I feel it like a separate power spreading throughout the room. "You have no idea what he is actually here to do. He isn't here to save me but to end me. He is a fool because he didn't do it right away." I bite the words out.

The double nature I am battling? It's winning. Khitaen will be too late.

"I—I don't understand." She's a monster, and soon she'll realize I am one too. The last puzzle piece slips into place, and I feel the light in my soul begin to waver. Suffocated by the shadows wrapping around it. When I open my eyes, she screams.

I smell blood again.

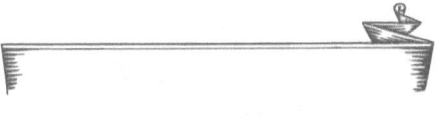

Thirty-Eight

Adrian

A cold wind howls against my face as I slip on fresh, wet snow. The last time I came through here I was in the house immediately. This time Marcus and I find ourselves standing on the front porch of Darci's house with a northern wind blowing against us. Something isn't right about it.

He swears and pulls his cloak tighter around his shoulders. "Is this her house?"

I scan the road in front of us and the fields in the distance before turning to face a rickety front door barely hanging on to its hinges. "Yes, I think it is."

"Well. What are you waiting for?" He moves to open the door.

"Wait." I hold my hand up and reach for the bond that connects us. To sense her presence in the house before we go in. It's quiet though.

I step forward and knock on the door instead. Marcus side eyes me but keeps his thoughts to himself for the time being.

No one answers the door. I don't even hear footsteps within. I'm about to open it myself when I see a shadow in the corner of my eye. Marcus must notice it the same moment I do.

"Meiora!" Eagerness radiates off him. "Is she here? Is she safe?" Hope—deadly and cruel—holds him captive.

"Marcus, we know she can't be." He frowns at me, but I ignore him and face the cryarsh. "We know something happened. We need to get to her." I know the cryarsh understands. Though they don't speak, it doesn't mean these aren't incredibly intelligent beings.

Meiora slips through the cracks in the door leaving us outside on the porch. I guess we are going into the house after all. I turn the knob and step inside, stomping snow off my boots. Marcus is close behind me.

The house is freezing. Only the wind whistling through the many cracks makes a sound. I walk farther in scouring the room for any evidence she might have left behind. A pile of clothes lay in the middle of the floor of the bedroom to the left. The fireplace is cold and empty, and blankets and curtains cover the back window facing the woods.

Marcus walks toward the kitchen and the other room with the door closed. I never saw the inside of the room. When I came here last time, I walked straight out of our world and into the living room. I sensed something there, but I didn't want to be rude.

The sensation is stronger now. A presence occupies the space, and I feel it calling to me in the same way Darci's magic calls to me. This presence is wilder and feels more dangerous.

"Stop." I don't know what makes me reach out to Marcus as his hand hovers above the doorknob.

"What? Did you hear something?" I'm transfixed on the door. Meiora forms a silhouette next to me, and wispy black tendrils stretch out towards the door. Is it pointing at the door for me to open?

"Do you feel it? There's something in the room."

Marcus' eyes dart back to the door. I can tell he doesn't feel it. I can tell it seems like any other room to him, but it's there. The part of her I always felt, it's right there.

"I need to open it. Not you, Marcus. It needs to be me." The commander's mask slips into place on my friend.

"I don't know, Adrian. If there is something that could harm you, I need to face it first. We can't risk your life." He stiffens his shoulders and moves to open it.

"No!" My voice is harsh and commanding. "It calls to me. If you open it, I think it will harm you. But—-I think I will be okay. It feels like Darci, but wilder." I swallow and move to the door before I can change my mind. He nods and stands at my back.

"I'm right here. I'm pulling you out if anything goes wrong."

"Okay."

The handle is cold in my hands, but I grip it tightly and turn. I shove the door open and step back quickly readying for something to attack us.

On the other side of the door, a massive cloud of black and writhing shadows consumes the space. They seep outward along the floor, set free from the chamber. As they dissipate, I see the symbols carved all over the walls. In the far corner, a blanket covers something large and misshapen.

We step into the room, and I hear Marcus swear under his breath.

"Those are—"

"I know." I interrupt. It's like a vault of history laid bare before us. The symbols of dragons and serpents winding around each other cover every surface. In the middle of the far wall, two dragons engaged in battle, with a black dagger pointed upward between them, ooze the shadows and black mist. We both know the symbol. In some ways we were right about Darci's magic. In the most important ways, we were so terribly wrong.

The beast inside of me drawn to this room, to this place, roars to life. That's exactly what it is too. A beast. A monster. This wasn't supposed to exist. The symbols are a corruption of the runes surrounding our world and the gods and goddesses of it. We have myrukim, but they are not these scaled and angry monsters.

I don't understand how I am drawn here. I don't know why there is a part of me pulled towards this place. Anger burns to life in my gut. Anger and betrayal.

"Do you think–do you think she knows?" Marcus looks gutted. He is usually not wrong about people and his first reactions to Darci were right. But I saw the whispers of goodness in her too. Too many questions and not enough time to hash them all out.

"Marcus, you and I both know there is no way she isn't who we think she is." But how? All our legends and histories had been vague. Foggy and shrouded in shadows. Just like her.

We're frozen staring at the symbol of nightmares on the wall.

We didn't expect the pale and beautiful green-eyed woman to be this. I see Meiora come into view. It makes sense now why the shadow creature was drawn to her. All shadows bow to their maker. Meiora doesn't seem evil though which confuses me even more.

"Is it true? Is what we are seeing true?" I don't know why I ask the shadow. I know I can't understand it. But the cryarsh slinks to the floor and rubs against my legs like a cat. It is soft and velvety. I've never felt the touch of one of these creatures. Then, it moves to the corner where the blanket hides more truths.

I walk over and yank the blanket back, stumbling at the sight before me.

"Araina, help us." Marcus prays as he helps me catch myself.

Perfectly   preserved   skeletons   blanketed   in   black chrysanthemums rest on the floor. Two smaller and one a full-size man. Magic glows around them and black flames burn consistently all over them. Burning but not catching anything on fire. Every inch is covered in the black flowers. A memorial. Perfectly preserved by death.

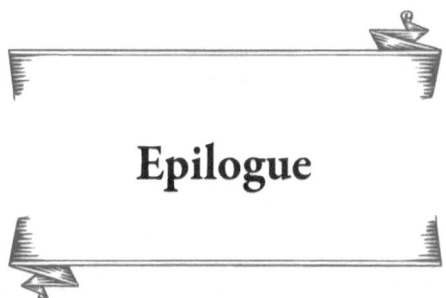

Epilogue

Darci

"I'm sorry, little snake." Nothing remains of Nidra. She probably deserved it. Her life force slips into me, but I don't release it like I'm supposed to. I think I'll keep hers with me for a while. I didn't even manage to get myself dirty. Suppressing magic and memories for a few decades has proven deadly for everyone in my path. I knew it wouldn't hold forever. The kernel of light inside of my soul flickers. It's so close to being snuffed out. If I look a little deeper, I can see my dark life force. One thought and I could extinguish it. Rid the world of the monster I am. The monster I have become.

It's a shame really. The good I could do and have done will always be overpowered by the wickedness of my nature.

I laugh a little under my breath. It is starting to feel good. Letting the shadows out a little at a time. Meiora wouldn't understand. Meiora was too good to be friends with me. My memories of Adrian and Marcus fade a little. Each moment I surrender them to the dark allows me to step farther away from the shame I had felt. The shame I do feel when I think too long on the lives lost to my hand—my power. A twinge of regret at never sitting down with Ginger and Gwenyth again hurts. Only for a moment though.

A crack sounds and Khitaen appears, and I laugh.

"You are as wicked as I remember you being." He growls.

"You should have taken care of me when you had the chance." I sneer. "What? Did you want me to help you rule Myzonia? You know it belongs to Markyr."

"If you would aid me, I could make a deal."

"Aid you? You were supposed to end me one thousand years ago."

"And I almost did." He snaps. His anger amuses me. "You could rule alongside me, though. We would be unstoppable."

"I didn't come to you to be a co-regent. I came to you for you to kill me." I grit out through clenched teeth. I guess not all the little flame has died out yet.

He narrows his eyes. "I wasn't sure you truly understood your past. You seemed awfully cozy with the sovereign."

A sadness coats my heart, and my smile dims a shade. But I quickly suppress the emotion and move on. Khitaen can't be killed by anyone but me. He's a god after all. But I don't know if I want him gone. War can be fun too.

He tilts his head, watching the conflicting emotions play out on my face.

"I didn't have to be all bad. I didn't have to want all of this." I whisper. "I didn't want to be demonized."

He thought this room would contain me, but my magic is far stronger than even the others realize. I hold a hand up and flick my wrist and instantly the room is gone. I think I might even hear a frustrated shout escape Khitaen when he realizes I've left.

They would have destroyed me long ago if they knew, or at least, they would have tried. But now, I will destroy them. They let my world waste away in ruin—forced the people to shun me and deny my existence and hid the true nature of death and its purpose. Demonizing me in the same breath they declared me not needed.

They have ruled the worlds for long enough. If I can't have peace and joy, then no one will. I think it's time to pay a visit to my sister Araina.

No one can kill a god or goddess. Except for me.
My name is Arawna.
I am the Goddess of Death.
I won't be forgotten any longer.

TO BE CONTINUED...

Acknowledgments

S pecial thanks to all who supported and encouraged me in this journey. For my oldest daughter who has been more pumped about this endeavor than anyone else I know. For my youngest being patient enough to leave me alone while I worked, and who also hit lots of random keys.

For my alpha and beta readers who gave me feedback and helped me refine the story.

For my husband who endured many hours of me lost in the pages of my story.

For Michaela Suver at MJ Design and her beautiful design of my author logo bringing to fruition my vision for this side of my life.

For my friend, Cheryl, who had to endure the random chapters sent to her each week that were so rough and awful, and you still gave feedback and encouragement along the way.

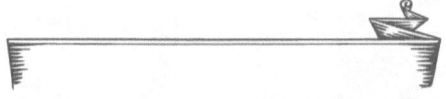

About the Author

Hi! I'm Olivia, and I have had a deep love of reading and all things books pretty much my entire life. I grew up on fantasy and magic, and the fact that I get to write stories full of those things boggles my mind. I hope to continue to grow as a writer and reader every year. I love a variety of genres and consume a diverse range of books.

I was born and raised in Kentucky, and I spend a lot of my time outside with my family, enjoying our garden and nature. My horses, cats, and dog also hold a dear place in my heart.

Thank you to every person who takes a chance on my book. I hope you like it, and even if you didn't, I'm still grateful you tried it out!

Happy Reading!

www.ingramcontent.com/pod-product-compliance
Lightning Source LLC
Chambersburg PA
CBHW030656260626
47157CB00007B/2675